MW01027121

THE

SEX
BOX

MAN

THE

SEX BOX

MAN

EDITED BY ANONYMOUS

CHRONICLE BOOKS
San Francisco

Copyright © 1996 by John Miller. All rights reserved. No part of this book may be reproduced in any form without written permission from the publisher.

Page 164 constitutes a continuation of the copyright page.

To maintain the authentic style of each writer included herein, quirks of spelling and grammar remain unchanged from their original state.

Printed in Singapore.

ISBN 0-8118-1405-X

Library of Congress Cataloging-in-Publication Data available.

Book and cover design: Big Fish Books
Composition: Big Fish Books
Cover photograph: *Torso*, from an Italian poster, circa 1920.

Distributed in Canada by Raincoast Books,
8680 Cambie Street
Vancouver BC V6P 6M9

10 9 8 7 6 5 4 3 2 1

Chronicle Books
275 Fifth Street
San Francisco, CA 94103

To my angel, K

CONTENTS

Anonymous

Sulumwoya Spell

[DATE UNKNOWN]

O, her sensual excitement!
O, her erotic swoon!
O, desire, O feminine swoon!

My clasping, thy clasping kindle our erotic swooning!

My embraces, thy embraces kindle our erotic swooning!

My copulation, thy copulation kindle our erotic swooning!

My horizontal motion, thy horizontal motion kindle our
erotic swooning!

My horizontal response, thy horizontal response kindle our
erotic swooning!

My erotic scratching, thy erotic scratching kindle our erotic swooning!

My erotic biting, thy erotic biting kindle our erotic swooning!

My nose rubbing, thy nose rubbing kindle our erotic swooning!

My eyelash biting, thy eyelash biting kindle our erotic swooning!

Ovid

In Summer's Heat

[22 B.C.]

In summer's heat and mid-time of the day,
To rest my limbs upon a bed a lay,
One window shut, the other open stood,
Which gave such light as twinkles in a wood
Like twilight glimpse at setting of the sun,
Or night being past and yet not day begun.
Such light to shamefaced maidens must be shown,
Where they may sport, and seem to be unknown.
Then came Corinna in a long, loose gown,
Her white neck hid with tresses hanging down,
Resembling fair Semiramis going to bed,

Or Lais of a thousand wooers sped.

I snatched her gown, being thin the harm was small,

Yet strived she to be covered therewithal,

And, striving thus as one that would be chaste,

Betrayed herself, and yielded at the last.

Stark naked as she stood before mine eye,

Not one wen in her body could I spy.

What arms and shoulders did I touch and see?

How apt her breasts were to be pressed by me?

How smooth a belly under her waist saw I?

How large a leg, and what a lusty thigh?

To leave the rest, all liked me passing well;

I clinged her naked body, down she fell.

Judge you the rest. Being tired, she bade me kiss.

Jove send me more such afternoons as this.

Shaykh Umar ibn Muhammed al-Nefzawi

*The Perfumed Garden, or
Concerning Everything that is
Favourable to the Act of Coition*

[1500s]

Know, O Vizir (God be good to you!), if you would have pleasant coition, which ought to give an equal share of happiness to the two combatants and be satisfactory to both, you must first of all toy with the woman, excite her with kisses, by nibbling and sucking her lips, by caressing her neck and cheeks. Turn her over in the bed, now on her back, now on her stomach, till you see by her eyes that the time for pleasure is near, as I have mentioned in the preceding chapter, and certainly I have not been sparing with my observations thereupon.

Then when you observe the lips of the woman to tremble and get red, and her eyes become languishing, and her sighs to become quicker, know that she is hot for coition; then get between her thighs, so that your member can enter into her vagina. If you follow my advice, you will enjoy a pleasant embrace, which will give you the greatest satisfaction, and leave you with a delicious remembrance.

Someone has said:

If you desire coition, place the woman on the ground, cling closely to her bosom, with her lips close to yours; then clasp her to you, suck her breath, bite her; kiss her breasts, her stomach, her flanks, press her close in your arms, so as to make her faint with pleasure; when you see her so far gone, then push your member into her. If you have done as I said, the enjoyment will come to both of you simultaneously. This it is which makes the pleasure of the woman so sweet. But if you neglect my advice the woman will not be satisfied, and you will not have procured her any pleasure.

The coition being finished, do not get up at once, but come down softly on her right side, and if she has conceived, she will bear a male child, if it please God on high!

Sages and Savants (may God grant to all his forgiveness!) have said:

If anyone placing his hand upon the vulva of a woman that is with child pronounces the following words: "In the name of God! may he grant salutation and mercy to his Prophet (salutation and mercy be with him). Oh! my God! I pray to thee in the name of the Prophet to let a boy issue from this conception," it will come to pass by the will of God, and in consideration of our lord Mohammed (the salutation and grace of God be with him), the woman will be delivered of a boy.

Do not drink rain water directly after copulation, because this beverage weakens the kidneys.

If you want to repeat the coition, perfume yourself with sweet scents, then close with the woman, and you will arrive at a happy result.

Do not let the woman perform the act of coition mounted upon you, for fear that in that position some drops of her seminal fluid might enter the canal of your verge and cause a sharp urethritis.

Do not work hard directly after coition as this might affect your health adversely, but go to rest for some time.

Do not wash your verge directly after having withdrawn it from the vagina of the woman, until the irritation has gone down somewhat; then wash it and its opening carefully. Otherwise, do not wash your member frequently. Do not leave the vulva directly after the emission, as this may cause canker.

Sundry Positions for the Coitus

The ways of doing it to women are numerous and variable. And now is the time to make known to you the different positions which are usual.

God, the magnificent, has said: "Women are your field. Go upon your field as you like." According to your wish you can choose the position you like best, provided, of course, that coition takes place in the spot destined for it, that is, in the vulva.

Manner the first—Make the woman lie upon her back, with her thighs raised, then, getting between her legs, introduce your member into her. Pressing your toes to the ground, you can rummage her in a convenient, measured way. This is a good position for a man with a long verge.

Manner the second—If your member is a short one, let the woman lie on her back, lift her legs into the air, so that her right leg be near her right ear, and the left one near her left ear, and in this posture, with her buttocks lifted up, her vulva will project forward. Then put in your member.

Manner the third—Let the woman stretch herself upon the ground, and place yourself between her thighs; then putting one of her legs upon your shoulder, and the other under your arm, near the armpit, get into her.

Manner the fourth—Let her lie down, and put her legs on your shoulders; in this position your member will just face her vulva, which must not touch the ground. And then introduce your member.

Manner the fifth—Let her lie down on her side, then lie yourself down by her on your side, and getting between her thighs, put your member in her vagina. But sidelong coition predisposes for rheumatic pains and sciatica.

Manner the sixth—Make her get down on her knees and elbows, as if kneeling in prayer. In this position the vulva is projected backwards; you then attack her from that side, and put your member into her.

Manner the seventh—Place the woman on her side, and squat between her thighs, with one of her legs on your shoulder and the other between your thighs, while she remains lying on her side. Then you enter her vagina, and make her move by drawing her towards your chest by means of your hands, with which you hold her embraced.

Manner the eighth—Let her stretch herself upon the ground on her back, with her legs crossed; then mount her like a cavalier on horseback, being on your knees, while her legs are placed under her thighs, and put your member into her vagina.

Manner the ninth—Place the woman so that she leans with her front, or, if you prefer it, her back upon a moderate elevation, with her feet set upon the ground. She thus offers her vulva to the introduction of your member.

Manner the tenth—Place the woman near to a low divan, the back of which she can take hold of with her hands; then, getting under her, lift her legs to the height of your navel, and let her clasp you with her legs on each side of your body; in this position plant your verge into her, seizing with your hands the back of the divan. When you begin the action your movements must respond to those of the woman.

Manner the eleventh—Let her lie upon her back on the ground with a cushion under her posterior; then getting between her legs, and letting her place the sole of her right foot against the sole of her left foot, introduce your member.

There are other positions besides the above named in use of the peoples of India. It is well for you to know that the inhabitants of those parts have multiplied the different ways to enjoy women, and they have advanced farther than we in the knowledge and investigation of coitus.

Amongst those manners are the following, called:

1. *El asemeud*, the stopperage.
2. *El modefadâ*, frog fashion.
3. *El mokefâ*, with the toes cramped.
4. *El mokeurmeutt*, with legs in the air.
5. *El setouri*, he-goat fashion.

6. *El loulabi*, the screw of Archimedes.

7. *El kelouci*, the somersault.

8. *Hachou en nekanok*, the tail of the ostrich.

9. *Lebeuss el djoureb*, fitting on of the sock.

10. *Kechef el astine*, reciprocal sight of the posteriors.

11. *Neza el kouss*, the rainbow arch.

12. *Nesedj el kheuzz*, alternative piercing.

13. *Dok el arz*, pounding on the spot.

14. *Nik el kohoul*, coition from the back.

15. *El keurchi*, belly to belly.

16. *El kebachi*, ram-fashion.

17. *Dok el outed*, driving the peg home.

18. *Sebek el heub*, love's fusion.

19. *Tred ech chate*, sheep-fashion.

20. *Kalen el miche*, interchange in coition.

21. *Rekeud el aïr*, the race of the member.

22. *El modakheli*, the fitter-in.

23. *El khouariki*, the one who stops in the house.

24. *Nik el haddadi*, the blacksmith's coition.

25. *El moheundi*, the seducer.

FIRST MANNER—*El asemeud* (the stopperage). Place the woman on her back, with a cushion under her buttocks, then get between her legs, resting the points of your feet against the ground; bend her two thighs against her chest as far as you can; place your hands under her arms so as to enfold her or cramp her shoulders. Then introduce your member, and at the moment of ejaculation draw her towards you. This position is painful for the woman, her thighs being bent upwards and her buttocks raised by the cushion, the walls of her vagina tighten, and the uterus tending forward there is not much room for movement, and scarcely space enough for the intruder; consequently the latter enters with difficulty and strikes against the uterus. This position should therefore not be adopted, unless the man's member is short or soft.

SECOND MANNER—*El modefedâ* (frog fashion). Place the woman on her back, and arrange her thighs so that they touch the heels, which latter are thus coming close to the buttocks; then down you sit in this kind of merry thought, facing the vulva, in which you insert your member; you then place her knees under your armpits; and taking firm hold of the upper part of her arms, you draw her towards you at the crisis.

THIRD MANNER—*El mokefâ* (with the toes cramped). Place the woman on her back, and squat on your knees, between her thighs, gripping the ground with your toes; raise her knees as high as your sides, in order that she may cross her legs over your back, and then pass her arms round your neck.

FOURTH MANNER—*El mokeurmeutt* (with legs in the air). The woman lying on her back, you put her thighs together and raise her legs up until the soles of her feet look at the ceiling; then enfolding her within your thighs you insert your member, holding her legs up with your hands.

FIFTH MANNER—*El setouri* (he-goat fashion). The woman being crouched on her side, you let her stretch out the leg on which she is resting, and squat down between her thighs with your calves bent under you. Then you lift her uppermost leg so that it rests on your back, and introduce your member. During the action you take hold of her shoulders, or, if you prefer it, by the arms.

SIXTH MANNER—*El loulabi* (the screw of Archimedes). The man being stretched on his back the woman sits on his member, facing him; she then places her hands upon the bed so that she can keep her stomach from touching the man's, and moves up and downwards, and if the man is supple he assists her from below. If in this position she wants to kiss him, she need only stretch her arms along the bed.

SEVENTH MANNER—*El kelouci* (the somersault). The woman must wear a pair of pantaloons, which she lets drop upon her heels; then she stoops, placing her head between her feet, so that her neck is in the opening of her pantaloons. At that moment, the man, seizing her legs, turns her upon her back, making her perform a somersault; then with her legs curved under him he brings his member right against her vulva, and, slipping it between her legs, inserts it.

It is alleged that there are women who, while lying on their back, can place their feet behind their head without the help of pantaloons or hands.

EIGHTH MANNER—*Hachou en nekanok* (the tail of the ostrich). The woman lying on her back along the bed, the man kneels in front of her, lifting up her legs until her head and shoulders only are resting on the bed; his member having penetrated into her vagina, he seizes and sets into motion the buttocks of the woman who, on her part, twines her legs around his neck.

NINTH MANNER—*Lebeuss el djoureb* (fitting on of the sock). The woman lies on her back. You sit down between her legs and place your member between the lips of her vulva, which you fit over it with your thumb and first finger; then you move so as to procure for your member, as far as it is in contact with the woman, a lively rubbing, which action you continue until her vulva gets moistened with the liquid emitted from your verge. When she is thus amply prepared for enjoyment by the alternate coming and going of your weapon in her scabbard, put it into her full length.

TENTH MANNER—*Kechef el astine* (reciprocal sight of the posteriors). The man lying stretched out on his back, the woman sits down upon his member with her back to the man's face, who presses her sides between his thighs and legs, whilst she places her hands upon the bed as a support for her movements, lowering her head, her eyes are turned towards the buttocks of the man.

ELEVENTH MANNER—*Neza el kouss* (the rainbow arch). The woman is lying on her side; the man also on his side, with his face towards her back, pushes in between her legs and introduces his member, with his hands lying on the upper part of her back. As to the woman, she then gets hold of the man's feet, which she lifts up as far as she can, drawing him close to her; thus she forms with the body of the man an arch, of which she is the rise.

TWELFTH MANNER—*Nesedj el kheuzz* (the alternate movement of piercing). The man in sitting attitude places the soles of his feet together, and lowering his thighs, draws his feet nearer to his member; the woman sits down upon his feet, which he takes care to keep firm together. In this position the two thighs of the woman are pressed against the man's flanks, and she puts her arms round his neck. Then the man clasps the woman's ankles, and drawing his feet nearer to his body, brings the woman, who is sitting on them, within range of his member, which then enters her vagina. By moving his feet he sends her back and brings her forward again, without ever withdrawing his member entirely.

The woman makes herself as light as possible, and assists as well as she can in this come-and-go movement; her co-operation is, in fact, indispensable for it. If the man apprehends that his member may come out entirely, he takes her round the waist, and she receives no other impulse than that which is imparted to her by the feet of the man upon which she is sitting.

THIRTEENTH MANNER—*Dok el arz* (pounding on the spot). The man sits down with his legs stretched out; the woman then places herself astride on his thighs, crossing her legs behind the back of the man, and places her vulva opposite his member, which latter she guides into her vagina; she then places her arms round his neck, and he embraces her sides and waist, and helps her to rise and descend upon his verge. She must assist in his work.

FOURTEENTH MANNER—*Nik el kohoul* (coitus from the back). The woman lies down on her stomach and raises her buttocks by help of a cushion; the man approaches from behind, stretches himself on her back and inserts his tool, while the woman twines her arms round the man's elbows. This is the easiest of all methods.

FIFTEENTH MANNER—*El keurchi* (belly to belly). The man and the woman are standing upright, face to face; she opens her thighs; the man then brings his feet forward between those of the woman, who advances hers a little. In this position the man must have one of his feet somewhat in advance of the other. Each of the two has the arms round the other's hips; the man introduces his verge, and the two move thus intertwined after a manner called *neza' el dela*, which I shall explain later, if it please God Almighty. (See FIRST MANNER.)

SIXTEENTH MANNER—*El kebachi* (after the fashion of the ram). The woman is on her knees, with her forearms on the ground; the man approaches from behind, kneels down, and lets his member penetrate into her vagina, which she presses out as much as possible; he will do well in placing his hands on the woman's shoulders.

SEVENTEENTH MANNER—*Dok el outed* (driving the peg home). The woman enlaces with her legs the waist of the man, who is standing, with her arms passed around his neck, steadying herself by leaning against the wall. Whilst she is thus suspended the man insinuates his pin into her vulva.

EIGHTEENTH MANNER—*Sebek el heub* (love's fusion). While the woman is lying on her right side, extend yourself on your left side; your left leg remains extended, and you raise your right one till it is up to her flank, when you lay her upper leg upon your side. Thus her uppermost leg serves the woman as a support for her back. After having introduced your member you move as you please, and she responds to your action as she pleases.

NINETEENTH MANNER—*Tred ech chate* (coitus of the sheep). The woman is on her hands and knees; the man, behind her, lifts her thighs till her vulva is on a level with his member, which he then inserts. In this position she ought to place her head between her arms.

TWENTIETH MANNER—*Kaleb el miche* (interchange in coition). The man lies on his back. The woman, gliding in between his legs, places herself upon him with her toe-nails against the ground; she lifts up the man's thighs, turning them against his own body, so that his virile member faces her vulva, into which she guides it; she then places her hands upon the bed by the sides of the man. It is, however, indispensable that the woman's feet rest upon a cushion to enable her to keep her vulva in concordance with his member.

In this position the parts are exchanged, the woman fulfilling that of the man, and vice-versa.

There is a variation to this manner. The man stretches himself out upon his back, while the woman kneels with her legs under her, but between his legs. The remainder conforms exactly to what has been said above.

TWENTY-FIRST MANNER—*Rekeud el aïr* (the race of the member). The man on his back, supports himself with a cushion under his shoulders, but his posterior must retain contact with the bed. Thus placed, he draws up his thighs until his knees are on a level with his face; then the woman sits down, impaling herself on his member; she must not lie down, but keep seated as if on horseback, the saddle being represented by the knees and the stomach of the man. In that position she can, by the play of her knees, work up and down and down and up. She can also place her knees on the bed, in which case the man accentuates the movement by plying his thighs, whilst she holds with her left hand on to his right shoulder.

TWENTY-SECOND MANNER—*El modakheli* (the fitter-in). The woman is seated on her coccyx, with only the points of her buttocks touching the ground; the man takes the same position, her vulva facing his member. Then the woman puts her right thigh over the left thigh of the man, whilst he on his part puts his right thigh over her left one.

The woman, seizing with her hands her partner's arms, gets his member into her vulva; and each of them leaning alternately a little back, and holding each other by the upper part of the arms, they initiate a swaying movement, moving with little concussions, and keeping their movements in exact rhythm by the assistance of their heels, which are resting on the ground.

TWENTY-THIRD MANNER—*El khouariki* (the one who stops at home). The woman being couched on her back, the man lies down upon her, with cushions held in his hands.

After his member is in, the woman raises her buttocks as high as she can off the bed, the man following her up with his member well inside; then the woman lowers herself again upon the bed, giving some short shocks, and although they do not embrace, the man must stick like glue to her. This movement they continue, but the man must make himself light and must not be ponderous, and the bed must be soft; in default of which the exercise cannot be kept up without break.

TWENTY-FOURTH MANNER—*Nik el haddadi* (the coition of the blacksmith). The woman lies on her back with a cushion under her buttocks, and her knees raised as far as possible towards her chest, so that her vulva stands out as a target; she then guides her partner's member in.

The man executes for some time the usual action of coition, then draws his tool out of the vulva, and glides it for a moment between the thighs of the woman, as the smith withdraws the glowing iron from the furnace in order to plunge it into cold water. This manner is called *sferdgeli*, position of the quince.

TWENTY-FIFTH MANNER—*El moheundi* (the seducer). The woman lying on her back, the man sits between her legs, with his croupe on his feet; then he raises and separates the woman's thighs, placing her legs under his arms, or over his shoulders; he then takes her round the waist, or seizes her shoulders.

The preceding descriptions furnish a large number of procedures, that cannot well be all put into proof; but with such a variety to choose from, the man who finds one of them difficult to practice, can easily find plenty of others more to his convenience.

I have not made mention of positions which it appeared to me impossible to realize, and if there be anybody who thinks that those which I have described are not exhaustive, he has only to look for new ones.

Hippocrates

Orgasm

[4 0 0   B . C .]

During intercourse, once a woman's genitals are vigorously rubbed and her womb titillated, a lustfulness [*an itch*] overwhelms her down there, and the feeling of pleasure and warmth pools out through the rest of her body. A woman also has an ejaculation, furnished by her body, occurring at the same time inside the womb, which has become wet, as well as on the outside because the womb is now gaping wide open.

A woman feels pleasure right from the start of intercourse, through the entire time of it, right up until the moment when the man pulls out; if she feels an orgasm coming on, she ejaculates with him, and then she no longer feels pleasure. But if she feels no oncoming orgasm, her pleasure stops when his does. It's like when one throws cold water onto boiling water, the boiling ceases immediately. The same with the man's sperm falling into the womb, it extinguishes the warmth and pleasure of the woman.

Her pleasure and warmth, though, surge the moment the sperm descends in the womb, then it fades. Just as when wine is poured on a flame, it gives a spurt before it goes out for good.

Neil Jordan

Seduction

[1993]

Y ou don't believe me, do you," he said, "you don't believe anything, but I've seen her"—and he repeated it again, but I didn't have to listen this time, I could imagine it so vividly. The naked woman's clothes lying in a heap under the drop from the road where the beach was clumsy with rocks and pebbles, her fat body running on the sand at the edge of the water, the waves splashing round her thick ankles. The imagining was just like the whole summer, it throbbed with forbidden promise. I had been back in the town two days and each day we had hung around till twilight, when the hours seemed longest, when the day would extend its dying till it seemed ready to burst, the sky like a piece of stretched gauze over it, grey, melancholy, yet infinitely desirable and unknown. This year I was a little afraid of him, though he was still smaller than me. I envied and loved his pointed shoes that were turned up and scuffed white and his hair that curled and dripped with oil that did its best to contain it in a duck's tail. I loved his assurance, the nonchalant way he let the vinegar run from the chip bag onto the breast of his off-white shirt. But I kept all this quiet knowing there were things he envied about me too. I think each of us treasured this envy, longing to know how the other had changed but disdaining to ask. We loved to talk in monosyllables conscious of the other's envy, a hidden mutual delight underneath it like blood. Both of us stayed in the same guest-house as last year. My room faced the sea, his the grounds of the convent, the basketball pitch with the tennis-net running through it where the nuns swung rackets with brittle, girlish laughter. We sniffed the smell of apples that came over the town from the monastery orchard behind it and the smell of apples in late August meant something different to me this year, as did the twilight. Last year it would have meant an invitation to rob. I wondered did it mean the same to him. I concluded that it must, with his hair like that. But then he was tougher, more obscene.

"Look, she's coming out now." He nodded his head sideways towards the chip-shop and I stared in through the dripping steamed glass. It looked warm inside, warm and greasy. I saw the woman coming out of the tiny corridor in which the chips were fried, leaning against the steel counter. Some older boys waiting for orders threw jibes at her. She laughed briefly, then took out a cigarette, put it in her mouth and lit it. I knew that when the cigarette came out its tip would be covered in lipstick, the way it happens in films. When she took the coins from them two gold bangles slipped down onto her fat wrist. There was something mysterious, hard and tired about her, some secret behind those layers of make-up which those older boys shared. I watched them laughing and felt the hard

excitement of the twilight, the apples. And I believed him
then, though I knew how much he lied. I believed him
because I wanted to believe it, to imagine it, the nakedness
of this fat blonde woman who looked older than her
twenty-five years, who sang every Saturday night at the
dance in the local hotel.

"Leanche's her name. Leanche the lion."

"Lioness," I said, being the erudite one. He looked at
me and spat.

"When'll you ever dry up." I spat too. "Here." He
held out the chip bag.

I took one. It was like when I came to the guest-
house and he had already been there a day. He stood in
the driveway pulling leaves off the rhododendron bush as
we took things off the rack of our Ford car. I looked over
at him, the same as last year, but with a new sullenness
in his face. I hoped my face was even more deadpan. He
turned his face away when I looked but stayed still,
pulling the oily leaves till the unpacking was finished.
Then I went over to talk to him. He said that the town

was a dump this year, that there was an Elvis playing in the local cinema. He said that Ford cars with high backs had gone out since the ark. I asked him had his people got a car yet and he said no. But somehow it seemed worse to have a car with a high back and rusted doors than no car at all. He said "Come on, we'll go to town" and we both walked to the gate, to the road that ran from the pier towards the town where every house was painted white and yellow and in summer was a guest-house.

"Let's go inside" he said, just as it was getting dark and the last of the queue filed from the chipper. "We've no money" I said. "Anyway, I don't believe you." I hoped my fright didn't glare through. "It's true," he said. "The man in the cinema told me." "Did he see her?" I asked. "No, his brother did." There was disdain in the statement that I couldn't have countered.

We pushed open the glass door, he took out a comb as he was doing so and slicked it through his hair. I went over to the yellow jukebox and pushed idly at the buttons "Are ye puttin' money in it son." I heard. I turned and saw her looking at me, the ridiculously small curls of her hair tumbling round her large face. Her cheeks were red and her dress was low and her immense bosom showed white through it, matching the grease-stains on her apron. "No" I said and began to blush to the roots, "we just wanted to know . . ."

"Have you got the time," Jamie burst in. "Have you eyes in your head," she countered. She raised her arm and pointed to a clock in the wall above her. Twenty past ten.

We had walked past the harbour and the chip-shop and the Great Northern Hotel that were all the same as last year. The rich hotelier's son who had left the priest-hood and had gone a little mad was on the beach again, turning himself to let his stomach get the sun now that his back was brown. Jamie told me about the two Belfast sisters who wore nylons and who were Protestants, how they sat in the cinema every night waiting for something. He asked me had I ever got anything off a girl that wore nylons. I asked him had he. He said nothing, but spat on the ground and stirred the spittle with the sole of his shoe.

The difference in the town was bigger now, lurid, hemming us in. I borrowed his comb and slicked it through my hair but my hair refused to quiff, it fell back each time on my forehead, incorrigibly flat and sandy-coloured.

The woman in the chip-shop smiled and crooked her arm on the counter, resting her chin on her fist. The folds of fat bulged round the golden bangles. "Anything else you'd like to know." I felt a sudden mad urge to surpass myself, to go one better than Jamie's duck-tailed hair. "Yeah," I began, "do you . . ." Then I stopped. She had seemed a little like an idiot to me but something more than idiocy stopped me. "Do I!" she said and turned her head towards me, looking at me straight in the eyes. And in the green irises underneath the clumsy mascara there was a mocking light that frightened me. I thought of the moon with a green mist around it like the Angel of Death in the Ten Commandments. I saw her cheeks and heard the wash of the sea and imagined her padding feet on the sand. And I shivered at the deeper, infinite idiocy there, the lurid idiocy that drew couples into long grass to engage in something I wasn't quite sure of. I blushed with shame, with longing to know it, but was saved by her banging hand on the silver counter. "If you don't want chips, hop it." "Don't worry," said Jamie, drawing the comb through his hair. "Don't worry," I said, listening to his hair click oilily, making for the glass door. "I still don't believe you," I said to him outside. "Do you want to wait up and see then." I didn't answer. Jamie drew a series of curves that formed a naked woman in the window-dew. We both watched them drip slowly into a mess of watery smudges.

We had gone to the cinema that first night, through the yellow-emulsioned doorway into the darkness of the long hall, its windows covered with sheets of brown paper. I smelt the smells of last year, the sweaty felt brass of the seats and the dust rising from the aisle to be changed into diamonds by the cone of light above. There was a scattering of older couples there, there was Elvis on the screen, on a beach in flowered bathing-trunks, but no Belfast sisters. "Where are they?" I asked him, with the ghost of a triumphant note in my voice. He saved himself by taking out a butt, lighting it and pulling harshly on it. We drank in Elvis silently. Later the cinema projectionist put his head between both our shoulders and said "Hey boys, you want to see the projection-room?" His breath smelt the same as last year, of cigarettes and peppermint. But this year we said no.

Later again I sat in my room and watched the strand, where two nuns were swinging tennis-rackets on a court they had scrawled on the sand. It was ten past nine and the twilight was well advanced, the balance between blue and grey almost perfect. I sat on my bed and pulled my knees to my chest, rocking softly, listening to the nuns' tinkling laughter, staring at the billows their habits made with each swing of their arms. Soon even the nuns left and the strand was empty but for the scrawled tennis-court and the marks of their high-heeled boots. But I watched on, hearing the waves break, letting the light die in the room around me, weeping for the innocence of last year.

We pressed ourselves against the wall below the road, trying to keep our feet from slipping off the large round pebbles. My father was calling my name from the drive of the guest-house. His voice seemed to echo right down the beach, seeming worried and sad. Soon even the echo died away and Jamie clambered up and peeped over the top and waved to me that no-one was there. Then we walked down the strand making a long trail of footsteps in the half-light. We settled ourselves behind an upturned boat and began to wait. We waited for hours, till Jamie's face became pinched and pale, till my teeth began to chatter. He stared at the sea and broke the teeth from his comb, one by one, scattering them at his feet. I spat in the sand and watched how my spittle rolled into tiny sandballs. The sea washed and sucked and washed and sucked but remained empty of fat women. Then Jamie began to talk, about kisses with the mouth open and closed, about the difference between the feel of a breast under and over a jumper, between nylons and short white socks. He talked for what seemed hours and after a while I stopped listening. I knew he was lying anyway. Then suddenly I noticed he had stopped talking. I didn't know how long he had stopped, but I knew it had been some time before I noticed it. I turned and saw he was hunched up, his face blank like a child's. All the teeth were broken from his comb, his hand was clutching it insensibly and he was crying softly. His hair was wild with curls, the oil was dripping onto his forehead, his lips were purple with the cold. I touched him on the elbow and when his quiet sobbing didn't stop I took off my coat and put it gingerly round his shoulders. He shivered and moved in close to me and his head touched my chest and lay there. I held him there while he slept, thinking how much smaller than me he was after all.

There was a thin rim of light round the edge of the sea when he woke. His face was pale, —though not as grey as that light, and his teeth had begun to chatter. "What happened?" he asked, shaking my coat off. "You were asleep," I said, "you missed it," and began a detailed account of how the woman had begun running from the pier right up past me to the end of the strand, how her breasts had bobbed as the water splashed round her thick ankles. "Liar" he said. "Yes" I said. Then I thought of home. "What are we going to do?" I asked him. He rubbed his eyes with his hand and drew wet smudges across each cheek. Then he got up and began to walk towards the sea. I followed him, knowing the sea would obliterate his tears and any I might have. When he came near the water he began to run, splashing the waves round him with his feet and I ran too, but with less abandon, and when he fell face down in the water I fell too. When I could see him through the salt water he was laughing madly in a crying sort of way, ducking his head in and out of the water the way swimmers do. I got to my feet and tried to pull him up but his clothes were clinging to every bone of his thin body. Then I felt myself slipping, being pulled from the legs and I fell in the water again and I felt his arms around my waist, tightening, the way boys wrestle, but more quietly then, and I felt his body not small any longer, pressing against mine. I heard him say "this is the way lovers do it" and felt his mouth on my neck but I didn't struggle, I knew that in the water he couldn't see my tears or see my smile.

Gustave Flaubert

Egyptian Belly Dancers

[1850]

CAIRO

I'll have this marvelous Hasan el-Belbeissi come again. He'll dance The Bee for me. Done by such a bardash [*a homosexual*] as he, it can scarcely be a thing for babes.

Speaking of bardashes, this is what I know about them. Here it is quite accepted. One admits one's sodomy, and it is spoken of at table in the hotel. Sometimes you do a bit of denying, and then everybody teases you and you end up confessing. Travelling as we are for educational purposes, and charged with a mission by the government,

41

we have considered it our duty to indulge in this form of ejaculation. So far the occasion has not presented itself. We continue to seek it, however. It's at the baths that such things
take place. You reserve the bath for yourself (five francs
including masseurs, pipe, coffee, sheet and towel) and you
skewer your lad in one of the rooms. Be informed, furthermore, that all the bath-boys are bardashes. The final
masseurs, the ones who come to rub you when all the rest is
done, are usually quite nice young boys. We had our eye on
one in an establishment very near our hotel. I reserved the
bath exclusively for myself. I went, and the rascal was away
that day! I was alone in the hot room, watching the daylight
fade through the great circles of glass in the dome. Hot water
was flowing everywhere; stretched out indolently I thought
of a quantity of things as my pores tranquilly dilated. It is
very voluptuous and sweetly melancholy to take a bath like
that quite alone, lost in those dim rooms where the slightest
noise resounds like a cannon shot, while the naked kellaas
call out to one another as they massage you, turning you over
like embalmers preparing you for the tomb. That day (the

day before yesterday, Monday) my kellaa was rubbing me gently, and when he came to my noble parts, he lifted up my boules d'amour to clean them, then continued rubbing my chest with his left hand he began to pull with his right on my prick, and as he drew it up and down he leaned over my shoulder and said, "baksheesh, baksheesh" ["*tip, tip*"]. He was a man in his fifties, ignoble, disgusting—imagine the effect, and the word "baksheesh, baksheesh." I pushed him away a little, saying, "lah, lah" ["*no, no*"]—he thought I was angry and took on a craven look—then I gave him a few pats on the shoulder saying, "lah, lah" again but more gently—he smiled a smile that meant, "You're not fooling me—you like it as much as anybody, but today you've decided against it for some reason." As for me, I laughed aloud like a dirty old man, and the shadowy vault of the bath echoed with the sound.

. . . A week ago I saw a monkey in the street jump on a donkey and try to jack him off—the donkey brayed and kicked, the monkey's owner shouted, the monkey itself squealed—apart from two or three children who laughed and me who found it very funny, no one paid any attention.

When I described this to M. Belin, the secretary at the consulate, he told me of having seen an ostrich try to violate a donkey. Max had himself jacked off the other day in a deserted section among some ruins and said it was very good.

Enough lubricities.

Automedon

Turkish. Belly-dancer. Sexy Tricks.

[90-50 B.C.]

Turkish. Belly-dancer. Sexy tricks.
(That quivering! Those fingernails!)
What do I like best? Hands here, here,
Soft, soft, stroking—or better,
Piping that little old man of mine,
Fondling each foldlet, tonguing,
Tickling, easing, teasing,
Then slipping on top, and . . .
I tell you, she could raise the dead.

Vatsyayana

The Kama Sutra

[100]

he ways of enlarging the lingam must be now related.

When a man wishes to enlarge his lingam, he should rub it with the bristles of certain insects that live in trees, and then, after rubbing it for ten nights with oils, he should again rub it with the bristles as before. By continuing to do this a swelling will be gradually produced in the lingam, and he should then lie on a cot, and cause his lingam to hang down through a hole in the cot. After this he should take away all the pain from the swelling by using cool concoctions. The swelling, which is called

'Suka,' and is often brought about among the people of the Dravida country, lasts for life.

If the lingam is rubbed with the following things, the plant physalis flexuosa, the shavara-kandaka plant, the jalasuka plant, the fruit of the egg-plant, the butter of a she buffalo, the hastri-charma plant, and the juice of the vajrarasa plant, a swelling lasting for one month will be produced.

By rubbing it with oil boiled in the concoctions of the above things, the same effect will be produced, but lasting for six months.

The enlargement of the lingam is also effected by rubbing it or moistening it with oil boiled on a moderate fire along with the seeds of the pomegranate, and the cucumber, the juices of the valuka plant, the hasti-charma plant, and the egg-plant.

In addition to the above, other means may be learnt from experienced and confidential persons.

Sam Keen

The Tantric Vision

[1983]

antra, tantric yoga, or kundalini yoga is an ancient philosophy and practice linking sexuality and consciousness that has appeared in widely separated times and places.[1] It has cropped up in different forms in India, Tibet, and Mexico as well as in the writings of the alchemists, in mystical Christianity, and in theosophy. Its central idea, which seems to have occurred independently to a large number of early thinkers and spiritual adventurers, is that the body contains a number (usually seven) of physio-psychic centers that may become suffused by a current of "sexual" energy that leads to an expansion of consciousness or enlightenment. Although there is a lush variety of symbols in the various traditions, we can identify a common core of beliefs.

In Tantra, as in most forms of sophisticated mysticism, there is a fundamental belief that the human spirit and body are united with the cosmos. It can be stated in several ways: As below, so above; deeper in is further out; the microcosm reflects the macrocosm; every level of the hierarchy of being can be found within man; the human mind is a hologram of the universe.

In the concrete symbolism of religion, this belief is frequently presented in a pictorial way by showing how the human spine, with its seven ascending centers of energy (or chakras), is analogous to the seven-story cosmic mountain—Mt. Meru, Mt. Sinai, or Mt. Analogue. This mountain-spine forms a world pole (*axis mundi*) uniting the lower realms (Hades, the unconscious), middle earth (the everyday world of the ego), and the heavens (the ideal but unseen structures, powers, and presences that underlie and in-form all visible reality). Each of the seven centers of the body vibrates with its cosmic counterpart. We tune in to different levels of reality.

Physical/mental/spiritual illness results from any blockage that prevents us from communication or resonance. Health is being full-bodied, allowing the entire range of cosmic rhythms and intentions to inhabit and harmonize the various physio-psycho-spiritual systems within the body. The story of how we move from dis-ease to health is identical with the account of the ascent of consciousness and the metamorphosis of eros. We become whole by becoming citizens of each of the seven kingdoms of love.

The tantric consensus is that there is a single primal energy-spirit-consciousness that flows through all the cosmos and informs each person. The path of maturation, enlightenment, or transformation involves allowing this power (which is called kundalini or serpent power in the East) to rise up the spine and infuse each of the centers.

In tantric imagery, the food that nourishes the nervous system during the elevation of consciousness is the seminal fluid in men and the erotic fluids in women. The sexual fluid streams up the hollow channel in the middle of the spine (the susumna) and floods each of the chakras until it reaches the brain, at which point enlightenment occurs, with accompanying ecstasy. As the concentrated energy (called variously prana, chi, holy spirit, libido, or orgone) passes through the chakras, it purifies the body and mind and reunites sexuality and spirituality.

Among some scholars and esoteric aspirants, there is a tendency to take the symbolism so literally that it makes nonsense out of Tantra. Much of the interpretive literature discusses quite seriously whether there really is a channel in the spine through which sexual fluid might rise. Such literalism misses the point. The most valuable thing we may learn from tantric symbolism is a vision of how eros may be transformed, of how sexuality matures, of how desire expands, of how motivation changes, in the course of an authentic life journey.

Consider, for instance, the symbolic meaning hidden in the image of the sexual fluid as the fuel of consciousness.

It is a fact of science as well as an abiding mystery that the intention and history of the entire evolutionary process is carried in the genes and chromosomes that flow together with the union of sperm and ovum. Whatever Nature or God is striving to create through this long drama of evolution is implicit in our drive to reproduce. The sexual organs do respond to the entire symphony of being. There is an intentionality, a telos, a purpose, a meaning, a direction encoded within our quest for pleasure. If we understand eros in its fullest sense, we may discover in sexual experience an impulse that may guide us in the unfoldment of consciousness. Perhaps our deepening desire is our surest path toward the sacred. Why should it be so startling to suggest that the cortex (a late-comer in the evolutionary story) might eventually fully understand the cosmic inten-tion that is programmed into the sexual fluids? (Might the image of the kundalini serpent winding its way up the spine be an intuitive prefiguration of the helix of the DNA?)

We make best use of Tantra if we play with its symbolism. I suggest that the seven chakras are symbols of different stages of life and the philosophies and erotic practices that accompany them. The kundalini symbolism is an early developmental psychology. Each chakra represents an orientation to life that is appropriate to a certain stage of the pilgrimage of the psyche. These stages and their correlation to the progression of consciousness and the transformations of eros suggested in this work are as follows:

1. *Anal chakra.* Symbolizes bonding or possession, being held or grasping.

2. *Genital chakra.* Symbolizes the orientation to life as pleasure, play, and game.

Chakras 1 and 2 are parallel to the psychological development of the child, and the sexual awakening of adolescence. The rebel impulse is not encouraged within Eastern philosophy or culture.

3. *The solar plexus chakra.* Symbolizes the orientation to life as power.

Chakra 3 is parallel to the psychological development of the adult.

4. *The heart chakra.* Symbolizes falling in love with the ideal, romance, passion.

5. *The throat chakra.* Symbolizes purgatory, repentance, eating one's projections.

Chakras 4 and 5 parallel the psychological development of the outlaw, the first love affair with a transpersonal self, and the process of metanoia necessary to free the spirit from the myths, roles, and defense mechanisms that were a part of the adult life with its orientation to power and position.

6. *The third eye chakra.* Symbolizes the single vision.

7. *The crown chakra.* Symbolizes the homecoming, return of the Bodhisattva to the world, to live by the rule of compassion.

Chakras 6 and 7 parallel the psychological development of the lover, the unitive glimpse, and the return to the world to follow the vocation of the healer.

---

[1]For more complete information, see Arthur Avalon, *The Serpent Power* (New York: Down Publications, 1974), or Mircea Eliade, *Yoga, Immortality and Freedom* (New York: Bollingen, 1958).

Ernest Hemingway

An Affair

[1952]

I started *The Sun Also Rises* in Valencia on my birthday because I had never completed a novel and everyone else my age had and I felt ashamed. So I wrote it in 6 weeks. I wrote it in Valencia, Madrid, St. Sebastian, Hendaye and Paris. Toward the last it was like a fever. Toward the last I was sprinting, like in a bicycle race, and I did not want to lose my speed making love or anything else and so had my wife go on a trip with two friends of hers down to the Loire. Then I finished and was hollow and lonely and needed a girl very badly. So I was in bed with a no good girl when my wife came home and had to get the girl out onto the roof of the sawmill (to cut lumber for picture frames) and change the sheets and come down to open the door of the court. Everybody happy at the surprise return except the girl on the roof of the sawmill. All small tactical problems you have to work out.

W. Dugdale, *editor*

The Battles of Venus

[c. 1850-1860]

he Battles of Venus a Descriptive Dissertation
of the Various Modes of Enjoyment of the
Female Sex, As Practised in different
Countries, with some curious Information on the
Resources of Lust, Lechery, & Licentiousness, to Revive
the Drooping Faculties and Strengthen the Voluptuous
and Exhausted. From the French.

The first and most obvious mode of enjoyment was
undoubtedly that practised by the generality of mankind,
and which is perhaps the most conducive to generation.

To behold the naked body of a beautiful woman *in front*, her juicy mouth, her heaving breasts, her firm pouting belly, will be allowed part of the finest gratifications of a voluptuous fancy; and consequently to feel and enjoy those parts must be ranked amongst the sweetest delights of sensual fruition.

Now, supposing that in the other modes of fruition, a man is in actual enjoyment of the ultimatum in a woman, and experiences emission either in or out of her body, yet he enjoys not that delightful pressure on those parts above mentioned, he feels not that delicious heaving, neither can insinuate his tongue within her warm lips, kiss or suck them, nor catch her ardent sighs created by her convulsive motion.

The next in degree of pleasure to this mode is perhaps that of enjoying her in the rear.

In this species it must be confessed that, besides the pleasure of novelty and variety, the breast and belly of the woman are not unenjoyed by the roving and pressure of the man's hands; and moreover there are certainly two additional gratifications not known in the former instance, namely, the feeling of her plump, warm buttocks planted in his lap, and the pleasure of handling the delightful mount of Venus, at the same time that he is fixed in, and enjoying it behind.

A woman may be enjoyed by two men at the same time:

The performance would, doubtless, require an extent of parts; but whoever reflects on their proverbial extensive quality, will not doubt of their admitting with ease two guests, after a trial or two, and with sufficiency of natural or artificial lubrication, provided themselves could accommodate their entrance to the convenience of each other.

And in the way above alluded to, I am confident that might be effected. The woman must lie straight, on either side, and the man who attacks her in front must, after entering her, lift her uppermost leg on his buttock. The antagonist in the rear must then accommodate himself to her posture, and glide in likewise.

The men may knock her as hard as they will; so as the woman is careful to keep herself exactly straight, and not to withdraw from one or the other, their violent shocks will only serve to make her more fixed and steady.

Is the prevalent desire of enjoying female virginity, in preference to charms that have been already surrendered, an original dictate of natural lust? or is it a symptom of refined experience, or impotent fastidiousness?

For my part, I am disposed to impute this to observable desire, to the two last causes; since any man may, I fancy, recollect the time when, upon the birth of his first and earliest wishes after woman, all he sighed for was the possession of one of the sex, abstractedly from the circumstance of her virginity. The object of his warm imagination was only fruition; and one handsome woman at that time would have been the same to him as another. Nay, I question whether a youth not initiated into the mysteries of Venus, would not prefer a woman who had been accustomed to dalliance, before one as shy and modest as himself. For in men (as well as women) there is at first a timidity towards familiarity with the other sex, which requires to be dissipated by the lively airs of a courtezan, ere the stripling can enjoy or exert his vigour, and which would damp his efforts, if encountered by a female equally reserved and inexperienced.

The youth himself is conscious of that shame respecting certain actions, implanted by education and custom, he secretly wishes to receive confirmation and encouragement in what he is going about, and he is gradually warmed into delight by the boldness and familiarities of the practised fair, in the same manner as the innocent yet wishful virgin is artfully seduced into enjoyment by the contrivance of her fortunate admirer.

That this eagerness after virginity is not an original lust, I must, indeed, prove from opinion of a certain remote people, who esteem the taking of a maidenhead, as a laborious and illiberal practice, which they delegate to men hired for that purpose, ere themselves condescend to lie with their wives; who are returned with disgrace to their friends, if it is discovered that they have brought their virginity with them.

How fortunate would the men of pleasure esteem themselves, in countries where the opinion chances to differ, to act as the *precursors* even without fee or reward, of these squeamish and delicate gentlemen!

This lust, then, after the *untouched* morsel, I take not to be an original dictate of nature; but consequently to result from much experience with women, which has been demonstrated to lead to novelty of wishes, from fastidious impotence, which, indeed, is only a farther degree or effect of that experience, or from both united.

Yet, in truth, I esteem the fruition of a virgin to be, with respect both to the mind and body of the enjoyer, the highest aggravation of sensual delight.

In the first place his fancy is heated with the prospect of enjoying a woman, after whom he has perhaps long sighed and had been in pursuit, who he thinks has never before been in bed with man, (in whose arms never before man has laid) and in triumphing in the first sight of her virgin beauties, and first fruition of her virgin charms. This precious operation, then, of fancy, has been shown in the highest degree to prepare the body for enjoyment.

Secondly, his body perceives, in that of a virgin, the cause of the greatest aggravation of delight. I mean not only in the coyness and resistance which she makes to his efforts, but when he is on the point of accomplishing them: when arrived, as the poet sings, 'on the brink of giddy rapture,' when in pity to a tender virgin's sufferings, he is intreated not to break fiercely in, but to spare 'fierce dilaceration and dire pangs.' The resistance which the small, and as yet unopened mouth of bliss makes to his eager endeavours, serves only, and that on a physical principle, to strengthen the instrument of his attack, and concurs with the instigation of his ardent fancy, to reinforce his efforts, to unite all the co-operative powers of enjoyment, and to produce an emission copious, rapid, and transporting.

Fancy has been repeatedly observed to heighten fruition. In this case, part of the delight arises from considering that the lewdest part of your body is fixed in the delicious centre of *her* body, that you feel the convulsive wrigglings of the chaste nymph you have so long adored, and at last feel her diffuse her warm juice throughout her dewy sheath, and moisten the hot, ruby crest of your firm-fixed instrument.

Leo Tolstoy

The Relations of the Sexes

[1870]

Attacks of sexual lust engender confusion of thought. The absence of thought rather. The whole world darkens. Man loses his relation to it. Chance, blackness, failure!

■

You have suffered very much poor fellow, from this dreadful passion, especially when you have let it loose and given it headway. I know how it overshadows everything, destroys temporarily all by which the heart and reason live. But the one deliverance is to know that it is a dream, an allurement, which will pass and you will return to true life, to the point at which it seized you. This you can know even during the moments of its power. God help you.

■

. . . You ask what aids there are for struggling with passion. Amongst the minor measures such as labour, fasting, the most effective is poverty, the absence of money, the external appearance of destitution; a position in which, it is evident, one cannot be attractive to any woman. But the chief and best means I know of is incessant struggle, the consciousness that the struggle is not an incidental temporary state, but a constant, unalterable condition of life.

■

It seems to me that being in love is that steam pressure which would burst the engine if the safety valve did not act. The valve opens only under strong pressure; at other times it is closely, tightly, closed; and our object should be to deliberately keep it closed as tightly as possible, applying as many weights as we can, in the desire that it shall not open. It is in this sense I understand the words "He that is able to receive it, let him receive it" (Matt. xix. 12). That is to say, let everyone strive not to marry, but, having married, to live with one's wife as brother and sister. The steam *will* accumulate, the valves *will* lift, but we should not open them ourselves, as we do when we regard intercourse as a lawful pleasure. It is allowable only when we cannot withhold, and when it breaks through against our wish.

Dafydd ap Gwilym

The Penis

[1300s]

By God penis, you must be guarded
with eye and hand
because of this lawsuit, straight-headed pole,
more carefully for evermore;
net-quill of the cunt, because of
complaint a bridle must be put on your snout
to keep you in check so that you are not indicted
again, take heed you despair of minstrels.

I consider you the vilest of rolling-pins,
horn of the scrotum, do not rise up or wave about;

gift of the noble ladies of Christendom,

nut-pole of the lap's cavity,

snare shape, gander

sleeping in its yearling plumage,

neck with a wet head and milk-giving shaft,

tip of a growing shoot, stop your awkward jerking;

crooked blunt one, accursed pole,

the centre pillar of the two halves of a girl,

head of a stiff conger with a hole in it,

blunt barrier like a fresh hazel-pole.

You are longer than a big man's thigh,

a long night's roaming, chisel of a hundred nights;

auger like the shaft of the post,

leather-headed one who is called 'tail'.

You are a sceptre which causes lust,

the bolt of the lid of a girl's bare arse.

There is a pipe in your head,

a whistle for fucking every day.

There is an eye in your pate

which sees every woman as fair;

round pestle, expanding gun,

it is a searing fire to a small cunt;

roof-beam of girls' laps,

the swift growth is the clapper of a bell;

blunt pod, it dug a family,

snare of skin, nostril with a crop of two testicles.

You are a trouserful of wantonness,

your neck is leather, image of a goose's neckbone;

nature of complete falsity, pod of lewdness,

door-nail which causes a lawsuit and trouble.

Consider that there is a writ and an indictment,

lower your head, stick for planting children.

It is difficult to keep you under control,

cold thrust, woe to you indeed!

Often is your lord rebuked,

obvious is the rottenness through your head.

Wilhelm Bolsche

Mystery of the Ovum-cell and the Sperm-cell

[1919]

Whoso an eagle is,
Can swing aloft his pinions,
Outfly the seraphim,
Pierce heavenly dominions.

ANGELUS SILESIUS (1657)

An artificial light of extraordinary power will serve to illuminate an underworld for us in which, but for this light, deep darkness is brooding. As the objects suddenly emerge into brightness, they are to appear fabulously magnified.

Your gaze loses itself in a huge shaft. From the background you see a strange thing moving, a great glistening sphere, without light of its own, but made luminous by our artificial day. It is not moving freely, like a star balanced by gravity in open space. It seems to be shoved downward along the shaft. As you look more closely, you see gleaming up from the bottom something resembling ears of a gigantic wheat-field glistening in the dew. An elastic ball, our sphere glides slowly along this field, help up by the dew and moved by the soft waves of the sea of wheat.

Being perfectly transparent, the ball, as it thus moves along, affords a view into its internal parts. Its outermost layer, which is rather thick, seems as clear and colourless as the crystal of a watch. The only structure of this envelope that we seem to distinguish consists of narrow canals running straight through the cover of the ball, appearing to form an open connection between the free air around the ball and the inside of it.

The inside, the chief portion of the ball, which is sharply divided from the glass envelope by an interspace, shows a very faint opacity only at the centre. Minute particles, like very fine grains, seem to be swimming about in it, but they are very indistinct. The general impression you get is that the entire hollow space is filled with a more or less elastic, sluggish inland water. At one place, not in the middle, another body is observable floating in the sea of the large ball. The second body is quite distinct and, strangely enough, also has the shape and transparency of a glass ball, though its glass wall seems much more delicate, scarcely discernible. It may be compared to a dainty little diving-bell equilibrated by water pressure. This diaphanous little ball, like the larger one, reveals, through all the fluid enveloping it, certain details of its interior structure. An extremely fine network or scaffolding delicate as foam spreads through it.

Perhaps our light is still not bright enough. No matter how you strain your eyes, you cannot for the time being discover anything further, whether on or in our mysterious ball. But your interest is growing, for presently you perceive changes going on within. Considering that the substances inside are soft, you are prepared for such changes. But what you see is remarkable in the extreme and indicates that highly mysterious powers are evidently at work in this fermenting structure of the Underworld.

First we are struck by the fact that the supposed network in the little diving-bell is in active motion. It seems to be separating, as we look at it, into loose strands. We think we can count twenty-four strands. But we have no time to pause very long.

All of a sudden a bright little point appears near the bell in the surrounding fluid. Perhaps it was there before, but until now it was not noticeable. It turns out to be, not so much a real body, as rather an eddy in the sea. Though you perceive no actual motion, you get the impression that an invisible little turbine has begun to work in the middle of the water. The effect of its action soon becomes apparent in the form of a little sun radiating rays of water round about. But no sooner have you become aware of this, than you observe two turbines producing a double eddy. This quickly grows more evident.

The two turbine centres, each with its radiating sun, draw apart, and now they actually go through distinct motions. But again how strange! Their suns do not fully detach themselves. On the side where the rays of the whirling suns at first overlapped, a sort of connecting current remains, even when they have moved further apart, as if longer and longer streaks were thrown out in that direction, so that, as the distance between them increases, the pivots should not wholly loose touch with each other in their action. As the field enlarges, the whirling picture finally assumes the form of a spindle. In the middle are parallel wave columns extending from turbine head to turbine head; and from these heads, as the ends of the spindle, the two little suns emit rays on each side.

You have concentrated your attention exclusively upon this play of forces with its rapidly changing phases.

Of a sudden you observe that something else, without your having noticed it, has entered the whirl. The bright little diving-bell, which was swimming close by in the same sea, now suddenly grown so turbulent, is all at once drawn into the commotion. Can it be that the turbine rays have struck it directly and stirred it up? In speaking of turbines and eddies I am, of course, only using an image. It may be that in the miraculous scene here enacted powers are at work, radiating and overlapping each other, far finer than the crude comparison with turbines and eddies implies. But that something in this play of forces is now seizing and overpowering the diving-bell is certain.

Suddenly its glass wall breaks and shivers into invisible bits. Its entire contents, the original pieces of that delicate net which seemed to be woven of foam, empty into the open sea, which the turbines are restlessly ploughing. For a while the pieces curl wildly and wind about one another like a torn net quivering in the water. All at once, however, a new order sets in in this play of loose shreds. Though the loose strands are not rewoven into the old net, they seem, under the guidance of a strange power, to be pushed and gathered together into systematic order by a very definite kind of current, each part remaining loose.

Absorbed by this new drama of the bursting and emptying of the diving-bell, we have for a while quite forgotten our free turbines. Now they force themselves upon our attention. We recognize that the turbines, which previously may have produced the bursting of the diving-bell by their wild gyrations, are the restorers of order among the defenceless, tiny parts of the net. In the midst of the general shipwreck the whirling spindle traversed the entire area formerly occupied by the diving-bell. While the pieces of net were wildly curling and serpentining, it assumed such a position that now the suns at its ends emit their rays precisely above and below the place where the wreck occurred, and the great connecting rays of the spindle pass directly across the place of the catastrophe where the pieces of net are quivering.

The moment they have the drifting remnants of the catastrophe, the net fragments, within their field, they begin to exercise their force upon them, which arranges them in systematic order. The fragments are driven into the middle of the connecting strand of the spindle and are there jammed up as if at a point of perfect equilibrium. For a moment it seems that the force waves of the spindle between sun and sun are about to form a new diving-bell, in which the old pieces of net will remain in a new rigid arrangement. The drama seems to have passed the climax. But no. The pieces thus jammed together, and, as it were, rescued, now begin a new unexpected performance.

We have paid no attention to their number. Now we are surprised to see that there are so many. We thought we counted only two dozen at first. Now we count carefully and find there are forty-eight. Each of the little strands must have quietly divided into two, each must have reeled off from itself a piece equal to half its length. On nearing the middle of the spindle, these forty-eight arrange themselves prettily, like a regiment of soldiers, into two rows of twenty-four each, one behind the other. But we no sooner perceive this and count the number in a row, than the regiment begins to move of its own accord within the region of the spindle. The two rows separate and move away from each other, one advancing to the under sun, the other to the upper sun. The middle of the spindle becomes empty? What will happen now?

While we are still looking at these things with intense interest, a glance around discloses the fact that in the meantime a change has taken place in the entire structure in the sea. Spindle and suns together with the forty-eight pieces of net under their aegis have slowly floated away from their position in the sea toward the envelope of the ball, which still encompasses the whole. The magic ship with its crew of two regiments at the turbine ends seems to be wanting to land. A moment longer and one end touches the envelope. The upper turbine swimming in advance will soon have to spread its rays flat against the surface. In fact, a sort of wave is seen arching at that point, and a small part of the current is already visibly crowded by the turbine against the surface.

You expect that in the next instant the glass cover will be broken through. But that does not happen. You again observe that this cover and the contents of the ball, which it envelops, are not in immediate contact but separated by a narrow interspace, into which the wart-like elevation can crowd without bursting the upper envelope.

Will the whole spindle-shaped body press after it and enter the space between? It seems a difficult thing to do and as a matter of fact is not done. The onward march has ceased. All at once the spindle snaps in the middle. Its one half, which, with the advance part at the edge, formed a sort of wave or wart on the main body of the ball, entirely severs its connection with it. The wart unreels itself loose, as it were, and is finally seen lying as a separate little ball in the narrow interspace between the transparent glass envelope and the main part of the ball. In the wart have entered a part of the substance of the sea, one of the turbine pivots, and one of the rows of twenty-four, which in the meantime have crowded more and more closely against the forward turbine of the little ship, while making for land.

The other half of the spindle, with its turbine and with the other row of twenty-four assembled around it, has dived back into the ball. As if vehemently rebounding from the violence of the break, it keeps sinking, sinking, without halt until it has reached the middle. But even there it does not come to rest. A new phase of the puzzling drama begins.

The half of the spectral little ship left in the waters begins to rebuild itself into a whole. Its remaining pivot doubles. Two turbines are formed and then, as they move away from each other without becoming completely detached, a new spindle. Again this spindle arranges the remaining twenty-four pieces of net in its middle and with them begins a journey towards the surface of the sea. But this time one thing does not happen. The twenty-four fragments of net do not again double into forty-eight. In order to form two parts, they arrange themselves in rows of twelve, one behind the other. Again the slow voyage begins; again the two members separate, as before, to withdraw to the two opposite turbine pivots. But now there are only twelve fragments, not twenty-four, at each end of the little ship. As for the rest precisely the same thing as before takes place at the surface of the large ball. The wart wave swells, the spindle snaps, its one head slips with its crew of twelve into the interspace under the glass envelope, the other head with its crew of twelve returns to the depths of the sea. Compared with the tiny little balls lying out there on the outskirts, the large ball is still a giant. This time the sinking half of the permanent submarine boat seems to remain at rest. It does not double its turbine, but is apparently bringing it to a complete standstill. In fact, it is forming a new diving-bell round its fragments of net, which immediately weave themselves into a reticulum. The whole seems to have returned to about the position from which it originally started: There is only one exception. The net itself, without any addition from the outside, cannot furnish more than twelve pieces of the original size. Even if they double, they can yield only twenty-four, never again forty-eight. There must be a mystery in this. It must have a significance.

In the meantime quiet has been restored in the whole ball. Only the soft beating of the waves on the wet surface of the wheat-field upon which it lies still remains outwardly as active as before, driving it incessantly further down the colossal arch of the shaft.

To what world has our fancy carried us? Were we looking into the phantom turmoils of a primaeval world, one of those cosmic nebulae at the beginning of things dreamt of by astronomers? Or were we looking into the convulsions of a planet still not quite cooled, around which a white cloud envelope floats, like bubbling, steaming water, an envelope such as surrounds the colossus of our solar system, Jupiter, whose real globe seems to be the dusky red spot but occasionally seen glowing as through a veil? Are those two little bodies to which we saw the ball give birth, without liberating them entirely, offshoots of a star in labour, like our moon, concerning which there is a suspicion that once upon a time it wrenched loose bodily, like a young shoot, from the great ball of the earth, without being able to escape entirely from the earth's force of attraction, in which it is held captive?

Nothing of the kind.

In our boldest flights of fancy we never left the earth. We remained on its inhabited surface, in the very thick of the welter of humanity. From this humanity we picked out one human female in good health and of mature years. We simply looked into the depths of certain organs of this female body while the body 'lived' in its normal condition and while these organs were developing a very remarkable activity. How we managed to do it is immaterial. Perhaps the next century will invent an apparatus for it, which, on the analogy of our Roentgen rays, will suffuse the whole human body with light without disturbing its vital activities, will perhaps project upon a white wall a faithful picture of even the finest internal parts and at the same time vastly magnify those parts and their movements. In the meantime our imagination serves us. It magnified everything for us at will and threw light upon everything.

The mystery that was unfolded before us, without seeming to have been brought to a final solution, was the process that takes place in and on the human female egg, shortly or immediately preceding the act of impregnation by the male semen.

For the process of generation the female of the human species produces eggs just like a hen. The human eggs, however, are not deposited outside the body like those of a hen. The evolution of the new little human being takes place entirely inside the mother, in the 'womb.' But the human eggs originate in precisely the same way as those of the hen, in a special organ of the female body, the ovary. From childhood on every nor-mally developed woman carries in her body two ovaries, just as she carries two lungs, two kidneys, two brain halves. In these ovaries many thousands of eggs develop, each of which, when mature and fertilized, produces a new human being. For reproduction, fertilization is absolutely essential, and in order to be fertilized (for which a second being, a male, is required) the egg undergoes peculiar processes, the agitated course of which we have just followed with our imagination.

The vault into which we have been transported is, very highly magnified, one of the two so-called oviducts of the female. The oviducts, or Fallopian tubes, connect the ovaries with the larger passage of the uterus.

The ball that moved along in it is the egg itself.

The actual size of the egg is not quite one-fifth of a millimetre, hence to the naked eye a barely perceptible point.

The transparent envelope encloses the yolk, or vitellus, which in the human egg is as strikingly transparent as the envelope. Within the substance of the egg floats the so-called germinal vesicle or nucleus.

We must imagine that the egg has just made its escape from the ovary, where it was previously imbedded like a bud in a special sheath, the so-called Graafian follicle.

It is now on its way from the ovary to the uterus in the intermediate shaft of the oviduct.

The wet ears of wheat, which seem to project into this shaft and sweep our ball downward with their soft wave beat, are in reality the fine hair-like processes, or so-called ciliated cells, which line the walls of the female organs of generation and by their movements through the oviduct convey to the uterus the escaped egg rushing to impregnation.

In the meantime the egg itself undergoes the last maturing process necessary before the expected impregnation. We have seen what happens. The nucleus of the egg or the germinal vesicle temporarily leaves its place, changes, and by dividing twice helps to produce the two little bodies between the transparent envelope and the yolk. For the sake of precision I was careful to observe that in our panorama the relations of both size and time were rather arbitrarily chosen. In all probability these processes do not follow each other so rapidly. The expulsion of the two little parts of the body in the egg begins when it is still attached to the ovary in its Graafian follicle, and its final act is synchronous with the beginning of the process of impregnation. Nevertheless, in this, as in all other instances, the time of development no doubt varies greatly in individual cases. We therefore assume a case with somewhat retarded development, but with a certain excess of speed to make up for the retardation and gain a slight start in advance. Such a case probably gives the most vivid idea of what actually takes place.

The extruded minute bodies are called 'polar globules,' a name now antiquated and therefore inappropriate. When they were first discovered their significance was not known. It was evident to the view that when the egg reached its highest degree of maturity, it rid itself of something. It threw out two minute secondary eggs, each of which received a little piece of yolk and a considerable part of nucleus from the general contents. These secondary products as such had no connection whatever with the subsequent development of the child from the egg. Now, was the extrusion of these two little bodies really no more than a removal of waste? Or was it due, perhaps, to a superfluity of force developed in the egg during its short period of waiting before the great act, which made it gambol and sport and lay a few wind-eggs, later playing no rôle in fertilization? Or, finally, was it merely a result of some old tradition, something which once in former stages of evolution, God knows when, had a significance, but which now is utterly useless and merely drags on as an inheritance from the past, just as man still possesses certain ear-muscles which he does not use, though the animals do; or as blind cave animals still often possess the remnants or rudiments of eyes. All these were possibilities so long as we saw merely the first division, the formation of the first wart and the separation of but one-half of the spindle. This left the large egg essentially the same as before.

But we cannot pass over so lightly the separation of the second 'polar globule,' or secondary egg. Here the large egg, that is, the egg that alone undergoes the subsequent development, really loses something of its original capital. At first it had in its germinal vesicle or nucleus a fine network. This net tore into twenty-four parts. The twenty-four increased by self-division to forty-eight, an act which, when taking place in normal time, is accomplished long before the extrusion of the first globule. 'When the egg laid the egg' the first time, twenty-four of those forty-eight pieces were lost. Accordingly, there again remained the original number of twenty-four. Now comes the second division. But this time the number is not doubled. Of the remaining twenty-four parts, twelve are lost. The result is that the germinal vesicle, the nucleus of the egg, has, at the conclusion of this last act, half of what it had in the beginning.

Of late biologists have been devoting very careful study to these pieces of net. They have arrived at the conclusion that of all the contents and capital of the egg they are probably, in fact, almost certainly, the greatest and most important treasure.

In observing the processes that take place in an egg under a microscope the scientist to-day frequently applies certain colouring matters by means of which important parts in the transparent mass are rendered more visible. Since these pieces of net stain readily and thus are especially conspicuous, they were given the name of chromatin filaments or chromosomes. The name has nothing to do with the point I wish to make. The fact of cardinal importance is, that in all probability the chromosomes are the only agents of hereditary transmission in the eggs.

All the 'hereditary characters' that the female egg inherited from its parents and ancestors, from all the human beings and animals from which it has come down in a direct line of physical descent, are contained in the chromosomes, the tiny net threads of its nucleus. The full significance of heredity is a question about which we shall have a good deal to say later. In the meantime your own experience will suffice. Every child has inherited much from its parents, grandparents, etc. Think of the similarities of feature. This egg, too, is a sort of child. It is to become a child, just as the warm living egg of a hen becomes a chick. Somehow and somewhere the hereditary qualities must already be contained in the egg. And the probabilities are that they are contained in the chromosomes, and in the chromosomes only.

But if it is so, then the fact that the egg at first has twenty-four such chromosomes, twenty-four hereditary certificates, so to speak, and at the conclusion of that process has only twelve cannot be immaterial. In the first case, when the first polar globule was formed, our egg gave away, one may say, merely copies or duplicates of its hereditary portion. But upon the formation of the second globule, it gave away part of the capital itself; it reduced its capital by half. What does that mean? The nucleus of the egg, with its twelve remaining chromosomes, settled down to rest at the conclusion of our little drama. Will it be permanently satisfied with 'half its hereditary portion'? Is it really possible that it had half a fortune too much to be able to squander it so lightly? It seems very improbable.

Or is something to follow, something else to happen? Perhaps the egg expects a stranger to help it, a partner, who will reimburse it from his own capital?

Exactly. What we witnessed was only the first act.

Let us return from the dry province of explanations to the actualities of the things themselves.

The egg has in the meantime approached the narrow cleft of the oviduct leading into the uterus. Now comes a highly dramatic and absorbing second act, the act of impregnation.

Our great ball is floating quite in the foreground of the colossal shaft. At this moment strange guests of a peculiar shape are approaching it.

Compared with the ball they are dwarfs. But to make up for their size, they advance in imposing numbers, with extremely animated movements. At first glance it might be supposed that an army of ghosts of tadpoles was advancing. There is a thick head, to which a rather long tail is almost directly joined. If we look more closely, we find that the supposed head is simply a longish disc, sharp in front. Seen from the side, it is somewhat pear-shaped. No inner organs, or any structure whatever, are at first distinguishable. With this disc, evidently the principal part of the little monster, is connected the apparent tail, somewhat thick at the base, but abruptly tapering down to a very thin delicate stalk, which runs along for some length and terminates in a still finer filament.

All of them are coming from the same direction, but they are a disorganized, irregular squad.

They advance with a hopping motion, the principal part forward, the little tail vibrating behind. Now they are near the great ball, and of a sudden they all seem to be making for the same goal as if some breath, some fragrance, wafted to them from the ball, draws them to it, as the voluptuous perfume of the honeysuckle on sultry summer evenings attracts the butterflies.

They throng around the ball. Now that they are in close proximity to it, we can clearly see how small they are by contrast. The narrow canals in the taut glass roof of the ball, which we observed at the beginning, give the caudate arrivals room enough to penetrate to the inside. That is apparently what they are striving for. Immediately several simultaneously stretch out length-wise in the canals, and creep like dachshunds into the pot. There seems to be a race as to who shall first reach the inner space between the envelope and the soft con-tents of the ball, the interspace in which the polar glob-ules were deposited.

One of the robbers has got ahead. Suddenly, we see him working his little head out of the canal into the open interspace, and the contents of the ball are again set in commotion, strangely astir with life.

Some suddenly awakened sense seems to announce the nearness of the first bold intruder. Precisely oppo-site the point where it stretches its little head out of the canal, the substance in the ball as if to meet it, bulges out in a hill-like elevation into the free interspace. A moment afterwards, and the head of the strange being seizes the hand that was extended to it, and sinks straight into the elevation of the soft substance. As if glad of it, the substance embraces it tight on all sides, never to let it go again.

In vain do the other, somewhat belated robbers crawling through the canals await a similar reception. The ball stretches no inner hand out to them. On the contrary, scarcely has the first fortunate guest plunged its entire head in, when instantly the whole substance covers itself over with a hard envelope, which thenceforth absolutely prevents every intrusion into its soft body. Those who remain outside of the new sheath must, after waiting hopelessly in the ante-chamber, finally perish miserably.

On the other hand, the bold victor, the first intruder, seems to be having an extremely good time of it inside. For a short while his little tail wiggles about the spot where his head has sunk, then it seems to separate from the rest of the body, as if superfluous. Now everything that follows is apparently the exclusive work of the head within. And very intensive work it is that the head is doing inside.

We can distinctly see in the bright illuminated mass how the small but energetic guest, sinking deeper and deeper, digs up and churns the substance with its tiny body and granule glistening in various hues. But it does not stop with stirring things up at random. You recognize something that you observed before. The little stranger also carries on his submarine boat one of those mysterious turbines with which we have become familiar in the nucleus of the egg, his apparent tail, that is, the short, thick part connecting the head with the real, extremely delicate, tail having been transformed into a turbine. At first it sits behind the head like the screw of a ship; then the boat turns around on its axis and sends the turbine in advance.

The presence of such a turbine evidently signifies new life in the economy of the ball; for the old nucleus of the ovum seems to have ceased its turbine activities since its last attempt at landing. It lies quietly at anchor in the middle of the sea, as if it never had possessed a turbine. But apparently the strange invader does possess one all the more effective. Behold! It is already surrounded by an entire sun, again a sun of waves driven in all directions of the wind.

James Joyce

Ulysses

[1922]

d love a big juicy pear now to melt in your mouth
like when I used to be in the longing way then Ill
throw him up his eggs and tea in the moustachecup
she gave him to make his mouth bigger I suppose hed like my
nice cream too I know what Ill do Ill go about rather gay not
too much singing a big now and then mi fa pietà Masetto then
Ill start dressing myself to out presto non son più fort Ill put
on my best shift and drawers let him have a good eyeful out
of that to make his micky stand for him Ill let him know if
thats what he wanted that his wife is fucked yes and damn
well fucked too up to my neck nearly not by him 5 or 6 times

handrunning theres the mark of his spunk on the clean sheet I wouldnt bother to even iron it out that ought to satisfy him if you dont believe me feel my belly unless I made him stand there and put him into me Ive a mind to tell him every scrap and make him do it in front of me serve him right its all his own fault if I am an adulteress as the thing in the gallery said O much about it if thats all the harm ever we did in this vale of tears God knows its not much doesnt everybody only they hide it I suppose thats what a woman is supposed to be there for of He wouldnt have made us the way He did so attractive to men then if he wants to kiss my bottom Ill drag open my drawers and bulge it right out in his face as large as life he can stick his tongue 7 miles up my hole as hes there my brown part then Ill tell him I want £1 or perhaps 30/-Ill tell him I want to buy underclothes if he gives me that well he wont be too bad I dont want to soak it all out of him like other women do I could often have written out a fine cheque for myself and write his name on it for a couple of pounds a few times he forgot to lock it up besides he wont spend it Ill let him do it off on me behind provided he doesnt smear all my good drawers O I suppose that cant be helped Ill do the indifferent 1 or 2 questions Ill know by the answers when hes like that he cant keep a thing back I know every turn in him Ill tighten my bottom well and let out a few smutty words smellrump or lick my shit or the first mad thing comes into my head then Ill suggest about yes O wait now sonny my turn is coming Ill be quite gay and friendly over it O but I was forgetting this bloody pest of a thing pfooh you wouldnt know which to laugh or cry were such a mixture of plum and apple no Ill have to wear the old things so much the better itll be more pointed hell never know whether he did it nor not there thats good enough for you any old thing at all then Ill wipe him off me just like a business his omission then Ill go out Ill have him eying up at the ceiling where is she gone now make him want me thats the only way a quarter after what an unearthly hour I suppose theyre just getting up in China now combing out their pigtails for the day well soon have the nuns ringing the angelus theyve nobody coming in to spoil their sleep

except an odd priest or two for his night office the alarm-
clock next door at cockshout clattering the brains out of
itself let me see if I can doze off 1 2 3 4 5 what kind of flowers are those they invented like the stars the wallpaper in
Lombard street was much nicer than the apron he gave me
like that something only I only wore it twice better lower
this lamp and try again so as I can get up early Ill go to
Lambes there beside Findlaters and get them to send us
some flowers to put about the place in case he brings him
home tomorrow today I mean no no Fridays an unlucky
day first I want to do the place up someway the dust grows
in it I think while Im asleep then we can have music and
cigarettes I can accompany him first I must clean the keys
of the piano with milk whatll I wear shall I wear a white
rose or those fairy cakes in Liptons I love the smell of a rich
big shop at 71/2d a lb or the other ones with the cherries
in them and the pinky sugar 11d a couple of lbs of course
a nice plant for the middle of the table Id get that cheaper
in wait wheres this I saw them not long ago I love flowers
Id love to have the whole place swimming in roses God of

heaven theres nothing like nature the wild mountains then the sea and the waves rushing then the beautiful country with fields of oats and what and all kinds of things and all the fine cattle going about that would do your heart good to see rivers and lakes and flowers all sorts of shapes and smells and colours springing up even out of the ditches primroses and violets nature it is as for them saying theres no God I wouldnt give a snap of my two fingers for all their learning why dont they go and create something I often asked him atheists or whatever they call themselves go and wash the cobbles off themselves first then they go howling for the priest and they dying and why why because theyre afraid of hell on account of their bad conscience ah yes I know them well who was the first person in the universe before there was anybody that made it all who ah that they dont know neither do I so there you are they might as well try to stop the sun from rising tomorrow the sun shines for you he said the day we were lying among the rhododendrons on Howth head in the grey tweed suit and his straw hat the day I got him to propose to me yes first I gave him the bit of seedcake out of my mouth and it was leapyear like now yes 16 years ago my God after that long kiss I near lost my breath yes he said I was a flower of the mountain yes so we are flowers all a womans body yes that was one true thing he said in his life and the sun shines for you today yes that was why I liked him because I saw he understood or felt what a woman is and I knew I could always get round him and I gave him all the pleasure I could leading him on till he asked me to say yes and I wouldnt answer first only looked out over the sea and sky I was thinking of so many things he didnt know of Mulvey and Mr Stanhope and Hester and father and old captain Groves and the sailors playing all birds fly and I say stoop and washing up dishes they called it on the pier and the sentry in front of the governors house with the thing round his white helmet poor devil half roasted and the Spanish girls laughing in their shawls and their tall combs and the auctions in the morning the Greeks and the jews and the Arabs and the devil knows who else from all ends of Europe and Duke street and the fowl market all clucking outside Larby

Sharons and the poor donkeys slipping half asleep and the vague fellows in the cloaks asleep in the shade on the steps and the big wheels of the carts of the bulls and the old castle thousands of years old yes and those handsome Moors all in white and turbans like kings asking you to sit down in their little bit of a shop and Ronda with the old windows of the posadas glancing eyes a lattice hid for her lover to kiss the iron and the wineshops half open at night and the castanets and the night we missed the boat at Algeciras the watchman going about serene with his lamp and O that awful deepdown torrent O and the sea the sea crimson sometimes like fire and the glorious sunsets and the figtrees in the Alameda gardens yes and all the queer little streets and pink and blue and yellow houses and the rosegardens and the jessamine and geraniums and cactuses and Gibraltar as a girl where I was a Flower of the mountain yes when I put the rose in my hair like the Andalusian girls used or shall I wear a red yes and how he kissed me under the Moorish wall and I thought well as well him as another and then I asked him with my eyes to ask again yes

and then he asked me would I yes to say yes my mountain
flower and first I put my arms around him and drew him
down to me so he could feel my breasts all perfume yes and
his heart was going like mad and yes I said I will Yes.

Lucretius

The Proper Position for Women

[60 B.C.]

The sexual position is also important. For wives who imitate the manner of wild beasts and quadrupeds—that is, breast down, haunches up—are generally thought to conceive better, since the semen can more easily reach the proper place.

And it is absolutely NOT necessary for wives to move at all. For a woman prevents and battles pregnancy if in her joy, she answers the man's lovemaking with her buttocks, and her soft breasts billow forward and back; for she diverts the ploughshare out of the furrow and makes the seed miss its mark. Whores practice such movements for their own reasons, to avoid conception and pregnancy, and also to make the lovemaking more enjoyable for men, which obviously isn't necessary for our wives.

W. L. Howard

Aphrodisiacs

[1896]

It must be remembered that the early history of this subject is more or less inextricably commingled with folk-lore practices of magical origin, not necessarily founded on actual observation of the physiological effects of consuming the semen or testes. Thus, according to W. H. Pearse (*Scalpel*, December, 1897), it is the custom in Cornwall for country maids to eat the testicles of the young male lambs when they are castrated in the spring, the survival, probably, of a very ancient religious cult. (I have not myself been able to hear of this custom in Cornwall.) In Burchard's Penitential (Cap. CLIV,

Wasserschleben, *op. cit.*, p. 660) seven years' penance is assigned to the woman who swallows her husband's semen to make him love her more. In the seventeenth century (as shown in William Salmon's *London Dispensatory*, 1678) semen was still considered to be good against witchcraft and also valuable as a love-philter, in which latter capacity its use still survives. (Bourke, *Scatalogic Rites*, pp. 343, 355.) In an earlier age (Picart, quoted by Crawley, *The Mystic Rose*, p. 109) the Manichæans, it is said, sprinkled their eucharistic bread with human semen, a custom followed by the Albigenses.

The belief, perhaps founded in experience, that semen possesses medical and stimulant virtues was doubtless fortified by the ancient opinion that the spinal cord is the source of this fluid. This was not only held by the highest medical authorities in Greece, but also in India and Persia.

The semen is thus a natural stimulant, a physiological aphrodisiac, the type of a class of drugs which have been known and cultivated in all parts of the world from time immemorial. (Dufour has discussed the aphrodisiacs used in ancient Rome, *Histoire de la Prostitution*, vol. II, ch. 21.) It would be vain to attempt to enumerate all the foods and medicaments to which has been ascribed an influence in heightening the sexual impulse. (Thus, in the sixteenth century, aphrodisiacal virtues were attributed to an immense variety of foods by Liébault in his *Thresor des Remèdes Secrets pour les Maladies des Femmes*, 1585, pp. 104, *et seq.*) A large number of them certainly have no such effect at all, but have obtained this credit either on some magical ground or from a mistaken association. Thus the potato, when first introduced from America, had the reputation of being a powerful aphrodisiac, and the Elizabethan dramatists contain many references to this supposed virtue. As we know, potatoes, even when taken in the largest doses, have not the slightest aphrodisiac effect, and the Irish peasantry, whose diet consists very largely of potatoes, are even regarded as possessing an unusually small measure of sexual feeling. It is probable that the mistake arose from the fact that potatoes were originally a luxury, and luxuries frequently tend to be regarded as aphrodisiacs, since they are consumed under circumstances which tend to arouse the sexual desires. It is possible also that, as has been plausibly suggested, the misunderstanding may have been due to sailors—the first to be familiar with the potato—who attributed to this particular element of their diet ashore the generally stimulating qualities of their life in port. The eryngo (*Eryngium maritimum*), or sea holly, which also had an erotic reputation in Elizabethan times, may well have acquired it in the same way. Many other vegetables have a similar reputation, which they still retain. Thus onions are regarded as aphrodisiacal, and were so regarded by the Greeks, as we learn from Aristophanes. It is noteworthy that Marro, a reliable observer, has found that in Italy, both in prisons and asylums, lascivious people are fond of onions (*La Pubertà*, p. 297), and it may perhaps be worth while to recall the observation of Sérieux that in a woman in whom the sexual instinct only awoke in middle age there was a horror of leeks. In some countries, and especially in Belgium, celery is popularly looked upon as a sexual stimulant. Various condiments, again, have the same reputation, perhaps because they are hot and because sexual desire is regarded, rightly enough, as a kind of heat. Fish—skate, for instance, and notably oysters and other shellfish—are very widely regarded as aphrodisiacs, and Kisch attributes this property to caviar. It is probable that all these and other foods which have obtained this reputation, in so far as they have any action whatever on the sexual appetite, only possess it by virtue of their generally nutritious and stimulating qualities, and not by the presence of any special principle having a selective action on the sexual sphere. A beefsteak is probably as powerful a sexual stimulant as any food; a nutritious food, however, which is at the same time easily digestible, and thus requiring less expenditure of energy for its absorption, may well exert a specially rapid and conspicuous stimulant effect. But it is not possible to draw a line, and, as Aquinas long since said, if we wish to maintain ourselves in a state of purity we shall fear even an immoderate use of bread and water.

Anonymous

Melanesian Erotic Chant

[DATE UNKNOWN]

Beautiful will my face remain,
Flashing will my face remain,
Buoyant will my face remain!
No more it is my face,
My face is as the full moon.
No more it is my face,
My face is as the round moon.
I pierce through,
As the creamy shoot of the areca leaf,
I come out,
As a bud of the white lily.

D. H. Lawrence

Once—!

[1912]

The morning was very beautiful. White packets of mist hung over the river, as if a great train had gone by leaving its stem idle, in a trail down the valley. The mountains were just faint grey-blue, with the slightest glitter of snow high up in the sunshine. They seemed to be standing a long way off, watching me, and wondering. As I bathed in the shaft of sunshine that came through the wide-opened window, letting the water slip swiftly down my sides, my mind went wandering through the hazy morning, very sweet and far-off and still, so that I had hardly wit enough to dry myself. And as soon as I had got on my dressing gown, I lay down again idly on the bed, looking out at the morning that still was greenish from the dawn, and thinking of Anita.

I had loved her when I was a boy. She was an aristocrat's daughter, but she was not rich. I was simply middle-class. Then, I was much too green and humble-minded to think of making love to her. No sooner had she come home from school than she married an officer. He was rather handsome, something in the Kaiser's fashion, but stupid as an ass. And Anita was only eighteen. When at last she accepted me as a lover, she told me about it.

"The night I was married," she said, "I lay counting the flowers on the wall-paper, how many on a string; he bored me so."

He was of good family, and of great repute in the army, being a worker. He had the tenacity of a bull-dog, and rode like a centaur. These things look well from a distance, but to live with they weary one beyond endurance, so Anita says.

She had her first child just before she was twenty: two years afterwards, another. Then no more. Her husband was something of a brute. He neglected her, though not outrageously, treated her as if she were a fine animal. To complete matters, he more than ruined himself owing to debts, gambling and otherwise, then utterly disgraced himself by using government money and being caught.

"You have found a hair in your soup," I wrote to Anita.

"Not a hair, a whole plait," she replied.

After that, she began to have lovers. She was a splendid young creature, and was not going to sit down in her rather elegant flat in Berlin, to run to seed. Her husband was officer in a crack regiment. Anita was superb to look at. He was proud to introduce her to his friends. Then moreover she had her relatives in Berlin, aristocratic but also rich, and moving in the first society. So she began to take lovers.

Anita shows her breeding: erect, rather haughty, with a good-humoured kind of scorn. She is tall and strong, her brown eyes are full of scorn, and she has a downy, warm-coloured skin, brownish to match her black hair.

At last she came to love me a little. Her soul is unspoiled. I think she has almost the soul of a virgin. I think, perhaps, it frets her that she has never really loved. She has never had the real respect—Ehrfurcht—for a man. And she has been here with me in the Tyrol these last ten days. I love her, and I am not satisfied with myself. Perhaps I too shall fall short.

"You have never *loved* your men?" I asked her.

"I loved them—but I have put them all in my pocket," she said, with just the faintest disappointment in her good-humour. She shrugged her shoulders at my serious gaze.

I lay wondering if I too were going into Anita's pocket, along with her purse and her perfume and the little sweets she loved. It would almost have been delicious to do so. A kind of voluptuousness urged me to let her have me, to let her put me in her pocket. It would be so nice. But I loved her: it would not be fair to her: I wanted to do more than give her pleasure.

Suddenly the door opened on my musing, and Anita came into my bedroom. Startled, I laughed in my very soul, and I adored her, she was so natural. She was dressed in a transparent lacy chemise, that was slipping over her shoulder, high boots, upon one of which her string-coloured stocking had fallen, and she wore an enormous hat, black, lined with white, and covered with a tremendous creamy-brown feather, that streamed like a flood of brownish foam, swaying lightly. It was an immense hat on top of her shamelessness, and the great, soft feather seemed to spill over, fall with a sudden gush, as she put back her head.

She looked at me, then went straight to the mirror.

"How do you like my hat?" she said.

She stood before the panel of looking glass, conscious only of her hat, whose great feather-strands swung in a tide. Her bare shoulder glistened, and through the fine web of her chemise, I could see all her body in warm silhouette, with golden reflections under the breasts and arms. The light ran in silver up her lifted arms, and the gold shadow stirred as she arranged her hat.

"How do you like my hat?" she repeated.

Then, as I did not answer, she turned to look at me. I was still lying on the bed. She must have seen that I had looked at her, instead of at her hat, for a quick darkness and a frown came into her eyes, cleared instantly, as she asked, in a slightly hard tone:

"Don't you like it?"

"It's rather splendid," I answered. "Where did it come from?"

"From Berlin this morning—or last evening," she replied.

"It's a bit huge," I ventured.

She drew herself up.

"Indeed not!" she said, turning to the mirror.

I got up, dropped off my dressing gown, put a silk hat quite correctly on my head, and then, naked save for a hat and a pair of gloves, I went forward to her.

"How do you like my hat?" I asked her.

She looked at me and went off into a fit of laughter. She dropped her hat onto a chair, and sank onto the bed, shaking with laughter. Every now and then she lifted her head, gave one look from her dark eyes, then buried her face in the pillows. I stood before her clad in my hat, feeling a good bit of a fool. She peeped up again.

"You are lovely, you are lovely!" she cried.

With a grave and dignified movement I prepared to remove the hat, saying:

"And even then, I lack high-laced boots and one stocking."

But she flew at me, kept the hat on my head, and kissed me.

"Don't take it off," she implored. "I love you for it."

So I sat down gravely and unembarrassed on the bed.

"But don't you like my hat?" I said in injured tones. "I bought it in London last month."

She looked up at me comically, and went into peals of laughter.

"Think," she cried, "if all those Englishmen in Piccadilly went like that!"

That amused even me.

At last I assured her her hat was adorable, and, much to my relief, I got rid of my silk and into a dressing gown.

"You *will* cover yourself up," she said reproachfully. "And you look so nice with nothing on—but a hat."

"It's that old Apple I can't digest," I said.

She was quite happy in her shift and her high boots. I lay looking at her beautiful legs.

"How many more men have you done that to?" I asked.

"What?" she answered.

"Gone into their bedrooms clad in a wisp of mist, trying a new hat on?"

She leaned over to me and kissed me.

"Not many," she said. "I've not been *quite* so familiar before, I don't think."

"I suppose you've forgotten," said I. "However, it doesn't matter." Perhaps the slight bitterness in my voice touched her. She said almost indignantly:

"Do you think I want to flatter you and make you believe you are the first that ever I really—*really*—"

"I don't," I replied. "Neither you nor I is so easily deluded."

She looked at me peculiarly and steadily.

"I know all the time," said I, "that I am 'pro tem.', and that I shan't even last as long as most."

"You are sorry for yourself?" she mocked.

I shrugged my shoulders, looking into her eyes. She caused me a good deal of agony, but I didn't give in to her.

"I shan't commit suicide," I replied.

"'On est mort pour si longtemps'," she said, suddenly dancing on the bed. I loved her. She had the courage to live, almost joyously.

"When you think back over your affairs—they are numerous, though you are only thirty-one—"

"Not numerous—only several—and you *do* under-line the thirty-one—," she laughed.

"But how do you feel, when you think of them?" I asked.

She knitted her eyebrows quaintly, and there was a shadow, more puzzled than anything, on her face.

"There is something nice in all of them," she said. "Men are really fearfully good," she sighed.

"If only they weren't all pocket-editions," I mocked.

She laughed, then began drawing the silk cord through the lace of her chemise, pensively. The round cap of her shoulder gleamed like old ivory: there was a faint brown stain towards the arm-pit.

"No," she said, suddenly lifting her head and looking me calmly into the eyes, "I have nothing to be ashamed of—that is, —no, I have nothing to be ashamed of!"

"I believe you," I said. "And I don't suppose you've done anything that even *I* shouldn't be able to swallow— have you—?"

I felt rather plaintive with my question. She looked at me and shrugged her shoulders.

"I know you haven't," I preached. "All your affairs have been rather decent. They've meant more to the men than they have to you."

The shadows of her breasts, fine globes, shone warm through the linen veil. She was thinking.

"Shall I tell you," she asked, "one thing I did?"

"If you like," I answered. "But let me get you a wrap." I kissed her shoulder. It had the same fine, delicious coldness of ivory.

"No—yes you may," she replied.

I brought her a Chinese thing of black silk with gorgeous embroidered dragons, green as flame, writhing upon it.

"How white against that black silk you are," I said, kissing the half globe of her breast, through the linen.

"Lie there," she commanded me. She sat in the middle of the bed, whilst I lay looking at her. She picked up the black silk tassel of my dressing gown, and began flattening it out like a daisy.

"Gretchen!" I said.

"'Marguerite with one petal,'" she answered in French, laughing. "I am ashamed of it, so you must be nice with me—"

"Have a cigarette!" I said.

She puffed wistfully for a few moments.

"You've got to hear it," she said.

"Go on!"

"I was staying in Dresden in quite a grand hôtel;
—which I rather enjoy: ringing bells, dressing three
times a day, feeling half a great lady, half a cocotte.
Don't be cross with me for saying it: look at me! The
man was at a garrison a little way off. I'd have married
him if I could—"

She shrugged her brown, handsome shoulders, and
puffed out a plume of smoke.

"It began to bore me after three days. I was always
alone, looking at shops alone, going to the opera alone—
where the beastly men got behind their wives' backs to
look at me. In the end I got cross with my poor man,
though of course it wasn't his fault, that he couldn't come."

She gave a little laugh as she took a draw at her cigarette.

"The fourth morning I came downstairs—I was feeling fearfully good-looking and proud of myself. I know I
had a sort of café au lait coat and skirt, very pale—and its
fit was a *joy!*"

After a pause, she continued: "—And a big black hat with a cloud of white ospreys. I nearly jumped when a man almost ran into me. O jeh!, it was a young officer, just bursting with life, a splendid creature: the German aristocrat at his best. He wasn't over tall, in his dark blue uniform, but simply firm with life. An electric shock went through me, it slipped down me like fire, when I looked into his eyes. O jeh!, they just flamed with consciousness of me—And they were just the same colour as the soft-blue revers of his uniform. He looked at me—ha!—and then, he bowed, the sort of bow a woman enjoys, like a caress.

"'Verzeihung, gnädiges Fräulein!'

"I just inclined my head, and we went our ways. It felt as if something mechanical shifted us, not our wills.

"I was restless that day, I could stay nowhere. Something stirred inside my veins. I was drinking tea on the Brühler Terrasse, watching the people go by like a sort of mechanical procession, and the broad Elbe as a stiller background, when he stood before me, saluting, and taking a seat, half apologetically, half devil-may-care. I was not nearly so much surprised at him, as at the mechanical parading people. And I could see he thought me a Cocotte—"

She looked thoughtfully across the room, the past roused dangerously in her dark eyes.

"But the game amused and excited me. He told me he had to go to a Court ball tonight and then he said, in his nonchalant yet pleadingly passionate way:

"'And afterwards—?'

"'And afterwards—!' I repeated.

"'May I—?' he asked.

"Then I told him the number of my room.

"I dawdled to the hôtel, and dressed for dinner, and talked to somebody sitting next to me, but I was an hour or two ahead, when he would come. I arranged my silver and brushes and things, and I had ordered a great bunch of lilies of the valley; they were in a black bowl. There were delicate pink silk curtains, and the carpet was a cold colour, nearly white, with a tawny pink and turquoise ravelled border, a Persian thing, I should imagine. I know I liked it. —And didn't that room feel fresh, full of expectation, like myself!

"That last half hour of waiting—so funny—I seemed to have no feeling, no consciousness. I lay in the dark, holding my nice pale blue gown of crêpe de chine against my body for comfort. There was a fumble at the door, and I caught my breath. Quickly he came in, locked the door, and switched on all the lights. There he stood, the centre of everything, the light shining on his bright brown hair. He was holding something under his cloak. Now he came to me, and threw on me from out of his cloak a whole armful of red and pink roses. It was delicious! Some of them were cold, when they fell on me. He took off his cloak: I loved his figure in its blue uniform, and then, oh jeh!, he picked me off the bed, the roses and all, and kissed me—*how* he kissed me!"

She paused at the recollection.

"I could feel his mouth through my thin gown. Then, he went still and intense. He pulled off my saut-de-lit, and looked at me. He held me away from him, his mouth parted with wonder, and yet, as if the Gods would envy him—wonder and adoration and pride! I liked his worship. Then he laid me on the bed again, and covered me up gently, and put my roses on the other side of me, a heap just near my hair, on the pillow.

"Quite unashamed and not the least conscious of himself, he got out of his clothes. And he *was* adorable— so young, and rather spare, but with a *rich* body, that simply glowed with love of me. He stood looking at me, quite humbly; and I held out my hands to him.

"All that night we loved each other. There were crushed, crumpled little rose-leaves on him when he sat up, almost like crimson blood! Oh and he was fierce, and at the same time, tender—!"

Anita's lips trembled slightly, and she paused. Then, very slowly, she went on:

"When I woke in the morning he was gone, and just a few passionate words on his dancing-card with a gold crown, on the little table beside me, imploring me to see him again in the Brühler Terrasse in the afternoon. But I took the morning express to Berlin—"

We both were still. The river rustled far off in the morning.

"And—?" I said.

"And I never saw him again—"

We were both still. She put her arms round her bright knee, and caressed it, lovingly, rather plaintively, with her mouth. The brilliant green dragons on her wrap seemed to be snarling at me.

"And you regret him?" I said at length.

"No," she answered, scarcely heeding me. —"I remember the way he unfastened his sword-belt and trappings from his loins, flung the whole with a jingle on the other bed—"

I was burning now with rage against Anita. Why should she love a man for the way he unbuckled his belt!

"With him," she mused, "everything felt so inevitable."

"Even your never seeing him again," I retorted.

"Yes!" she said, quietly.

Still musing, dreaming, she continued to caress her own knees.

"He said to me, 'We are like the two halves of a walnut.'"

And she laughed slightly.

"He said some lovely things to me. —'Tonight, you're an Answer.' And then 'Whichever bit of you I touch, seems to startle me afresh with joy.' And he said, he should never forget the velvety feel of my skin. —Lots of beautiful things he told me."

Anita cast them over pathetically in her mind. I sat biting my finger with rage.

"—And I made him have roses in his hair. He sat so still and good while I trimmed him up, and was quite shy. He had a figure nearly like yours—."

Which compliment was a last insult to me.

"—And he had a long gold chain, threaded with little emeralds, that he wound round and round my knees, binding me like a prisoner, never thinking."

"And you wish he had kept you prisoner," I said.

"No," she answered. "He couldn't!"

"I see! You just preserve him as the standard by which you measure the amount of satisfaction you get from the rest of us."

"Yes," she said, quietly.

Then I knew she was liking to make me furious.

"But I thought you were rather ashamed of the adventure?" I said.

"No," she answered, perversely.

She made me tired. One could never be on firm ground with her. Always, one was slipping and plunging on uncertainty. I lay still, watching the sunshine streaming white outside.

"What are you thinking?" she asked.

"The waiter will smile when we go down for coffee."

"No—tell me!"

"It is half past nine."

She fingered the string of her shift.

"What are you thinking?" she asked, very low.

"I was thinking, all you want, you get."

"In what way?"

"In love."

"And what do I want?"

"Sensation."

"Do I?"

"Yes."

She sat with her head drooped down.

"Have a cigarette," I said. "And are you going to that place for sleighing today?"

"Why do you say I only want sensation?" she asked quietly.

"Because it's all you'll take from a man. —You *won't* have a cigarette?"

"No thanks—and what else could I take—?"

I shrugged my shoulders.

"Nothing, I suppose—" I replied.

Still she picked pensively at her chemise string.

"Up to now, you've missed nothing—you haven't felt the lack of anything—in love," I said.

She waited awhile.

"Oh yes I have," she said gravely.

Hearing her say it, my heart stood still.

Burchard of Worms

Medieval Sexual Menu

[1012]

QUESTIONS FOR MEN

Nuns

Have you committed fornication with a nun, that is to say, a bride of Christ? If you have done this, you shall do penance for forty days on bread and water, which they call a "carina," and [*repeat it*] for the next seven years; and so long as you live, you shall observe all six holy days on bread and water.

"Retro, Canino"

Have you had sex with your wife or with another woman from behind, doggy style? [*Latin: "retro canino"*] If you have done this, you shall do penance for ten days on bread and water.

Sunday

Have you had sex with your wife on a Sunday? You shall do penance for four days on bread and water.

Sister-in-law

If in your wife's absence, without your or your wife's knowledge, your wife's sister entered your bed and you thought that she was your wife and you had sex with her, if you have done this, then if you complete the penance, you can keep your lawful wife, but the adulterous sister must suffer the appropriate punishment and be deprived of a husband for all time.

Stepdaughter

Have you fornicated with your stepdaughter? If you have done this, you shall have neither mother nor daughter, nor shall you take a wife, nor shall she take a husband, but you shall do penance until death. But your wife, if she only learnt afterwards that you committed adultery with her daughter, shall not sleep with you but marry again in the Lord if she wishes.

Son's Fiancée

Have you fornicated with your son's fiancée, and afterwards, your son took her to wife? If you have done this, because you concealed the crime from your son, you shall do penance until death and remain without hope of marriage. but your son, because he was ignorant of your sin, if he wishes, may take another wife.

Mother

Have you fornicated with your mother? If you have done this, you shall do penance for fifteen years on the legitimate holy days, and one of these [*years*] on bread and water, and you shall remain without hope of marriage, and you shall never be without penitence. But your mother, if she was not consenting, shall do penance according to the decision of the priest; and if she cannot live chastely may marry in the Lord.

Sodomy

Have you fornicated as the Sodomites did, such that you inserted your penis into the rear of a man and into his posterior, and thus had intercourse with him in the Sodomite manner? If you had a wife and did this only once or twice, you should do penance for ten years on the legitimate holy days, and for one of these on bread and water. If you did this as a manner of habit, then you should do penance for twelve years on the legitimate holy days. If you committed this sin with your brother, you should do penance for fifteen years on the legitimate holy days.

Interfemoral

Have you fornicated with a man, as some are accustomed to do, between the thighs, that is to say, you inserted your member between the thighs of another and by thus moving it about ejaculated semen? If you did this, you shall do penance for forty days on bread and water.

Homosexual Mutual Masturbation

Have you fornicated, as some are accustomed to do, such that you took another's penis in your hand, while he took yours in his and thus in turn you moved each other's penises in your hands with the result that by this enjoyment you ejaculated semen? If you have done this, you shall do penance for thirty days on bread and water.

Masturbation

Have you fornicated with yourself alone, as some are accustomed to do, that is to say, you yourself took your penis in your hands and thus held your foreskin and moved it with your own hand so that by this enjoyment you ejaculated semen? If you have done this, you shall do penance for twenty days on bread and water.

Masturbation with Sex Aid

Have you fornicated, as some are accustomed to do, such that you inserted your penis into a hollowed-out piece of wood or some such device, so that by this movement and enjoyment you ejaculated semen? If you have done this, you shall do penance for twenty days on bread and water.

Kiss

Have you kissed some woman due to foul desire and thus polluted yourself? If you have done this, you shall do penance for three days on bread and water. But if this happened in a church, you shall do penance for twenty days on bread and water.

Bestiality

Have you fornicated against Nature, that is, you have had intercourse with animals, that is, with a horse or a cow or a donkey or with some other animal? If you did this only once or twice, and if you had no wife, so that you could to relieve your lust, you must do penance for forty days on bread and water, which is called a "carina," as well as [repeating it] for the seven following years, and never be without penitence. If, however, you had a wife, you must do penance for ten years on legitimate holy days; and if you were in the habit of this crime, you must do penance for fifteen years on the legitimate holy days. If, however, this occurred during your childhood, you must do penance on bread and water for one hundred days.

QUESTIONS FOR WOMEN

Lesbians with Sex Aids

Have you done what certain women are accustomed to do, that is, to make some sort of device or implement in the shape of the male member, of a size to match your desire, and you have fastened it to the area of your genitals or those of another with some form of fastenings and you have fornicated with other women or others have done with a similar instrument or another sort with you? If you have done this, you shall do penance for five years on legitimate holy days.

Female Masturbation with Sex Aid

Have you done what certain women are accustomed to do, that is, you have fornicated with yourself with the aforementioned device or some other device? If you have done this, you shall do penance for one year on legitimate holy days.

Mother with Son

Have you done what certain women are accustomed to do, that is, have you fornicated with your young son, that is to say, placed your son above your "indecency" and thus imitated fornication? If you have done this, you must do penance for two years on legitimate holy days.

Bestiality

Have you done what certain women are accustomed to do, that is, you have lain with an animal and incited that animal to coitus by whatever ability you possess so that it will thus have intercourse with you? If you have done this, you shall do penance for one "carina," along with [*each of*] the seven following years, and you shall never be without penitence.

APHRODISIACS AND SUPERSTITIOUS PRACTICES

Semen Swallowing

Have you tasted your husband's semen in the hope that because of your diabolical deed he might burn the more with love for you? If you have done this, you should do penance for seven years on the legitimate holy days.

Live Fish and Childbirth

Have you done what certain women are accustomed to do? They take a live fish and place it in their afterbirth and hold it there until it dies, and then after boiling and roasting it, they give it to their husbands to eat in the hope that they will burn all the more with love for them. If you have done this, you shall do penance for two years on the legitimate holy days.

Bread and Buttocks

Have you done what certain women are accustomed to do? They prostrate themselves face-down and uncover their buttocks, then they order that bread be prepared on their naked buttocks; when it's baked, they give it to their husbands to eat so they will burn more for love of them. If you have done this, you shall do penance for two years on legitimate holy days.

Menstrual Blood

Have you done what certain women are accustomed to do? They take their menstrual blood and mix it into food or drink and give it to their husbands to eat or drink so that they might be more attentive to them. If you have done this, you shall do penance for five years on legitimate holy days.

Selective Impotence Spell

Have you done what some adulterous women are accustomed to do? When they first find out that their lovers want to take legitimate wives, they then by some trick of magic extinguish the man's lust, so that they are impotent and cannot consummate their marriage with their legitimate wives. If you have done this or taught others to do this, you should do penance for forty days on bread and water.

Aphrodisiac Loaf

Have you done what certain women are accustomed to do? They take off their clothes and smear honey all over their naked body and then lay down their honey-drenched body onto some wheat scattered upon a linen on the ground; they then roll around a lot this way and that, and then carefully collect all the grains of wheat which stick to their wet body, and place them in a mill and make the mill go backwards against the sun and grind it to flour; and they make bread from the flour and then give it to their husbands to eat that they may become feeble and waste away. If you have done this, you shall do penance for forty days on bread and water.

Tahltan Tale

The Penis

[1840s]

An old man had a remarkable penis with teeth on the end that chewed like mice. It could reach long distances, crossing water like a snake and going underground like a mole. If it met roots or any other obstruction, it simply gnawed them to bits and went onward. The man could extend it or distend it at will, and most of the time he kept it looking normal. He would attack women when they were asleep, but he did not impregnate them, for the penis simply fed from them, gnawing on their insides. Women who were thus attacked felt sick in the morning, but usually recovered. One girl felt something gnawing on her breeches one night. In the morning she found her breeches looking as if mice had been after them. The next night she put on thicker clothes and waited. Pretty soon the man's penis came and began to gnaw on them. She grabbed hold of it and called for a knife. The man tried to pull back, but she held tightly. Finally, the men of the village came with sharp knives and cut off the toothed penis. Because the old man was sick the next day, they found him out. He said he couldn't eat as he had lost his teeth. He admitted that women's insides were his food and he didn't care if he died or not. The village let him die, and so men look the way they do now. Had they given him back the parts they cut off and let him live, men would have teeth today where the old man had teeth.

Milan Kundera

The Book of Laughter and Forgetting

[1980]

Ten years earlier Jan had received irregular visits from a married woman. They had known each other for years, but hardly ever saw each other because the woman had a job, and even when she took time off to be with him, they had to be quick about it. First they would sit and talk a while, but only a very short while. Soon Jan would get up, walk over to her, give her a kiss, and take her in his arms.

When he released her, they would separate and begin to undress quickly. He threw his jacket on the chair. She took off her sweater and put it over the back of the chair.

She bent down and began sliding off her pantyhose. He undid his trousers and let them drop. They were in a hurry. They stood opposite each other, leaning forward, he lifting first one, then the other leg out of his trousers (he would raise them high in the air like a soldier on parade), she bending to gather up the pantyhose at her ankles and pull her feet out of them, raising her legs as high in the air as he did.

Each time it was the same. And then one day something happened. He would never forget it: she looked up at him and smiled. It was a smile that was almost tender, a smile full of sympathy and understanding, a bashful smile that seemed to apologize for itself, but nonetheless a smile clearly brought on by a sudden insight into the absurdity of the situation as a whole. It was all he could do not to return it. For if the absurdity of the situation emerged from the semi-obscurity of habit—the absurdity of two people standing face to face, kicking their legs in the air in a mad rush—it was bound to have an effect on him as well. In fact, he was only a hair's breadth away from bursting out laughing. But he knew that if he did, they would not be able to make love. Laughter was like an enormous trap waiting patiently in the room with them, but hidden behind a thin wall. There was only a fraction of an inch separating intercourse from laughter, and he was terrified of overstepping it; there was only a fraction of an inch separating him from the border, and across the border things no longer had any meaning.

He controlled himself. He held back the smile. He threw off his trousers, went right up to her, and touched her body, hoping to drive away the demon of laughter.

Anonymous

Black Hair

[DATE UNKNOWN]

ast night my kisses drowned in the softness of black hair,
And my kisses like bees went plundering the softness
of black hair.

Last night my hands were thrust in the mystery of black hair,

And my kisses like bees went plundering the sweetness of
pomegranates

And among the scents of the harvest above my queen's neck,
the harvest of black hair;

And my teeth played with the golden skin of her two ears.

Last night my kisses drowned in the softness of black hair,

And my kisses like bees went plundering the softness
of black hair.

Your kisses went plundering the scents of my harvest,
O friend,
And the scents laid you drunk at my side. As sleep
overcame Bahram
In the bed of Sarasya, so sleep overcame you on my bed.
I know one that has sworn your hurt for stealing the
roses from my cheeks,
Has sworn your hurt even to death, the Guardian of
black hair.
Last night my kisses drowned in the softness of
black hair,
And my kisses like bees went plundering the softness of
black hair.
My hurt, darling? The sky will guard me if you wish
me guarded.
But now for my defence, dearest, roll me a cudgel of
black hair;

And give me the whiteness of your face, I am hungry
for it like a little bird.

Still, if you wish me there, loosen me among the
wantonness of black hair.
Last night my kisses drowned in the softness of
black hair,
and my kisses like bees went plundering the softness of
black hair.

Sweet friend, I will part the curtain of black hair and let
you into the white garden of my breast.
But I fear you will despise me and not look back when
you go away.
I am so beautiful and so white that the lamp-light faints
to see my face,
And also God has given me for adornment my heavy
black hair,
Last night my kisses drowned in the softness of
black hair,

And my kisses like bees went plundering the softness of black
  hair.

He has made you beautiful even among his most
  beautiful;
I am your little slave. O queen, cast me a little look.
I sent you the message of love at the dawn of day,
But my heart is stung by a snake, the snake of black hair.
Last night my kisses drowned in the softness of black hair,
And my kisses like bees went plundering the softness of
  black hair.

Fear not, dear friend, I am the Charmer,
My breath will charm the snake upon your heart;
But who will charm the snake on my honour, my sad honour?
If you love me, let us go from Pakli. My husband is horrible.
From this forth I give you command over black hair.
Last night my kisses drowned in the softness of black hair,
And my kisses like bees went plundering the softness of
  black hair.

Muhammadji has power over the poets of Pakli,

He takes tax from the Amirs of great Delhi.

He reigns over an empire and governs with a sceptre of
    black hair,

Last night my kisses drowned in the softness of black hair,

And my kisses like bees went plundering the softness of
    black hair.

Little is known of the **Anonymous** author of "Black Hair." The mysterious poem originates in Afghanistan; the date is unknown.

The **Anonymous** *Melanesian Erotic Chant* and *Sulumwoya Spell* were first recorded in Bronislaw Malinowski's *The Sexual Life of Savages* (1919).

The Greek poet **Automedon**'s satirical verse was highly popular during the Roman period (90-50 B.C.)

Wilhelm Bolsche's the "Mystery of the Ovum-cell and the Sperm-cell" is from his 1919 thesis *Love-Life in Nature*.

In 1012, the German Bishop **Burchard of Worms** compiled a hulking, 22 volume tome covering sin in its entirety. Volume 19 concerns itself with sexual transgressions.

Welsh Poet **Dafydd ap Gwilym** was one of the founders of the modern Welsh language. His classic "The Penis" was penned in the mid-1300s.

W. Dugdale privately published *The Battles of Venus: a Descriptive Dissertation of the Various Modes of Enjoyment of the Female Sex*. The manuscript was originally (and incorrectly) attributed to Voltaire.

French novelist **Gustave Flaubert** is known for a string of masterpieces, including *Madame Bovary*, *Salaambo* and *L'Education Sentimentale*. As a 28-year old, he traveled to Egypt, where he marvelled at the local entertainment.

Swashbuckling American novelist **Ernest Hemingway** is equally heralded for his novels *(The Sun also Rises, To Have and Have Not, The Old Man and the Sea)* and his manly, globetrotting adventures. In the included 1952 letter, he lives up to form.

The Greek Physician and Father of Medicine **Hippocrates** was always happy to theorize. In a paper delivered around 400 B.C., he explained orgasms.

W. L. Howard's vivid treatise on aphrodisiacs first appeared as "Sexual Perversion" in the ever-popular *Alienist and Neurologist* magazine, January, 1896.

Writer and director **Neil Jordan** is best known for his films *Mona Lisa* and *The Crying Game*. "Seduction" is from 1990.

Irish novelist and poet **James Joyce**'s experimental novels *Portrait of the Artist as a Young Man*, *Ulysses*, and *Finnegan's Wake* employed experimental techniques, such as free-wheeling stream of consciousness, evident in this excerpt from *Ulysses* (1922).

Sam Keen is the author of several books for the modern, sensitive male. His 1983 classic, *The Passionate Life*, boasts an intriguing appendix, "The Tantric Vision."

Czech novelist **Milan Kundera** regularly explores sexual antics in *The Joke*, *The Unbearable Lightness of Being*, and the 1980 masterpiece *The Book of Laughter and Forgetting*, from which this excerpt is taken.

English novelist **D. H. Lawrence** believed sex was the answer to many of man's ills. This is evidenced in his classics *Lady Chatterley's Lover, Women in Love, Sons and Lovers* and the early short story "Once—" (1912).

In 60 B.C., the Roman philosopher **Lucretius** took it upon himself to detail the proper position of women during intercourse.

The Roman Poet **Ovid** (43 B.C.-A.D. 17) is best known for his torrid writings *The Art of Love* and *Amores*. His poem "In Summer's Heat" was translated by Christopher Marlowe.

Shaykh Umar ibn Muhammed al-Nefzawi's *The Perfumed Garden*, or *Concerning Everything that is Favorable to the Act of Coition*, was written in the 16th century, and published privately by its translator, Sir Richard Burton, in 1886.

The alarming Native American **Tahltan Tale** "The Penis" dates to the 1840s.

In 1870, Russian Novelist **Leo Tolstoy** *(War and Peace, Anna Karenina)* penned *The Relations of the Sexes*, a frank and controversial collection of his thoughts on love and marriage.

The famous erotic manual, *Kama Sutra* (literally love-science) was written by Indian sage **Vatsyayana** in the 1st century. This 1883 translation is from Sir Richard Burton.

ACKNOWLEDGEMENTS

Excerpt from *The Neil Jordan Reader* by Neil Jordan ©1993 by Neil Jordan. Reprinted by permission of Vintage Books, a division of Random House.

Excerpt from *The Passionate Life: Stages of Loving* by Sam Keen. ©1983 by Sam Keen. Reprinted by permission of HarperCollins Publishers, Inc.

Letter excerpt from Ernest Hemingway ©1952 by Ernest Hemingway. Reprinted by permission of Scribner's, a division of Macmillan Inc.

Excerpt from *The Book of Laughter and Forgetting* by Milan Kundera, trans., M. Heim. English translation ©1980 by Alfred A. Knopf, Inc. Reprinted by permission of the publisher.

SEX
BOX

T H E

SEX BOX

WOMAN

EDITED BY ANONYMOUS

CHRONICLE BOOKS
San Francisco

Copyright © 1996 by John Miller. All rights reserved. No part of this book
may be reproduced in any form without written permission from the publisher.

Page 168 constitutes a continuation of the copyright page.

To maintain the authentic style of each writer included herein, quirks of
spelling and grammar remain unchanged from their original state.

Printed in Singapore.

ISBN 0-8118-1436-X

Library of Congress Cataloging-in-Publication Data available.

Book and cover design: Big Fish Books
Composition: Big Fish Books
Cover painting: Amedeo Modigliani, *Seated Nude*, 1911, Chinese ink.

Distributed in Canada by Raincoast Books,
8680 Cambie Street
Vancouver BC V6P 6M9

10 9 8 7 6 5 4 3 2 1

Chronicle Books
275 Fifth Street
San Francisco, CA 94103

To my angel, K

CONTENTS

Anonymous

Melanesian Erotic Spell

[DATE UNKNOWN]

His name be extinguished, his name be rejected;
Extinguished at sunset, rejected at sunrise;
Rejected at sunset, extinguished at sunrise.
A bird is on the *baku,*
A bird which is dainty about its food.
I make it rejected!
His mint-magic, I make it rejected.
His *kayro'iwa* magic, I make it rejected.
His *libomatu* magic, I make it rejected.
His copulation magic, I make it rejected.
His horizontal magic, I make it rejected.

His horizontal movement, I make it rejected.

His answering movement, I make it rejected.

His love dalliance, I make it rejected.

His erotic scratching, I make it rejected.

His caresses of love, I make it rejected.

His love embraces, I make it rejected.

His bodily embracing, I make it rejected.

My Kabisilova spell, I make it rejected.

It worms its way within you,

The way of the earth heap in the bush gapes open,

The way of the refuse heap in the village is closed.

Sappho

It Seems to Me That Man is Equal to the Gods

[600 B.C.]

It seems to me that man is equal to the gods,
that is, whoever sits opposite you
and, drawing nearer, savours, as you speak,
the sweetness of your voice

and the thrill of your laugh, which have so stirred the heart
in my own breast, that whenever I catch
sight of you, even if for a moment,
then my voice deserts me

and my tongue is struck silent, a delicate fire
suddenly races underneath my skin,
my eyes see nothing, my ears whistle like
the whirling of a top

and sweat pours down me and a trembling creeps over
my whole body, I am greener than grass,
at such times, I seem to be no more than
a step away from death. . . .

Kathy Acker

The Adult Life of Toulouse Lautrec
by Henri Toulouse Lautrec

[1975]

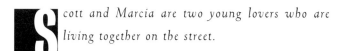

cott and Marcia are two young lovers who are living together on the street.

Being wet and dark with someone.

Being touched and being able to know the person will touch you again.

Being in a cave you don't want to leave and don't have to leave. Being in a place in which you're able to be open and stupid and boring.

You're open and wet and your edges are rough and hurt. You remember that you've always been this: totally vulnerable.

You don't want to forget who you are. Being with someone has made you remember that you're totally vulnerable.

Marcia and Scott now always felt these ways. Being out of control and not knowing it. Being in total danger and believing that you're safer than you've ever been in your life, you're inside and so you can open yourself and make yourself raw to the other person.

Suddenly seeing something you've never seen before. You're willing to compromise yourself for this person. Forget what you've just thought. You don't have any more thoughts of yourself. You want to know everything about the other person.

What was your childhood like?

What do you like to do the most?

Have you ever fucked any weirdos?

When did you start being an adult?

You think you are the other person. You begin to forget what you feel.

Scott and Marcia now were living on the street cause they didn't have any money. Caught between the devil and the deep blue sea: The other person's frightened of you. He's scared if he lets you into his wetness and heat, you'll disrupt everything. You want him wet and hot so badly, you act so heavy, he gets more scared, you put him out of your head. You want nothing to do with him. Finally you can think one thought which isn't about him. The second you see him again and his hand barely grazes your hand, your heart flops over, you almost faint, you feel like you're turning inside out. When he holds you, you forget the room exists. You can't act like he's the most casual fuck in the world. You can't tell him you're madly in love with him cause then he'll never see you again. You're screwed.

Marcia and Scott didn't even notice they didn't have any money. You're a man. You're not going to take anything from anyone cause you're a man. When you see her your mouth dries up and your eyes can't leave her face. You want her so much you can't handle it. You flee. You tell her you don't want her warmth. You tell

7

her to go fuck herself. You can't let her go because you and she are, at one point, one. The more she wants you, the crazier you get. You have to let her go and you want to sink into her body.

You tell her you're in love with other women. When you wake up in the morning, holding her warm sleeping body in the curve of your body, you tell her you want to fall in love with someone.

Marcia and Scott hardly had enough money to eat and they were sleeping on the street. They'd lie on top of one blue blanket and place newspapers over their huddling bodies. Being at ease and in paradise. Every person you see looks proud and interesting. Every person you meet gives you information you want to hear. Every object in the store windows looks beautiful and yet doesn't drive you crazy with desire. Doesn't torment you with the knowledge of how poor you are. Every new street, every alleyway you see is a new stage of the voodoo ritual you're part of: A series of rooms. In each room a new magic event which changes you takes place. You're fascinated and scared. One room contains swamps and alligators and floating moss and voodoo doctors. In another room your sex is cut open and you become a third weird sex. You feel freaked. In another room, a little table covered with a white cloth serves as an altar upon which offerings are placed, and a candle burns on the dirt floor as its base, where the vevers are drawn. For the greater part of the time, Ogoun, and then Ghede mount the houngenikon. You place your hand on the heads of lions and wolves whom you're now equal to and who stand next to you. You find yourself outside: in a green grassy world, outside the wooden building.

Marcia and Scott knew that if the cops ever noticed they were people and not pieces of garbage strewn on the street, the cops would beat them up and put them in jail. The cops would forcibly separate them. Being so happy that you forget everything. You don't know whether you love or don't love. Forget you ever felt anything. Forget you can feel anything. You sleep cause you

have to sleep and you piss in the streets. You're learning
to know everything a new way.

Anonymous

*Account of the Visit Made
to the Theatine Nuns*

[1619]

or two continuous years, two or three times a week, in the evening, after disrobing and going to bed waiting for her companion,[1] who serves her, to disrobe also, she would force her into the bed and kissing her as if she were a man she would stir on top of her so much that both of them corrupted themselves because she held her by force sometimes for one, sometimes for two, sometimes for three hours. And [she did these things] during the most solemn hours, especially the mornings, at dawn. Pretending that she had some need, she would call her, and taking her by force she sinned with her as was said above. Benedetta, in order to have greater pleasure, put her face between the other's breasts and kissed them, and wanted always to be thus on her. And six or eight times, when the other nun did not want to sleep with her in order to avoid sin, Benedetta went to find her in her bed and, climbing on top, sinned with her by force. Also at that time, during the day, pretending to be sick and showing that she had some need, she grabbed her companion's hand by force, and putting it under herself, she would have her put her fingers in her genitals, and holding it there she stirred herself so much that she corrupted herself. And she would kiss her and also by force would put her own hand under her companion and her fingers into her genitals and corrupted her. And when the latter would flee, she would do the same with her own hands. Many times she locked her companion in the study, and making her sit down in front of her, by force she put her hands under her and corrupted her; she wanted her companion to do the same to her, and while she was doing this she would kiss her. She always appeared to be in a trance while doing this. Her angel, Splenditello,[2] did these things, appearing as a boy of eight or nine years of age. This angel Splenditello through the mouth and hands of Benedetta, taught her companion to read and write, making her be near her on her knees and kissing her and putting her hands on her breasts. And the first time she made her learn all the letters without forgetting them; the second, to read the whole side of a page; the second day she made her take the small book of the Madonna and read the words; and Benedetta's two other angels listened to the lesson and saw the writing.

---

[1]Bartolomea Crivelli.

[2]Splenditello was the name which Benedetta gave to the angel who appeared to her regularly.

Sabina Sedgewick

Sabina's Sauerkraut

[1984]

My craving for sauerkraut in the raw goes back to when I was six years old. Propped up in bed (I had the flu), I spent my idle and listless hours watching the cows outside my window. Although they spent the whole day doing the same thing over and over, they never showed the slightest sign of boredom. On the contrary, their satisfaction showed with every mouthful of fresh green grass. I watched them circle clumps of grass with strong, fleshy tongues, then pull up a tasty bunch and munch steadily, without haste. Every so often they looked up dreamily just to chew, totally absorbed, totally content.

Knowing my mother would not let me out to graze, I begged her to get me a plate full of raw sauerkraut. I still remember how I masticated the tangy shreds, feeling very much in tune with the cows' intense eating experience.

Unfortunately, I never found a partner willing to share my passion for eating sauerkraut in bed. My husband finds it disgusting, so I do it secretly.

If raw sauerkraut is too kinky for the common tongue, I recommend this cooked version. Although not as elemental, it is equally earthy. Since the ingredients are ordinary kitchen staples, rather than fancy French delicacies, all the credit goes to the imaginative cook, not the gourmet grocer. It satisfies a voracious appetite, which usually follows vigorous exercise and therefore is best served at the conclusion of a seduction. Only hardy eaters will be able to consume this hearty meal before lovemaking. If, for reasons beyond the control of the cook, the food has to come first, I suggest a brisk walk in the woods as a transition, possibly an al fresco setting for the post-sauerkraut event.

Drain and rinse one pound of sauerkraut (or a twenty-seven-ounce can) in cold water. Place in a casserole with large smoked sausages or ham hocks. Add two lean pork chops, and top with a can of diced pineapple including the juice. Sprinkle with chopped walnuts, coarsely ground pepper, a bay leaf, and a dash of salt. Cover and simmer in a moderate oven for at least two hours. This should leave plenty of time for an unhurried erotic encounter enhanced by the tantalizing aroma from the kitchen. As soon as you are ready to return your attention to cooking—there are no exact time limits—brown four small breakfast sausages in a skillet, drain off the fat, and arrange them on top of the sauerkraut with the other pieces of meat. Serve with fluffy mashed potatoes, garnished with fried onions. (Smoked beef and veal frankfurters can be substituted for a kosher version, and dried fruit with small white beans instead of meat can turn this into a vegetarian meal.)

Recommended for active couples who are seeking a nourishing relationship. The flavor increases with reheating.

Pauline Réage

The Story of O

[1954]

he Ile Saint-Louis apartment O lived in was in the attic storey of an old building on a southern quay by the Seine. The rooms were mansarded, spacious and low, and the two of them that were on the façade side each opened out upon a balcony inset between sloping sections of roof. One of these last was O's bedroom; the other—where, on one wall, full-length bookcases framed the fireplaces—served as a living-room, as a study and could, if need be, function temporarily as a bedroom: there was a broad divan before the two windows, and a large antique table in front of the fireplace. Were her dinner guests too numerous, they would eat here instead of in the small dining-room, hung in dark green serge, which faced in upon the court. Another room, also on the court, was René's, where he kept his clothes and would dress in the morning. They shared the yellow bathroom and the tiny yellow kitchen. O had a cleaning woman in every day. The rooms overlooking the court were tiled in red—the tiles were the old six-sided sort one still finds on stair-treads and landings from the third floor up in old Paris hotels. Seeing them again caused O's heart to beat faster: they were the same as the tiles in the Roissy hallways. Her bedroom was small, the pink and black chintz curtains were drawn, the fire glistened behind the screen, the bed was made, the covers turned down.

'You didn't have a nylon blouse,' said René, 'so I bought you one.' True enough: there, unfolded on the side of the bed where O slept was a white nylon blouse, pleated, tailored, fine, like one of the garments that appear on Egyptian figurines, and nearly transparent. O tried it on: round her waist she put a thin belt to conceal the series of elastics inside, and the blouse was so sheer that the tips of her breasts turned it pink.

Everything, except for the curtains and the head-board panel overlaid with the same material and the two little armchairs upholstered in the same chintz, every-thing in this room was white: the walls were white, the fringe round the mahogany four-poster bed was white, so was the bearskin rug on the floor. Wearing her new white blouse, O sat down by the fire to listen to her lover. He told her that, to begin with, she mustn't think of herself as free. From now on, that is to say, she was not free; or rather she was free in one sense, only in one: to stop lov-ing him and to leave him immediately. But if she did love him, if she were going to, then she wasn't free at all. She listened to him without saying a word, calling it fortune, calling herself happy that he wanted to prove to himself, no matter how, that she belonged to him, but thinking also that there was a naïveté in his failing to realize that the degree to which he possessed her lay beyond the scope of any proof. Perhaps, though, he did realize it, and wished only to stress it? Perhaps it gave him pleasure to stress it to her? She gazed at the fire while he talked; but he, unwilling, not daring to meet her gaze, he was looking elsewhere. He was on his feet. He was pacing to and fro, staring at the floor. He suddenly said that, before anything else, in order that she hear what he was saying he wanted her, right away, to unlock her knees and unfold her arms—for she was sitting with her knees locked together and her arms folded. So she drew up her skirt and, kneeling, but sitting back on her heels, in the posture the Carmelites or the Japanese women adopt, she waited. Except that, her knees being spread, between her parted thighs she felt the faint needling of the white bearskin's fur; no, that wouldn't do, he insisted, she wasn't opening her legs wide enough. The word *open* and the expression *open your legs*, when uttered by her lover, would acquire in her mind such overtones of restiveness and of force that she never heard them without a kind of inward prostration, of sacred submission, as if they had emanated from a god, not from him. And so she remained perfectly still, her hands, palms turned upward, resting on either side of her knees, and her pleated skirt lay in a quiet circle around her. What her lover wanted of her was simple: that she be constantly and immediately accessible. It wasn't enough for him to know that she was: to her accessibility every obstacle had to be eliminated, and by her carriage and manner, in the first place, and in the second place by the clothing she wore, she would, as it were, signify her accessibility to those who knew what these signs implied. That he continued, involved doing two things. The first of them she already knew: for on the evening of her arrival at the château it had been made clear to her that she was never to cross her legs and was to keep her lips open at all times. All this, she probably thought, meant very little (she did in fact think exactly that), but she was wrong: to the contrary, she would discover that conformance to this discipline would require a continual effort of attention which would continually remind her, when the two and perhaps certain others were together even though in the midst of the most

everyday occupations and while amongst those who did
not share the secret, of what in reality her condition was.
As for her clothing, it was up to her to choose it and, if
need be, to devise a costume which would render unnecessary that half-undressing he had submitted her to in the
car while taking her to Roissy: tomorrow she would go
through her clothes-closets and bureau drawers and sort
out every last garter-belt and pair of panties, which she
would hand over to him; he would likewise take all the
brassieres, like the one whose shoulder-straps he'd had to
cut in order to get it off her, all the slips she had whose
upper part covered her breasts, all her blouses and
dresses which didn't open in front, any of her skirts
which were too narrow to be raised instantly, with a single quick motion. She'd have other brassieres, other
blouses and other dresses made. Between now and then
was she to go to her corset-maker with her breasts naked
under her blouse or sweater? Yes, he replied, that was
how she would go to her corset-maker, her breasts naked
under her blouse or sweater. And if anyone were to

notice and comment, she'd make whatever explanations she liked, or would make none; either way, that was her own affair and no concern of his. Now as to the rest of what he had to tell her, he preferred to wait a few days and when the next time she sat down to listen to him, he wanted her to be dressed in the way she should be. In the little drawer of her writing-desk she'd find all the money she'd need. When he had finished speaking, she murmured: 'I love you'—pronounced those words without stirring an eyelash. It was he who added wood to the fire, lit the pink opaline lamp by the bed. Then he told O to get into bed and to wait for him, as he was going to sleep with her. When he returned, O put out her hand to turn off the light: it was her left hand and before darkness engulfed everything the last thing she saw was her ring. Propped on one elbow, lying on one hip, she saw the dull glint of iron, then touched the switch; and at the same instant her lover's low voice summoned her by her name, she went to him, he laid his whole hand upon her womb and drew her the rest of the way.

The next morning, O was in the dining room, in her dressing-gown, having just finished breakfast and alone—René had gone early and wasn't to be back until evening to take her to dinner—when the telephone rang. The phone was in her room, on the bedside table by the lamp. O sat on the floor and picked up the receiver. It was René. The cleaning-woman, he asked, had she left? Yes, she'd gone just a moment ago, after serving breakfast, and she wasn't due back until the following day.

'Have you started to go through your things?' René asked.

'I was about to,' she replied, 'but I got up very late, didn't finish my bath till noon—'

'Are you dressed?'

'No, I'm in my nightgown and bathrobe.'

'Set the receiver down—no, don't hang up, set it on the bed. Take off your nightgown and your bathrobe.'

O obeyed, a little hastily, for the receiver slipped off the bed and fell onto the white rug; still more hastily, fearing the connection had been broken, she snatched it up, said: 'Hello.'

No, it wasn't broken.

'Are you naked?' René asked.

'Yes,' she said. 'Where are you calling from?'

He didn't reply to her question. 'You've still got your ring on?'

She had it on. Then he told her to stay as she was until he returned and, staying that way, to put the things she was discarding into a suitcase; and he hung up.

It was past one o'clock, the weather was clear. A patch of sunlight fell on the rug where, after taking them off, she had let fall the white nightgown and the velvet corduroy bathrobe, pale green in colour, like the hulls of fresh almonds. She collected them and started towards the bathroom to hang them in a closet; on the way she encountered a three-sided mirror formed by a glass mounted on a door to two others, one straight ahead and one on the right, in a bend in the hall: she encountered her reflection: she was naked save for the green leather clogs of the same green as her bathrobe and not much darker than the clogs she had worn at Roissy, and the ring. She was no longer wearing collar or leather wrist-bands, and she was alone, sole spectator to herself. Be that as it may, she had never felt so utterly subject to a foreign will, never so utterly a slave nor so happy to be one. When she bent to open a drawer, she saw her breasts sway softly. She was almost two hours at laying out on the bed the clothes she was supposed next to put in the suitcase. First of all, the panties; well, there was no problem here, they all went into a pile by the bedpost. The brassieres? The same thing, they all had to go: for they all crossed behind and hooked at the side. But she did see that the same model could perfectly well do if the catch were brought round to the front, just under the hollow between her breasts. Out went the garter-belts too, but she hesitated getting rid of the rose satin corset which laced up the back and which so closely resembled the bodice she'd worn at Roissy. So she set it aside, on the dressing-table. René'd decide. He'd also decide about the sweaters which, without exception, were the slipover sort and tight around the neck, hence unopenable. But they could, why not? they could be pulled up from the waist by anyone wanting to get at her breasts. Well, she'd wait and see. On the other hand, there was no doubt about the full-length slips: they were in a heap on the bed. In the bureau drawer remained one half-slip, black crêpe hemmed with fine lace at the bottom; she used to wear it beneath a pleated circular sun's-ray skirt in loose-woven wool, light enough to be transparent. She'd have to have other half-slips, light-coloured and short. She also realized that she'd have to give up wearing slipover dresses, but that she might be able to get the same effect from a dress which buttoned all the way down in front and it might be possible to have a built-in slip made which would unbutton at the same time the dress was unbuttoned. In connection with the half-skirts there wasn't likely to be any trouble, nor with the dresses, but what in the world would her dressmaker say about these underthings? She'd tell her she wanted a removable lining because she was sensitive to the cold. Come to think of it, she *was* sensitive to the cold and she

suddenly wondered how, with the light clothing she usually wore, she ever managed out-of-doors in the winter.
Finally, when she'd finished the job, and from her
wardrobe salvaged only those of the blouses which buttoned in front, her black pleated half-slip, her coats of
course, and the suit she'd worn back from Roissy, she
went to make some tea. She moved up the thermostat in
the kitchen; the woman hadn't remembered to fill the living-room firewood basket and O knew that her lover
would be delighted to find her in the living-room by the
fire when he came home that evening. Out in the corridor there was a big wood-box; she filled the basket, carried it into the living-room, and got a fire going. Thus
did she wait, curled up in a big chair, the tea-tray next to
her, thus did she await his return; but this time, as he
had ordered, she awaited him naked.

The first difficult O met with was at work. Difficulty?
Not quite; rather, she met with astonishment. O worked
in the fashion branch of a photograph agency. Which
meant that, in the studio where they posed hour after

hour, she took the pictures of the strangest—and pretti-est-looking—girls whom *couturiers* had selected to model their gowns. They were astonished, or at least surprised, that O had extended her vacation so far into the autumn and, in doing so, had absented herself at the very period when professional activity was at its height, when new styles were about to be released. That surprised them. But they were truly astonished at the change that had taken place in her. At first glance, you couldn't tell in just what way, but you sensed there'd been some sort of a change, and the more you looked at her, the surer of it you were. She stood straighter, her gaze was clearer, sharper, but what was downright striking was this faultless immobility when she was still and, when she moved, the measure, the sureness in her movements. Previously, she'd always dressed soberly, as working girls do when their work resembles men's work, but so cleverly that sobriety seemed quite right for her; and owing to the fact that the other girls, who constituted the very object of her work, had clothing and adornments by way of occupation and vocation, they were quick to detect what other eyes might not have seen. Sweaters worn next to the skin and which so softly outlined her breasts—René had ended up permitting sweaters—pleated skirts which, when she turned, swirled so readily, these took on the quality of a discreet uniform, so regularly was O seen wearing them. 'Very little-girl,' and that in a teasing manner, from a blond green-eyed mannequin with high Slavic cheek-bones and the Slavic olive tint, 'but you're wrong about the garterbelt, you're not going to do your legs any good wearing elastic-bands all the time'—for O, in front of her and without paying attention, had sat down a little too quickly and at an angle upon the arm of a heavy leather-upholstered chair and her skirt had, for a moment, flown up. The tall girl had caught a flash of naked thigh above the rolled-down stocking stopping just above the knee. O had seen her smile, smile so curiously that, at that very instant, she'd wondered what the girl had supposed or perhaps understood. She pulled her stockings up tight, first one stocking, then the other (it wasn't as easy keeping them tight that way as when they mounted to mid-thigh and when garters held them in place), and replied, as if to justify herself: 'It's practical.'

'Practical for what?' Jacqueline said.

'I don't like garter-belts,' O answered. But Jacqueline wasn't listening to her; her eyes fixed on the iron ring.

During the next few days O made some fifty photographs of Jacqueline. They were like none she had ever taken before. Perhaps she had never had such a model before. In any case, she had never been able to extract anything quite like this impassioned meaningfulness from a face or a body. Yet she had undertaken no more than to highlight the silks, the furs, the laces, with the fairy-tale loveliness, the suddenly awakened Sleeping Beauty surprise which swept over Jacqueline no matter what she was wearing, the simplest blouse or the most elegant mink. Her hair was cut short, it was thick and blonde, faintly waved, and, as they were readying the shot, she'd bend her head ever so slightly towards her left shoulder, leaning her cheek against the upturned collar of

her fur, if she was wearing a fur. O caught her once that
way, smiling and sweet, her hair faintly lifted as though
by some gentle breeze, and her soft but hard cheek graz-
ing silver-fox, as grey and delicate as fresh firewood ash.
Her lips were parted, her eyes half-closed. Under the cool
brilliance of glossy paper one would have thought this the
picture of some blessed victim of a drowning; pale, so very
pale. From the negative O had made a high-key print all
in soft greys. She had taken another photograph of
Jacqueline, even more stunning than the first: this one
was side-lit, her shoulders bare, her delicately-shaped
head and delicately-featured face too enveloped in a large-
mesh black veil, that surmounted by absurd-looking egret
feathers wafting upward in a crown of mist or smoke; she
was wearing an immense gown of heavy silk and brocade,
red, like what brides wore in the Middle Ages, going to
within a few inches of the floor, flaring at the hips, tight
at the waist, and whose armature sketched her breasts.
Nobody ever wore such dresses anymore, it was what the
couturiers called a show-gown. The very high-heeled san-

dals were also of red silk. And all the while Jacqueline was there before O in this dress and in those sandals and that veil, which was like a suggestion of mask, in mind O completed the image, modified it according to a prototype she had: just a shade of this, a shade of that—the waist constructed a little more tightly, the breasts a little more sharply uplifted—and it was the Roissy dress, the same dress Jeanne had been wearing, the same heavy silk, shining, smooth, cascading, the silk one seizes in great handfuls and raises when one's told to... And, yes, Jacqueline had hold of handfuls of it and was lifting it as she stepped down from the platform where she had been posing for a quarter of an hour. It was the same rustling, the same dry-leaves crackling. Nobody ever wears such dresses anymore? Oh, but there are still some who wear them. Round her neck, Jacqueline also was wearing a golden choker, two golden bracelets on her wrists. O caught herself in the midst of imagining that she'd be lovelier with a collar and with bracelets of leather. And now, doing something she'd never done before, she followed

Jacqueline out into the large dressing-room, adjacent to the studio, where the models dressed and made up and where they left their clothes and make-up when they left. She leaned against the doorjamb, her eyes riveted upon the hairdresser's mirror before which Jacqueline still wearing her dress, had sat down. The mirror was so tall—it reflected the entirety of the room, and the dressing-table was an ordinary table surfaced with black glass—that O could see both Jacqueline's and her own image, and the image also of the dressing-assistant who was detaching the egret plumes and removing the tulle veil. Jacqueline herself undid her choker, her naked arms lifted like two swans' necks; a trace of sweat glistened under her armpits, which were shaven (why shaven? What a pity, thought O, she is so fair), and O could smell the keen, pungent odour, somewhat vegetable and wondered what perfume Jacqueline ought to be wearing—what perfume they'd give Jacqueline to wear. Then Jacqueline undid her bracelets, posed them on the glass table-top where, for a fleet instant, they made a clicking like chains clicking. She was so fair-haired that her skin was of a darker hue than her hair, bistre, beige, like fine sand just after the tide has retreated. On the photo, the red silk would come out black. At that same moment, the thick eye-lashes Jacqueline painted only to satisfy the requirements of her job and reluctantly, lifted, and in the mirror O caught a glance so keen, so steady, that, the while unable to remove her own she sensed a warmth flow into her cheeks. That was all, just one glance.

'I beg your pardon, I must undress.'

'Excuse me,' O murmured, and closed the door.

The next day she took home the prints made the day before, not knowing whether she did or didn't desire to show them to her lover; with him she was dining out that evening. While making up before the dressing-table in her room, she gazed at them and would now and then interrupt what she was doing to touch her finger to the photo and trace the line of an eyebrow, the contour of a smile. But when she heard the sound of a key in the front-door lock, she slipped the prints away into the drawer.

Gabriella Parca

Italian Women Confess

[1963]

Puglie

I'm almost sixteen, and for three years I've been in love with a boy who I think loves me. I say, "I think," because from the way he acts on our dates, I'm not really sure. Every time we meet, my fiancé does nothing but kiss me and caress me, but I can't stand when he pulls up my dress and . . . (you understand), he touches my breasts, in fact he practically consumes me, and he pays no attention to what I say. I'm always threatening to have a fight with him if he doesn't change. And when he's busy kissing me, etc., he doesn't listen to me, on the contrary he overwhelms me with phrases full of love and affection. Then when he comes to his senses again, he tells me, "I didn't want to, but it's just that when I'm close to you, you make me lose my head, and I don't know how to control my desires."

Let me say first that my fiancé has never been engaged before except once, which I find hard to believe, to a girl with a bad reputation he only had two dates with. It was because I went to Milan when he'd told me not to, and for spite he went to Naples, his home town, and to get revenge he did this; but as soon as he came back, we made up. Being back with me, he was even more in love than before. I don't believe it, and I think he may have told me that just to make me jealous and so I won't act the same way this time. Coming back to what we were saying and what interests me, I would like to know, since I've never been engaged to anyone but him, if everybody does these things and if it's true that they're caused by love.

Campania

We're two nineteen year old girls, tall and blonde, and we're file clerks in an office. Quite often we go to dance at the house of our boss who I love madly and the other girl loves his brother who's a lawyer. The thing that hurts us the most is that they love us too and they're married. But we're not able to leave them because we were engaged to them before they got married, but then while they were traveling around the world they married two foreigners. You should know that it's been almost two years and now we find ourselves in danger and this is why we're begging you to answer us as soon as possible because in a little while they're going abroad on business and they've promised to take us with them. Should we believe them? What should we do?

Sardegna

First of all, I want to introduce myself. I'm twenty-four years old, and I'm married, I have one child, and I really love my husband.

Every week I read the answers in your column with great interest, by maybe you've never given an answer on this subject. Everybody, more or less, asks for advice about their fiancés or things like that. But my problem is quite different: it's something that for the moment I can only confide in you.

Well, it's about a girl who has fallen in love with me. Yes, it's really true, you've understood perfectly. To be exact, she's a girl who's the same age as I am and who has been living in my neighborhood for five months. When I first knew her, I didn't pay much attention to her compliments during the work break or when she came to see me at home. But a month ago when we were on our way home after work at ten in the evening as usual, she spoke to me and said that she couldn't sleep any more because I'd stolen her heart and she was in love with me. I told her there was nothing I could do for her; then taking me by the shoulders, she said that I could do something for her, and as she said this she kissed me on the mouth. I broke away from her, saying she was crazy, and then I slapped her across the face. But she didn't do anything, and she stood there in the street with her hand on her cheek. I screamed at her that I was going to tell her parents everything. "There's nothing they can do to keep you from me," she answered. "I love you too much, and I don't want to lose you, no matter how much you threaten me. But you'll see that in time you'll love me a little, and that's enough for me."

But now I feel that I really hate her. I can't stand the way she looks at me when I meet her, or during work, and she goes on making indecent propositions to me. A few days ago I wanted to tell her brother and her parents everything. But more than anything I don't want other people to know about it. There are lots of men who'd be interested in her, serious refined people, but she really doesn't want to have anything to do with them. To tell the truth, she's a beautiful girl, blonde, with a wistful expression in her eyes, very beautiful. And this is exactly why I'm afraid, maybe you'll understand . . . and I wouldn't want this to happen to me.

Sicilia

I'm desperate, help me, I beg you; what I'm about to write to you about is a terrible thing. If you can remember a letter signed Maria S., it was mine, and in that letter I wrote to you about all my anxiety and my love for my boyfriend, my desperation and doubts that he didn't love me. Well, I could be happy now, because he loves me, but my destiny is an unlucky one, and maybe I'll never be happy! Well, listen, and please advise me as if you were my sister. The other day I found out that he's not a normal boy. I'll explain more clearly: he's a man physically, but they say that inside he has the tendencies of a woman and a man at the same time. But they say that the male tendencies are stronger. I can't believe it; because I don't see anything effeminate about him either physically or morally; on the contrary, he's very masculine. Believe me, what I heard has really upset me. I don't know what to do. I feel as if I'm going mad because I believe that he won't love me the way a man can passionately love a woman, since he has this evil inside him. Help me, I want to die, I think of nothing but this terrible fact, and I don't know what to do but to cry, cry, cry. . . .

They say that his father is like "him" too, and that by having operations they can be cured, and it would be easy for him because, as I'm telling you, if you saw him, you'd fall in love with him. I won't leave him. I'm ready to give my life, my blood, anything, that he might be cured. Tell me, types like this, what character, what symptoms are they supposed to have? I'd like to find out by myself, without him realizing it; but how? My life has become a hell. . . . Will I be able to cure him with my infinite love? Next question: I haven't answered yes or no to his declaration. What should I say to him?

I know that if I tell him no, I'll lose him forever. My mother knows he's that way, but she doesn't know that we love each other, and she has told me that to marry one of "those men" means to make yourself unhappy for the rest of your life.

Piemonte

I'm a girl of sixteen, and for six months I've been engaged to a boy of eighteen. We love each other very much, and so we decided that he should come to my house. When I spoke to my parents they didn't say anything, except that I'm very young. So the next night he came, but when they saw him, they said no, and I saw my mother turn so pale I don't know how to describe it. After that night we saw each other just the same, but we kept wondering what the reason was for their behavior. Only two days ago, I talked to my mother, and I asked her why.

At first she didn't want to say, but then she told me. And she said that she hadn't given her permission *because he is my brother.* When she told me this, I began crying, and I thought that I couldn't go on without him. The next night I met him, I told him that I didn't love him any more and that I'd never loved him, but when I told him this, he slapped me twice. Why is destiny so cruel? What should I do, believe all this? I don't think my parents would lie to me, because they love me. I'm an only child.

Emilia

I'm thirty now, and for twelve years I've loved a man who has never returned my love, though his feeling for me is one of friendship. Through a combination of circumstances we meet every once in a while, and through these meetings my love for him has grown still stronger. Besides, he's married, and to forget him I tried to get interested in another man, but I didn't succeed, and I broke off the relationship with the other one.

Now once again because of work we're together from morning to night, most of the time alone. So often, during the time that we're alone, I don't know how to resist declaring my love to him, a love that's still strong in me, and I give myself to him. This offer is accepted every once in a while just to satisfy a whim; he doesn't hide this from me, and in spite of the fact that he keeps saying this relationship between us isn't right, I go on wanting it.

Now once again it looks as if we'll be separated, and this is why more and more often he tries to avoid relations with me, saying that it could be morally harmful to me, since all it does is intensify this love and make the separation even more difficult. If there's anything that consoles me a little, it's the hope that after the separation he might accept my offer of love sometimes, even if it's just to satisfy a whim of his. But I already know this won't happen, because he told me so and I know he'll keep his word.

All of this is a torment for me, and I'd like to hear some words from you that might help me to see the situation better from a point of view different from mine, and so I'd have a way of reasoning it out and understanding what would be the right way for me to act with him in the future.

Napoli

I'm a girl of twenty-five, and I feel very confused; that's why I'm turning to you, and I really hope that you won't throw this miserable letter of mine away. Excuse the way I write, because I only finished the third grade of grammar school. I'll go back a little bit. I was seventeen when I got engaged to my cousin, believing in his love, and then, because I was so young, he made me his. Afterwards there wasn't anything I could do; he didn't want to marry me, and my threats were in vain, because I shot at him with a revolver, and unfortunately I didn't hit him. After that day I closed myself up in my sorrow and loneliness, until I met love. For me he's the whole world and I'm very jealous, but for him it's different, he's just a Don Juan, and then I should tell you that he's also married and we work together. You can't believe what a torture it is for me, because I'd like him to be all mine, and at the same time I'd like to leave him; but it's stronger than I am, as if he'd cast a spell over me. To free myself from him I even got officially engaged to a boy who loves me very much, but not even this way can I get the other man out of my heart. I really don't know what to do, I feel too attached to him. Not even my fiancé can hold me back, I don't think about anything, it's enough for me to be near the man I love. What should I do? Help me, I feel so desperate, and I do nothing but spend my days crying. Sometimes I even think about suicide, and maybe I'll do it if I don't get a little understanding from somebody. I know it, what I'm doing isn't right for me, I deserve better, but there's a proverb that says: love is blind, and hunger is an ugly beast.

Napoli

I'm the girl who wrote you that she was engaged to a married man, and I followed your advice, but believe me I don't know how to resign myself to it. And now I want to tell you how our farewell took place.

He came back from his town, and his first thought was to come to my house. I refused to see him, and this went on for a week, but one day I called him to ask him for my photograph and he told me that he'd only give me the picture in person and that he wanted an explanation for my behavior. I told him that we'd already talked about it before, but he wouldn't listen to me; so after two months we saw each other again. I went right up to him and asked him for the photograph, but he said: "Have you really decided?" And again he told me that he'd suffered being away from me. Besides feeling my absence, he'd had some bad luck which cost him 30 million lire, and he said that exactly now, when he needed an affectionate person near him, I'd abandoned him. I said to him: "If you were a bachelor, I wouldn't have left you." But he answered very angrily: "I've never been married," because according to him a marriage in a civil ceremony doesn't count. To be brief, I'll tell you that when we parted, he cried a lot, saying that he's never loved a woman in his life the way he loves me and that in leaving him I've ruined him and he kept repeating over and over: "I beg you, don't leave me, have compassion, don't leave me now when I need a little affection," because, as I told you, he's had such bad luck.

When we parted I promised him I'd call him, and it's just been two days, and I already feel I can't go without seeing him, and now I'm waiting for some advice from you as to whether I should call him, but the way you'd call a dear friend. I'd like to try and forget him, but I don't think I ever will, since he always used to come to my house on

Sundays with his car and we'd go out together. It's Sunday now as I'm writing to you, and with great melancholy I'm waiting for tomorrow to come to go to work, so that in working I'll be able to distract myself a little. Advise me, if I mustn't see him any more, what should I do to kill these sad Sundays that are hanging over me? I'd have some place to go with my sisters, but I can't, I don't feel like going out alone, that is without him.

Anonymous

The Lustful Turk

[1828]

Never, oh never shall I forget the delicious transport that followed the stiff insertion; and then, ah me! by what thrilling degrees did he, by his luxurious movements, fiery kisses, and strange touches of his hand to the most crimson parts of my body, reduce me to a voluptuous state of insensibility. I blush to say so powerfully did his ravishing instrument stir up nature within me, that by mere instinct I returned him kiss for kiss, responsively meeting his fierce thrusts, until the fury of the pleasure and the ravishing became so overpowering that, unable longer to support the excitement I so luxuriously felt, I fainted in his arms with pleasure . . .'

Anais Nin

The Delta of Venus

[1940]

The wife of one of the modern painters was a nymphomaniac. She was tubercular, I believe. She had a chalk-white face, burning black eyes deeply sunk in her face, with eyelids painted green. She had a voluptuous figure, which she covered very sleekly in black satin. Her waist was small in proportion to the rest of her body. Around her waist she wore a huge Greek silver belt, about six inches wide, studded with stones. This belt was fascinating. It was like the belt of a slave. One felt that deep down she *was* a slave—to her sexual hunger. One felt that all one had to do was to grip the belt and open it for her to fall into one's arms. It was very much like the chastity belt they showed in the Musée Cluny, which the crusaders were said to have put on their wives, a very wide silver belt with a hanging appendage that covered the sex and locked it up for the duration of their crusades. Someone told me the delightful story of a crusader who had put a chastity belt on his wife and left the key in care of his best friend in case of his death. He had barely ridden away a few miles when he saw his friend riding furiously after him, calling out: "You gave me the wrong key!"

'Such were the feelings that the belt of Louise inspired in everyone. Seeing her arrive at a café, her hungry eyes looking us over, searching for a response, an invitation to sit down, we knew she was out on a hunt for the day. Her husband could not help knowing about this. He was a pitiful figure, always looking for her, being told by his friends that she was at another café and then another, where he would go, which gave her time to steal off to a hotel room with someone.

Then everyone would try to let her know where her husband was looking for her. Finally, in desperation, he began to beg his best friends to take her, so that at least she would not fall into strangers' hands.

'He had a fear of strangers, of South Americans in particular, and of Negroes and Cubans. He had heard remarks about their extraordinary sexual powers and felt that, if his wife fell into their hands, she would never return to him. Louise, however, after having slept with all his best friends, finally did meet one of the strangers.

'He was a Cuban, a tremendous brown man, extraordinarily handsome, with long, straight hair like a Hindu's and beautifully full, noble features. He would practically live at the Dome until he found a woman he wanted. And then they would disappear for two or three days, locked up in a hotel room, and not reappear until they were both satiated. He believed in making such a thorough feast of a woman that neither one wanted to see the other again. Only when this was over would he be seen sitting in the café again, conversing brilliantly. He was, in addition, a remarkable fresco painter.

'When he and Louise met, they immediately went off together. Antonio was powerfully fascinated by the whiteness of her skin, the abundance of her breasts, her slender waist, her long, straight, heavy blond hair. And she was fascinated by his head and powerful body, by his slowness and ease. Everything made him laugh. He gave one the feeling that the whole world was now shut out and only this sensual feast existed, that there would be no tomorrows, no meetings with anyone else—that there was only this room, this afternoon, this bed.

'When she stood by the big iron bed, waiting, he said, "Keep your belt on." And he began by slowly tearing her dress from around it. Calmly and with no effort, he tore it into shreds as if it were made of paper. Louise was trembling at the strength of his hands. She stood naked now except for the heavy silver belt. He loosened her hair over her shoulders. And only then did he bend her back on the bed and kiss her interminably, his hands over her breasts. She felt the painful weight both of the silver belt and of his hands pressing so hard on her naked flesh. Her sexual hunger was rising like madness to her head, blinding her. It was so urgent that she could not wait. She could not even wait until he undressed. But Antonio ignored her movements of impatience. He not only continued to kiss her as if he were drinking her whole mouth, tongue, breath, into his big dark mouth, but his hands mauled her, pressed deeply into her flesh, leaving marks and pain everywhere. She was moist and trembling, opening her legs and trying to climb over him. She tried to open his pants.

'"There is time," he said. "There is plenty of time. We are going to stay in this room for days. There is a lot of time for both of us."

'Then he turned away and got undressed. He had a golden-brown body, a penis as smooth as the rest of his body, big, firm as a polished wood baton. She fell on him and took it into her mouth. His fingers went everywhere, into her anus, into her sex; his tongue, into her mouth, into her ears. He bit at her nipples, he kissed and bit her belly. She was trying to satisfy her hunger by rubbing against his leg, but he would not let her. He bent her as if she were made of rubber, twisted her into every position. With his two strong hands he took whatever part of her he was hungry for and brought it up to his mouth like a morsel of food, not caring how the rest of her body fell into space. Just so, he took her ass between his two hands, held it to his mouth, and bit and kissed her. She begged, "Take me, Antonio, take me, I can't wait!" He would not take her.

'By this time the hunger in her womb was like a raging fire. She thought that it would drive her insane. Whatever she tried to do to bring herself to an orgasm, he defeated. If she even kissed him too long he would break away. As she moved, the big belt made a clinking sound, like the chain of a slave. She was now indeed the slave of this enormous brown man. He ruled like a king. Her pleasure was subordinated to his. She realised she could do nothing against his force and will. He demanded submission. Her desire died in her from sheer exhaustion. All the tautness left her body. She became as soft as cotton. Into this he delved with greater exultancy. His slave, his possession, a broken body, panting, malleable, growing softer under his fingers. His hands searched every nook of her body, leaving nothing untouched, kneading it, kneading it to suit his fancy, bending it to suit his mouth, his tongue, pressing it against his big shining white teeth, marking her as his.

'For the first time, the hunger that had been on the surface of her skin like an irritation, retreated into a deeper part of her body. It retreated and accumulated, and it became a core of fire that waited to be exploded by his time and his rhythm. His touching was like a dance in which the two bodies turned and deformed themselves into new shapes, new arrangements, new designs. Now they were cupped like twins, spoon-fashion, his penis against her ass, her breasts undulating like waves under his hands, painfully awake, aware, sensitive. Now he was crouching over her prone body like some great lion, as she placed her two fists under her ass to raise herself to his penis. He entered for the first time and filled her as none other had, touching the very depths of the womb.

'The honey was pouring from her. As he pushed, his penis made little sucking sounds. All the air was drawn from the womb, the way his penis filled it, and he swung in and out of the honey endlessly, touching the tip of the womb, but as soon as her breathing hastened, he would draw it out, all glistening, and take up another form of caress. He lay back on the bed, legs apart, his penis raised, and he made her sit upon it, swallow it up to the hilt, so that her pubic hair rubbed against his. As he held her, he made her dance circles around his penis. She would fall on him and rub her breasts against his chest, and seek his mouth, then straighten up again and resume her motions around the penis. Sometimes she raised herself a little so that she kept only the head of the penis in her sex, and she moved lightly, very lightly, just enough to keep it inside, touching the edges of her sex, which were red and swollen, and clasped the penis like a mouth. Then suddenly moving downwards, engulfing the whole penis, and gasping with the joy, she would fall over his body and seek his mouth again. His hands remained on her ass all the time, gripping her to force her movements so that she could not suddenly accelerate them and come.

'He took her off the bed, laid her on the floor, on her hands and knees, and said, "Move." She began to crawl about the room, her long blond hair half-covering her, her belt weighing her waist down. Then he knelt behind her and inserted his penis, his whole body over hers, also moving on its iron knees and long arms. After he had enjoyed her from behind, he slipped his head under her so that he could suckle her luxuriant breasts, as if she were an animal, holding her in place with his hands and mouth. They were both panting and twisting, and only then did he lift her up, carry her to the bed, and put her legs around his shoulders. He took her violently and they shook and trembled as they came together. She fell away suddenly and sobbed hysterically. The orgasm had been so strong that she had thought she would go insane, with a hatred and a joy like nothing she had ever known. He was smiling, panting; they lay back and fell asleep.'

Anonymous

Kitty's Atlantis for the Year 1766

[1766]

What's that in which good housewives take delight,
Which, though it has no legs, will stand upright,
'Tis often us'd, both sexes must agree,
Beneath the navel, yet above the knee;
At the end it has a hole; 'tis stiff and strong,
Thick as a maiden's wrist and pretty long:
To a soft place 'tis very oft apply'd,
And makes the thing 'tis us'd to, still more wide;
The women love to wriggle it to and fro,
That what lies under may the wider grow:
By giddy sluts sometimes it is abus'd,

But by good housewives rubb'd before it's us'd,

That it may fitter for their purpose be,

When they to occupy the same are free.

Now tell me merry lasses if you can,

What this must be, that is no part of man?

[Answer: A Rolling Pin]

Rey Anthony [pseudonym]

The Housewives' Handbook
on Selective Promiscuity

[1962]

I could be the woman next door to you, in a middle-class three-bedroom house. I belong to P.-T.A.s, I operate a publishing and printing house, I'm a member of a national business-woman's organization.

Age 28 . . . Houston

I met Dan Jacobs through a mutual friend. The mutual friend, and Dan, were both electronic technicians. Dan was a quiet fellow, gentle and kind. He made the atmosphere comfortable and soft to be in. We sat and listened to records. Rock was away on a ship.

We discussed sexual activities. I told him about the pictures that I used when I had sex. I couldn't remember if I had used them in my early sexual relations with Clint and Bill, but after I had used them during the mental masturbation I had come to use them in all my sex relations.

Dan said he thought sex should be performed between friends. He said he would only go to bed with a friend. He said too many people hang up on purely physical attractions and thereby find themselves in bed with people that they don't even enjoy talking to when the sex is over. Or before the next sex begins.

He said he preferred to go to bed with a friend—and therefore they could also talk. This seemed like a very nice idea to me. I had always thought of Larry as a very good friend, completely aside from our sexual relations. I am sure I had thought of Clint and Bill as friends during our associations. I didn't remember any time I had thought of Rock as a friend. Maybe at the very first, for one or two days, but not since then.

We made love. I told him how I liked to have sex. I explained that I had gotten to where I was ritualistic about cleanliness before having sex. I gave him information about how I liked the stimulation of the clitoris, and ultimately liked climax in that manner.

He said quietly, "Let's continue this ritual."

Dan prided himself on being a logician. He liked things to be orderly and understandable. Partly as a result of some of these qualities, and from attitudes of my own, we were able to achieve a singularly satisfying sexual relation.

I was able to reach orgasms that were of beautiful intensity. The sensuality flooded my body and I felt as though I were feeling it all around my body, even outside it.

By now I could move my body more capably for my lover's enjoyment. He commented on how really wonderful our sexual relations were.

Once he asked, "How can you possibly know just how to move in such perfect rhythm to meet me as you do?"

I laughed lightly and asked, "What gives you the impression that *you* are making the movements and that I am meeting *you*? Maybe I am making the motions and you are following—or maybe we're cocreating them."

After a while my logical lover began to have problems. Eventually these became problems of mine—we were so close and we shared each other's thoughts so intimately.

We had passed over the problem of natural lubrication for sexual purposes. He had had the idea that the vagina, with proper stimulation, is provided with lots of natural goo. I had found this to be true, at certain times; and at other times, no matter how stimulated I felt—no goo.

Even when this good was plentiful it had a consistency that I didn't consider suitable for sexual purposes. Never had I had any problem preferring what is *natural*. Man, Homo sapiens, talks a lot about doing what is natural, and not going against nature, but man as an intelligent creature has never functioned in this manner.

He builds houses to shut out the cold, kills animals for their skins to keep himself warm, makes floating machines that float on the sea and through the air. So why he should hang up on his sexual practices of more than I could see. Whatever would make the sexual affair a nicer and more enjoyable thing would be the most *natural* and plausible thing for me. So, with some of this attitude I got the goo situation under control— we used Vaseline. Having tried many things in the course of my life, from cold creams to sulfathiazole, I had settled for Vaseline.

But now his problem was that he didn't experience so tumultuous a climax as I did. He was a person who wrote some of these things out. I liked to do this too and we wrote pages on our mutual problems in this area. It helped us to understand what we were entangled in. He said he could understand and accept that he could never reach such an intense orgasm, but that by making me reach an orgasm with his finger made him feel so alone. He said it was as though I were alone on the universe and that he had only contributed by helping to make it happen, that he was not really a part of it at all.

From there he went to "normal" intercourse. Now, if I were to reach a climax by normal intercourse, then he could *share* the experience with me. I pointed out that some sexologists no longer referred to intercourse as *normal*, but as just another way of reaching a climax. Dr. Kinsey listed six sexual "outlets" for men. He didn't refer to any one of them as normal, but rather as ways men could experience orgasm. Dr. Kinsey also pointed out the increase in petting to climax among the more intelligent white males. All of this was of no avail in the final analysis. Dan wanted to *share* this experience of mine.

We had several heartbreaking scenes over this. We might have made it through this one, but we came to "spontaneity." Dan was not alone in this attitude. I had encountered it before, alone with ideas such as: "Sex isn't any fun unless it's sinful," "Sex isn't any fun if you're married," "Sex isn't any fun unless you're afraid of getting caught." The one of spontaneity turns out something like this: "Sex isn't any fun unless it occurs on the spur of the moment, without any previous planning."

Used in this context spontaneity means anything unplanned. The opposite of it turns out to be anything planned; anything planned becomes something premeditated, and therefore cold-blooded. Without *real* emotion.

■

Age 33 . . . Tucson

I had known Bill Iverson for several years and we had never been particularly fond of each other. When I had known him previously, he had been living with an interesting girl, but now they were separated. Bill came to visit us with another fellow we both knew. The two of them were around quite a bit.

As Bill and I got to know each other better our attitudes began to change. He said nice things to me, about me, and I liked this. He was courteous. Once he leaned toward me and I found this slightest of approaches exciting. I had been living in a state of enforced celibacy, with no sex at all, and now this man made verbal passes at me and it was fun.

I had the feeling that I was being seduced. This was something new for me. Usually when I felt that I wanted a man, I let him know in some manner I'm not completely sure of, and had then allowed him to make passes at me. In Bill's case it seemed that he had picked me, and was invading, and I was liking it.

He stood by a wall one day and held out his hands toward me. I moved toward him. He said, "If you stand that close I'll make love to you." I stood that close.

He kissed me and moved his hands over my back. He felt my breasts.

"I just can't kiss standing up," I said, "I feel too weak."

"I'll hold you."

He kissed me some more, and he held me.

Later he said, "You know, something is puzzling me. I'd say offhand that you enjoy having me kiss you. But why do you push me away?"

I said I didn't.

"I wondered if I'd done something wrong. You did push me away."

I said I didn't believe it.

When he kissed me again I liked it and felt caught

up in it. And I found that I had my hands on his chest and was pushing at him. I said, "Ohmigod!"

"That's right," he said.

"The only way I can understand it," I said, "is that I get to feeling it so much that I don't think I can let it go on. I think I can hold it away for a few seconds maybe—and then have another go at it."

Bill was in no rush. I saw him often. We made love. He told me we didn't have to hurry. "We know what we're doing. We'll do what we want to do when we want to."

He didn't push me. He never made me feel that he expected anything more of me than I wanted to give. It was more that he could make me want him so very much that I was *willing* to give.

He kissed my breasts. Once I masturbated him. We both had our clothes on. Though I didn't reach a climax at that time I felt completely relaxed. I was sure he would make me reach a climax when we got to that.

We had picked the pleasant easygoing way of gradually having sex.

Bill could *talk* about sex. He could say more than that was good, or that was fun, or I would like to have a little. Not since Clint Jameson had I met a man who could speak so freely on specific parts of the body and specific actions regarding these parts. Bill Sanford was a very free soul, but we had never been around each other for long periods of time.

Bill Iverson could tell me, "I want to lick your clitoris. I am going to kiss you on your thighs. You have lovely breasts."

He visited us one day and I drove him home. We sat and talked a few minutes. Then he said, "Come inside so that I can rape you gently."

I went inside and took a shower. I lay down on his bed. He came in and kissed me, regarded my breasts lovingly, and ran his tongue over my nipples. Then he pulled my body to the edge of the bed. He sat on the floor and put his face between my legs—I felt his tongue on my clitoris.

I felt the awkwardness of not knowing exactly what I was doing.

I asked, "Where am I going to put my legs?"

He paused and said casually, "Put them anywhere. You can put them on my shoulders." He returned to my clitoris.

When I reached a very wonderful climax I again had the feeling that my legs could just jerk his head off, as I had with Bill Sanford. The contractions of my vagina were so strong, the tendency of my legs to come together forcefully was so great, that I felt I could not keep them from it.

I moaned.

Bill had his arms around my legs. He stroked the pelvic area above the *mons Veneris*. He pulled his head free of my body briefly and said, "Let go."

All of the resistance to completely feeling the intensity of the climax swooshed out of me. I abandoned myself to the sensuous feelings. I pulled my legs tightly together and let my hips gyrate with the will of their own that they seemed to have.

When I was quite satiated, he smiled pleasantly and said, "That was nice."

He let me rest for a while, and then he loomed above me. The vaginal sensations were still present, the quivering excitement of the nerves at the entrance. Our intercourse was a lovemaking aftermath for me; for him it was a highly successful experience, obviously.

Christina Rossetti

Goblin Market

[1859]

Morning and evening
Maids heard the goblins cry:
'Come buy our orchard fruits,
Come buy, come buy:
Apples and quinces,
Lemons and oranges,
Plump unpecked cherries,
Melons and raspberries,
Bloom-down-cheeked peaches,
Swart-headed mulberries,
Wild free-born cranberries,

Crab-apples, dewberries,
Pine-apples, blackberries,
Apricots, strawberries;—
All ripe together
In summer weather,—
Morns that pass by,
Fair eves that fly;
Come buy, come buy:
Our grapes fresh from the vine,
Pomegranates full and fine,
Dates and sharp bullaces,
Rare pears and greengages,
Damsons and bilberries,
Taste them and try:
Currants and gooseberries,
Bright-fire-like barberries,
Figs to fill your mouth,
Citrons from the South,
Sweet to tongue and sound to eye;
Come buy, come buy.'

Evening by evening
Among the brookside rushes,
Laura bowed her head to hear,
Lizzie veiled her blushes:
Crouching close together
In the cooling weather,
With clasping arms and cautioning
    lips,
With tingling cheeks and finger tips.
'Lie close,' Laura said,
Pricking up her golden head:
'We must not look at goblin men,
We must not buy their fruits:
Who knows upon what soil they fed
Their hungry thirsty roots?'
'Come buy,' call the goblins
Hobbling down the glen.
'Oh,' cried Lizzie, 'Laura, Laura,
You should not peep at goblin men.'
Lizzie covered up her eyes,

Covered close lest they should look;
Laura reared her glossy head,
And whispered like the restless brook:
'Look, Lizzie, look, Lizzie,
Down the glen tramp little men.
One hauls a basket,
One bears a plate,
One lugs a golden dish
Of many pounds' weight.
How fair the vine must grow
Whose grapes are so luscious
How warm the wind must blow
Through those fruit bushes.'

'No,' said Lizzie: 'No, no, no;
Their offers should not charm us,
Their evil gifts would harm us.'
She thrust a dimpled finger
In each ear, shut eyes and ran;
Curious Laura chose to linger

Wondering at each merchant man.
One had a cat's face,
One whisked a tail,
One tramped at a rat's pace,
One crawled like a snail,
One like a wombat prowled obtuse
    and furry,
One like a ratel tumbled hurry skurry.
She heard a voice like voice of doves
Cooing all together:
They sounded kind and full of loves
In the pleasant weather.

Laura stretched her gleaming neck
Like a rush-imbedded swan,
Like a lily from the beck,
Like a moonlit poplar branch,
Like a vessel at the launch
When its last restraint is gone.

Backwards up the mossy glen
Turned and trooped the goblin men,
With their shrill repeated cry,
'Come buy, come buy.'
When they reached where Laura was
They stood stock still upon the moss,
Leering at each other,
Brother with queer brother;
Signalling each other,
Brother with sly brother.
One set his basket down,
One reared his plate;
One began to weave a crown
Of tendrils, leaves, and rough nuts
    brown
(Men sell not such in any town);
One heaved the golden weight
Of dish and fruit to offer her:
'Come buy, come buy,' was still
    their cry.

Laura stared but did not stir,
Longed but had no money.
The whisk-tailed merchant bade her
    taste
In tones as smooth as honey,
The cat-faced purr'd,
The rat-paced spoke a word
Of welcome, and the snail-paced
    even was heard;
One parrot-voiced and jolly
Cried 'Pretty Goblin' still for 'Pretty
    Polly';
One whistled like a bird.

But sweet-tooth Laura spoke in
    haste:
'Good Folk, I have no coin;
To take were to purloin:
I have no copper in my purse,
I have no silver either,

And all my gold is on the furze
That shakes in windy weather
Above the rusty heather.'
'You have much gold upon your
    head,'
They answered all together:
'Buy from us with a golden curl.'
She clipped a precious golden lock,
She dropped a tear more rare than
    pearl,
Then sucked their fruit globes fair
    or red.
Sweeter than honey from the rock,
Stronger than man-rejoicing wine,
Clearer than water flowed that juice;
She never tasted such before,
How should it cloy with length of
    use?
She sucked and sucked and sucked
    the more

Fruits which that unknown orchard
    bore;
She sucked until her lips were sore;
Then flung the emptied rinds away
But gathered up one kernel stone,
And knew not was it night or day
As she turned home alone.

Lizzie met her at the gate
Full of wise upbraidings:
'Dear, you should not stay so late,
Twilight is not good for maidens;
Should not loiter in the glen
In the haunts of the goblin men.
Do you not remember Jeanie,
How she met them in the moonlight,
Took their gifts both choice and
    many,
Ate their fruits and wore their
    flowers

Plucked from bowers
Where summer ripens at all hours?
But ever in the noonlight
she pined and pined away;
Sought them by night and day,
Found them no more, but dwindled
    and grew grey;
Then fell with the first snow,
While to this day no grass will grow
Where she lies low:
I planted daisies there a year ago
That never blow.
You should not loiter so.'
'Nay, hush,' said Laura:
'Nay, hush, my sister:
I ate and ate my fill,
Yet my mouth waters still:
To-morrow night I will
Buy more;' and kissed her.
'Have done with sorrow;

I'll bring you plums to-morrow
Fresh on their mother twigs,
Cherries worth getting;
You cannot think what figs
My teeth have met in,
What melons icy-cold
Piled on a dish of gold
Too huge for me to hold,
What peaches with a velvet nap,
Pellucid grapes without one seed:
Odorous indeed must be the mead
Whereon they grow, and pure the
    wave they drink
With lilies at the brink,
And sugar-sweet their sap.'

Golden head by golden head,
Like two pigeons in one nest
Folded in each other's wings,

They lay down in their curtained
    bed:
Like two blossoms on one stem,
Like two flakes of new-fall'n snow,
Like two wands of ivory
Tipped with gold for awful kings.
Moon and stars gazed in at them,
Wind sang to them lullaby,
Lumbering owls forebore to fly,
Not a bat flapped to and fro
Round their nest:
Cheek to cheek and breast to breast
Locked together in one nest.

Early in the morning—
When the first cock crowed his
    warning,
Neat like bees, as sweet and busy,
Laura rose with Lizzie:
Fetched in honey, milked the cows,

Aired and set to rights the house,
Kneaded cakes of whitest wheat,
Cakes for dainty mouths to eat,
Next churned butter, whipped up
    cream,
Fed their poultry, sat and sewed;
Talked as modest maidens should:
Lizzie with an open heart,
Laura in an absent dream,
One content, one sick in part;
One warbling for the mere bright
    day's delight,
One longing for the night.

At length slow evening came:
They went with pitchers to the
    reedy brook;
Lizzie most placid in her look,
Laura most like a leaping flame.

They drew the gurgling water from
  its deep.
Lizzie plucked purple and rich
  golden flags,
Then turning homeward said: 'The
  sunset flushes
Those furthest loftiest crags;
Come, Laura, not another maiden
  lags.
No wilful squirrel wags,
The beasts and birds are fast asleep.'
But Laura loitered still among the
  rushes,
And said the bank was steep.

And said the hour was early still,
The dew not fall'n, the wind not
  chill;
Listening ever, but not catching
The customary cry,

'Come buy, come buy,'
With its iterated jingle
Of sugar-baited words:
Not for all her watching
Once discerning even one goblin
Racing, whisking, tumbling, hobbling—
Let alone the herds
That used to tramp along the glen,
In groups or single,
Of brisk fruit-merchant men.

Till Lizzie urged, 'O Laura, come;
I hear the fruit-call, but I dare not
    look:
You should not loiter longer at this
    brook:
Come with me home.
The stars rise, the moon bends her
    arc,

Each glow-worm winks her spark,
Let us get home before the night
    grows dark:
For clouds may gather
Though this is summer weather,
Put out the lights and drench us
    through;
Then if we lost our way what should
    we do?'

Laura turned cold as stone
To find her sister heard that cry
    alone,
That goblin cry,
'Come buy our fruits, come buy.'
Must she then buy no more such
    dainty fruit?
Must she no more such succous
    pasture find,
Gone deaf and blind?

Her tree of life drooped from the
    root:
She said not one word in her heart's
    sore ache:
But peering thro' the dimness,
    nought discerning,
Trudged home, her pitcher dripping
    all the way;
So crept to bed, and lay
Silent till Lizzie slept;
Then sat up in a passionate yearning,
And gnashed her teeth for baulked
    desire, and wept
As if her heart would break.

Day after day, night after night,
Laura kept watch in vain
In sullen silence of exceeding pain.
She never caught again the goblin
    cry,

'Come buy, come buy;'—
She never spied the goblin men
Hawking their fruits along the glen:
But when the noon waxed bright
Her hair grew thin and grey;
She dwindled, as the fair full moon
    doth turn
To swift decay and burn
Her fire away.

One day remembering her kernel-stone
She set it by a wall that faced the
    south;
Dewed it with tears, hoped for a
    root,
Watched for a waxing shoot,
But there came none.
It never saw the sun,
It never felt the trickling moisture
    run:

While with sunk eyes and faded
    mouth
She dreamed of melons, as a
    traveller sees
False waves in desert drouth
With shade of leaf-crowned trees,
And burns the thirstier in the sandful
    breeze.

She no more swept the house,
Tended the fowls or cows,
Fetched honey, kneaded cakes of
    wheat,
Brought water from the brook:
But sat down listless in the chimney-nook
And would not eat.

Tender Lizzie could not bear
To watch her sister's cankerous care,
Yet not to share.

She night and morning
Caught the goblins' cry:
'Come buy our orchard fruits,
Come buy, come buy:'—
Beside the brook, along the glen,
She heard the tramp of goblin men,
The voice and stir
Poor Laura could not hear;
Longed to buy fruit to comfort her,
But feared to pay too dear.
She thought of Jeanie in her grave,
Who should have been a bride.
But who for joys brides hope to have
Fell sick and died
In her gay prime,
In earliest winter time,
With the first glazing rime,
With the first snow-fall of crisp
    winter time.
Till Laura dwindling

Seemed knocking at Death's door.
Then Lizzie weighed no more
Better and worse;
But put a silver penny in her purse,
Kissed Laura, crossed the heath
    with clumps of furze
At twilight, halted by the brook:
And for the first time in her life
Began to listen and look.

Laughed every goblin
When they spied her peeping:
Came towards her hobbling,
Flying, running, leaping,
Puffing and blowing,
Chuckling, clapping, crowing,
Clucking and gobbling,
Mopping and mowing,
Full of airs and graces,
Pulling wry faces,

Demure grimaces,
Cat-like and rat-like,
Ratel- and wombat-like,
Snail-paced in a hurry,
Parrot-voiced and whistler,
Helter skelter, hurry skurry,
Chattering like magpies,
Fluttering like pigeons,
Gliding like fishes,—
Hugged her and kissed her:
Squeezed and caressed her:
Stretched up their dishes,
Pranniers, and plates:
'Look at our apples
Russet and dun,
Bob at our cherries,
Bite at our peaches,
Citrons and dates,
Grapes for the asking,
Pears red with basking

Out in the sun,
Plums on their twigs;
Pluck them and suck them,—
Pomegranates, figs,'
'Good folk,' said Lizzie,
Mindful of Jeanie:
'Give me much and many:'
Held out her apron,
Tossed them her penny.
'Nay, take a seat with us,
Honour and eat with us,'
They answered grinning:
'Our feast is but beginning.
Night yet is early,
Warm and dew-pearly,
Wakeful and starry:
Such fruits as these
No man can carry;
Half their bloom would fly,
Half their dew would dry,

Half their flavour would pass by.
Sit down and feast with us,
Cheer you and rest with us.'—
'Thank you,' said Lizzie: 'But one
    waits
At home alone for me:
So without further parleying,
If you will not sell me any
Of your fruits though much and many,
Give me back my silver penny
I tossed you for a fee.'—
They began to scratch their pates,
No longer wagging, purring,
But visibly demurring,
Grunting and snarling.
One called her proud,
Cross-grained, uncivil;
Their tones waxed loud,
Their looks were evil,
Lashing their tails

They trod and hustled her,
Elbowed and jostled her,
Clawed with their nails,
Barking, mewing, hissing, mocking,
Tore her gown and soiled her
    stocking.
Twitched her hair out by the roots,
Stamped upon her tender feet,
Held her hands and squeezed their
    fruits
Against her mouth to make her eat.

White and golden Lizzie stood,
Like a lily in a flood,—
Like a rock of blue-veined stone
Lashed by tides obstreperously,—
Like a beacon left alone
In a hoary roaring sea,
Sending up a golden fire,—
Like a fruit-crowned orange-tree

White with blossoms honey-sweet
Sore beset by wasp and bee,—
Like a royal virgin town
Topped with gilded dome and spire
Close beleaguered by a fleet
Mad to tug her standard down.

One may lead a horse to water,
Twenty cannot make him drink.
Though the goblins cuffed and caught
    her,
Coaxed and fought her,
Bullied and besought her,
Scratched her, pinched her black as
    ink,
Kicked and knocked her,
Mauled and mocked her,
Lizzie uttered not a word;
Would not open lip from lip
Lest they should cram a mouthful in:

But laughed in heart to feel the drip
Of juice that syruped all her face,
And lodged in dimples of her chin,
And streaked her neck which quaked
    like curd.
At last the evil people,
Worn out by her resistance,
Flung back her penny, kicked their
    fruit
Along whichever road they took,
Not leaving root or stone or shoot;
Some writhed into the ground,
Some dived into the brook
With ring and ripple,
Some scudded on the gale without a
    sound,
Some vanished in the distance.

In a smart, ache, tingle,
Lizzie went her way;

Knew not was it night or day;
Sprang up the bank, tore thro' the
    furze,
Threaded copse and dingle,
And heard her penny jingle
Bouncing in her purse,—
Its bounce was music to her ear.
She ran and ran
As if she feared some goblin man
Dogged her with gibe or curse
Or something worse:
But not one goblin skurried after,
Nor was she pricked by fear;
The kind heart made her windy-paced
That urged her home quite out of
    breath with haste
And inward laughter.

She cried, 'Laura,' up the garden,
'Did you miss me?

Come and kiss me.
Never mind my bruises,
Hug me, kiss me, suck my juices
Squeezed from goblin fruits for you,
Goblin pulp and goblin dew.
Eat me, drink me, love me;
Laura, make much of me;
For your sake I have braved the glen
And had to do with goblin merchant
      men.'

Laura started from her chair,
Flung her arms up in the air,
Clutched her hair:
'Lizzie, Lizzie, have you tasted
Nor my sake the fruit forbidden?
Must your light like mine be hidden,
Your young life like mine be wasted,
Undone in mine undoing,
And ruined in my ruin,

Thirsty, cankered, goblin-ridden?'—
She clung about her sister,
Kissed and kissed and kissed her:
Tears once again
Refreshed her shrunken eyes,
Dropping like rain
After long sultry drouth;
Shaking with anguish fear, and pain,
She kissed and kissed her with a
    hungry mouth.

Her lips began to scorch,
That juice was wormwood to her
    tongue,
She loathed the feast:
Writhing as one possessed she leaped
    and sung,
Rent all her robe, and wrung
Her hands in lamentable haste,
And beat her breast.

Her locks streamed like the torch
Borne by a racer at full speed,
Or like the mane of horses in their
    flight,
Or like an eagle when she stems the
    light
Straight toward the sun,
Or like a caged thing freed,
Or like a flying flag when armies run.

Swift fire spread through her veins,
    knocked at her heart,
Met the fire smouldering there
And overbore its lesser flame;
She gorged on bitterness without a
    name:
Ah fool, to choose such part
Of soul-consuming care!
Sense failed in the mortal strife:
Like the watch-tower of a town

Which an earthquake shatters down,
Like a lightning-stricken mast,
Like a wind-uprooted tree
Spun about,
Like a foam-topped waterspout
Cast down headlong in the sea,
She fell at last;
Pleasure past and anguish past,
Is it death or is it life?

Life out of death.
That night long Lizzie watched by
    her,
Counted her pulse's flagging stir,
Felt for her breath,
Held water to her lips, and cooled
    her face
With tears and fanning leaves.
But when the first birds chirped
    about their eaves,

And early reapers plodded to the
place
Of golden sheaves,
And dew-wet grass
Bowed in the morning winds so brisk
to pass,
And new buds with new day
Opened of cup-like lilies on the
stream,
Laura awoke as from a dream,
Laughed in the innocent old way,
Hugged Lizzie but not twice or
thrice;
Her gleaming locks showed not one
thread of grey,
Her breath was sweet as May,
And light danced in her eyes.

Days, weeks, months, years
Afterwards, when both were wives

With children of their own;
Their mother-hearts beset with fears,
Their lives bound up in tender lives;
Laura would call the little ones
And tell them of her early prime,
Those pleasant days long gone
Of not-returning time:
Would talk about the haunted glen,
The wicked quaint fruit-merchant
    men,
Their fruits like honey to the throat
But poison in the blood
(Men sell not such in any town):
Would tell them how her sister
    stood
In deadly peril to do her good,
And win the fiery antidote:
Then joining hands to little hands
Would bid them cling together,—
'For there is no friend like a sister

In calm or stormy weather;
To cheer one on the tedious way,
To fetch one if one goes astray,
To lift one if one totters down,
To strengthen whilst one stands.'

Diane Ackerman

Kissing

[1994]

Sex is the ultimate intimacy, the ultimate touching when, like two paramecia, we engulf one another. We play at devouring each other, digesting each other, we nurse on each other, drink each other's fluids, get under each other's skin. Kissing, we share one breath, open the sealed fortress of our body to our lover. We shelter under a warm net of kisses. We drink from the well of each other's mouths. Setting out on a kiss caravan of the other's body, we map the new terrain with our fingertips and lips, pausing at the oasis of a nipple, the hillock of a thigh, the backbone's meandering riverbed. It is a kind of pilgrimage of touch, which leads to the temple of our desire.

We most often touch a lover's genitals before we actually see them. For the most part, our leftover puritanism doesn't condone exhibiting ourselves to each other naked before we've kissed and fondled first. There is an etiquette, a protocol, even in impetuous, runaway sex. But kissing can happen right away, and, if two people care for each other, then it's less a prelude to mating than a sign of deep regard. There are wild, hungry kisses or there are rollicking kisses, and there are kisses fluttery and soft as the feathers of cockatoos. It's as if, in the complex language of love, there were a word that could only be spoken when lips touch, a silent contract sealed with a kiss. One style of sex can be bare bones, fundamental and unromantic, but a kiss is the height of voluptuousness, an expense of time and an expanse of spirit in the sweet toil of romance, when one's bones quiver, anticipation rockets, but gratification is kept at bay on purpose, in exquisite torment, to build to a succulent crescendo of emotion and passion.

When I was in high school in the early sixties, nice girls didn't go all the way—most of us wouldn't have known how to. But man, could we kiss! We kissed for hours in the busted-up front seat of a borrowed Chevy, which, in motion, sounded like a a broken dinette set; we kissed inventively, clutching our boyfriends from behind as we straddled motorcycles, whose vibrations turned our hips to jelly; we kissed extravagantly beside a turtlearium in the park, or at the local rose garden or zoo; we kissed delicately, in waves of sipping and puckering; we kissed torridly, with tongues like hot pokers; we kissed timelessly, because lovers throughout the ages knew our longing; we kissed wildly, almost painfully, with tough, soul-stealing rigor; we kissed elaborately, as if we were inventing kisses; we kissed furtively when we met in the hallways between classes; we kissed soulfully in the shadows at concerts, the way we thought musical knights of passion like The Righteous Brothers and their ladies did; we kissed articles of clothing or objects belonging to our boyfriends; we kissed our hands when we blew our boyfriends kisses across the street; we kissed our pillows at night, pretending they were mates; we kissed shamelessly, with all the robust sappiness of youth; we kissed as if kissing could save us from ourselves.

Before I went off to summer camp, which is what fourteen-year-old girls in suburban Pennsylvania did to mark time, my boyfriend, whom my parents did not approve of (wrong religion) and had forbidden me to see, used to walk five miles across town each evening, and climb in through my bedroom window to kiss me. These were not open-mouthed "French" kisses, which we didn't know about, and they weren't accompanied by groping. They were just earth-stopping, soulful, on-the-ledge-of-adolescence kissing, when you press your lips together and yearn so hard you feel faint. We wrote letters while I was away, but when school started again in the fall the affair seemed to fade of its own accord. I still remember those summer nights, how my boyfriend would hide in my closet if my parents or brother chanced in, and then kiss me for an hour or so and head back home before dark, and I marvel at his determination and the power of a kiss.

A kiss seems the smallest movement of the lips, yet it can capture emotions wild as kindling, or be a contract, or dash a mystery. Some cultures don't do much kissing. In *The Kiss and Its History*, Dr. Christopher Nyrop refers to Finnish tribes "which bathe together in a state of complete nudity," but regard kissing "as something indecent." Certain African tribes, whose lips are decorated, mutilated, stretched, or in other ways deformed, don't kiss. But they are unusual. Most people on the planet greet one another face-to-face; their greeting may take many forms, but it usually includes kissing, nose-kissing, or nose-saluting. There are many theories about how kissing began. Some authorities believe it evolved from the act of smelling someone's face, inhaling them out of friendship or love in order to gauge their mood and well-being. There are cultures today in which people greet each other by putting their heads together and inhaling the other's essence. Some sniff hands. The mucous membranes of the lips are exquisitely sensitive, and we often use the mouth to taste texture while using the nose to smell flavor. Animals frequently lick their masters or their young with relish, savoring the taste of a favorite's identity. (Not only humans kiss. Apes and chimps have been observed kissing and embracing as a form of peace-making.) So we may indeed have begun kissing as a way to taste and smell someone. According to the Bible account, when Isaac grew old and lost his sight, he called his son Esau to kiss him and receive a blessing. But Jacob put on Esau's clothing and, because he smelled like Esau to his blind father, received the kiss instead. In Mongolia, a father does not kiss his son; he smells his son's head. Some cultures prefer just to rub noses (Inuits, Maoris, Polynesians, and others), while in some Malay tribes the word "smell" means the same as "salute." Here is how Charles Darwin describes the Malay nose-rubbing kiss: "The women squatted with their faces upturned; my attendants stood leaning over theirs, and commenced rubbing. It lasts somewhat longer than a hearty handshake with us. During this process they uttered a grunt of satisfaction."

Some cultures kiss chastely, some extravagantly, and some savagely, biting and sucking each other's lips. In *The Customs of the Swahili People*, edited by J.W.T. Allen, it is reported that a Swahili husband and wife kiss on the lips if they are indoors, and will freely kiss young children. However, boys over the age of seven usually are not kissed by mother, aunt, sister-in-law, or sister. The father may kiss a son, but a brother or father shouldn't kiss a girl. Furthermore,

> when his grandmother or his aunt or another woman comes, a child one or two years old is told to show his love for his aunt and he goes to her. Then she tells him to kiss her, and he does so. Then he is told by his mother to show his aunt his tobacco, and he lifts his clothes and shows her his penis. She tweaks the penis and sniffs and sneezes and says: "O, very strong tobacco."

Then she says, "Hide your tobacco." If there are four or five women, they all sniff and are pleased and laugh a lot.

How did mouth kissing begin? To primitive peoples, the hot air wafting from their mouths may have seemed a magical embodiment of the soul, and a kiss a way to fuse two souls. Desmond Morris, who has been observing people with a keen zoologist's eye for decades, is one of a number of authorities who claim this fascinating and, to me, plausible origin for French kissing:

> In early human societies, before commercial baby-food was invented, mothers weaned their children by chewing up their food and then passing it into the infantile mouth by lip-to-lip contact—which naturally involved a considerable amount of tonguing and mutual mouth-pressure. This almost bird-like system of parental care seems strange and alien to us today, but our species probably practiced it for a million

years or more, and adult erotic kissing today is almost certainly a Relic Gesture stemming from these origins. . . . Whether it has been handed down to us from generation to generation . . . or whether we have an inborn predisposition towards it, we cannot say. But, whichever is the case, it looks rather as though, with the deep kissing and tonguing of modern lovers, we are back again at the infantile mouth-feeding stage of the far-distant past. . . . If the young lovers exploring each other's mouths with their tongues feel the ancient comfort of parental mouth-feeding, this may help them increase their mutual trust and thereby their pair-bonding.

Our lips are deliciously soft and responsive. Their touch sensations are transmitted to a large part of the brain, and what a boon that is to kissing. We don't just kiss romantically, of course. We also kiss dice before we roll them, kiss our own hurt finger or that of a loved one, kiss a religious symbol or statue, kiss the flag of our homeland or the ground itself, kiss a good-luck charm, kiss a photograph, kiss the king's or bishop's ring, kiss our own fingers to signal farewell to someone. The ancient Romans used to deliver the "last kiss," which custom had it would capture a dying person's soul.[1] In America we "kiss off" someone when we dump them, and they yell "Kiss my ass!" when angry. Young women press lipsticked mouths to the backs of envelopes so all the imprinted tiny lines will carry like fingerprint kisses to their sweethearts. We even refer to billiard balls as "kissing" when they touch delicately and glance away. Hershey sells small foil-wrapped candy "kisses," so we can give love to ourselves or others with each morsel. Christian worship includes a "kiss of peace," whether of a holy object—a relic or a cross—or of fellow worshipers, translated by some Christians into a rather more restrained handshake. William S. Walsh's 1897 book, *Curiosities of Popular Customs*, quotes a Dean Stanley, writing in *Christian Institutions*, as reporting travelers who "have had their faces stroked and been kissed by the Coptic priest in the cathedral at Cairo, while at the same moment everybody else was kissing everybody throughout the church." In ancient Egypt, the Orient, Rome, and Greece, honor used to dictate kissing the hem or feet or hands of important persons. Mary Magdalen kissed the feet of Jesus. Kissing the pope's ring is a near-miss kiss. A sultan often required subjects of varying ranks to kiss varying parts of his royal body: high officials might kiss the toe, others merely the fringe of his scarf. The riffraff just bowed to the ground. Drawing a row of XXXXXs at the bottom of a letter to represent kisses began in the Middle Ages, when so many people were illiterate that a cross was acceptable as a signature on a legal document. The cross did not represent the Crucifixion, nor was it an arbitrary scrawl; it stood for "Saint Andrew's mark," and people vowed to be honest in his sacred name. To pledge their sincerity, they would kiss their signature. In time, the "X" became associated with the kiss alone.[2]

Perhaps the most famous buss in the world is Rodin's sculpture *The Kiss*, in which two lovers, sitting on a rocky ledge or outcropping, embrace tenderly with radiant energy, and kiss forever. Her left hand wrapped around his neck, she seems almost to be swooning, or to be singing into his mouth. As he rests his open right hand on her thigh, a thigh he knows well and adores, he seems to be ready to play her leg as if it were a musical instrument. Enveloped in each other, glued together by touch at the shoulder, hand, leg, hip, and chest, they seal their fate and close it with the stoppers of their mouths. His calves and knees are beautiful, her ankles are strong and firmly feminine, and her buttocks, waist, and breasts are all heavily fleshed and curvy. Ecstasy pours off every inch of them. Touching in only a few places, they seem to be touching in every cell. Above all, they are oblivious to us, the sculptor, or anything on earth outside of themselves. It is as if they have fallen down the well of each other; they are not only self-absorbed, but absorbing each other. Rodin, who often took secret sketch notes of the irrelevant motions made by his models, has given these lovers a vitality and thrill that bronze can rarely capture in its fundamental calm. Only the fluent, abstracted stroking and pressing of live lovers actually kissing could capture it. Rilke notes how Rodin was able to fill his sculptures "with this deep inner vitality, with the rich and amazing restlessness of life. Even the tranquility, where there was a tranquility, was composed of hundreds upon hundreds of moments of motion keeping each other in equilibrium. . . . Here was desire immeasurable, thirst so great that all the waters of the world dried in it like a single drop."

According to anthropologists, the lips remind us of the labia, because they flush red and swell when aroused, which is the conscious or subconscious reason women have always made them look even redder with lipstick. Today the bee-stung look is popular; models draw even larger and more hospitable lips, almost always in shades of pink and red, and then apply a further gloss to make them look shiny and moist. So, anthropologically at least, a kiss on the mouth, especially with all the plunging of tongues and the exchanging of saliva, is another form of intercourse. No surprise that it makes the mind and body surge with gorgeous sensations.

---

[1] Last-kiss scenes appear in Ovid's *Metamorphoses* (VIII, 860–61), Seneca's *Hercules Oetaeus*, and Virgil's *Aeneid* (IV, 684–85), among others, and in a more erotic form in the writings of Ariosto.

[2] It used to be fashionable in Spain to close formal letters with QBSP (*Que Besa Su Pies*, "Who kisses your feet") or QBSM (*Que Besa Su Mano*, "Who kisses your hand").

Emily Dickinson

Wild Nights—Wild Nights

[1861]

Wild Nights—Wild Nights!
Were I with thee
Wild Nights should be
Our luxury!

Futile—the Winds—
To a Heart in port—
Done with the Compass—
Done with the Chart!

Rowing in Eden—
Ah, the Sea!
Might I put moor—Tonight—
In Thee!

Trotula

A Gynecologist's Tips

[1075]

Vervain carried or drunk will not permit the penis to go stiff until it is laid aside, and vervain placed under the pillow makes an erection impossible for seven days, which prescription if you wish to test, give to a cock mixed with bran and the cock will not mount the hen. . . . Likewise, anoint the shoelaces with the juice of vervain and wear them against the flesh, and you will be effeminate; and if a man touches anyone he will be inept for such things because it weakens the pleasure of touching.

Hygiene

Whenever a woman is going to sleep with someone, let her wash out the inside of her pudenda, inserting her fingers wrapped in dry wool . . . then let her carefully wipe inside and out with a very clean cloth. Next, she should bind her legs so that all the wetness may flow out from her insides and then, inserting a cloth, she should vigorously dry her genitalia; then let her take some powder in her mouth, and chew, and rub her hands, chest, and nipples; let her sprinkle rose water on her pubis, genitals, and face. Thus nicely made up, let her approach the man.

Anonymous

The Autobiography of a Flea

[1880s]

Born I was—but how, when, or where I cannot say; so I must leave the reader to accept the assertion "per se," and believe it if he will. One thing is equally certain, the fact of my birth is not one atom less veracious than the reality of these memoirs, and if the intelligent student of these pages wonders how it came to pass that one in my walk—or perhaps, I should have said jump—in life, became possessed of the learning, observation and power of committing to memory the whole of the wonderful facts and disclosures I am about to relate. I can only remind him that there are intelligences, little suspected by the vulgar, and laws in nature, the very existence of which have not yet been detected by the advanced among the scientific world.

I have heard it somewhere remarked that my province was to get my living by blood sucking. I am not the lowest by any means of that universal fraternity, and if I sustain a precarious existence upon the bodies of those with whom I come in contact, my own experience proves that I do so in a marked and peculiar manner, with a warning of my employment which is seldom given by those in other grades of my profession. But I submit that I have other and nobler aims than the mere sustaining of my being by the contributions of the unwary. I have been conscious of this original defect, and, with a soul far above the vulgar instincts of my race. I jumped by degrees to heights of mental perception and erudition which placed me for ever upon a pinnacle of insect-grandeur.

It is this attainment to learning which I shall evoke in describing the scenes of which I have been a witness—nay, even a partaker. I shall not stop to explain by what means I am possessed of human powers of thinking and observing, but, in my lucubrations, leave you simply to perceive that I possess them and wonder accordingly.

You will thus perceive that I am not common flea; indeed, when it is borne in mind the company in which I have been accustomed to mingle, the familiarity with which I have been suffered to treat persons the most exalted, and the opportunities I have possessed to make the most of my acquaintances, the reader will no doubt agree with me that I am in very truth a most wonderful and exalted insect.

My earliest recollections lead me back to a period when I found myself within a church. There was a rolling of rich music and a slow monotonous chanting which then filled me with surprise and admiration, but I have long since learnt the true importance of such influences, and the attitudes of the worshippers are now taken by me for the outward semblance of inward emotions which are very generally non-existent. Be this as it may, I was engaged upon professional business connected with the plump white leg of a young lady of some fourteen years of age, the taste of whose delicious blood I well remember, and the flavour of whose—

But I am digressing.

Soon after commencing in a quiet and friendly way my little attentions, the young girl in common with the rest of the congregation rose to depart, and I, as a matter of course, determined to accompany her.

I am very sharp of sight as well as of hearing, and that is how I saw a young gentleman slip a small folded piece of white paper into the young lady's pretty gloved hand, as she passed through the crowded porch. I had noticed the name Bella neatly worked upon the soft silk stocking which had at first attracted me, and I now saw that the same word appeared alone upon the outside of the billet-doux. She was with her Aunt, a tall, stately dame, with whom I did not care to get upon terms of intimacy.

Bella was a beauty—just fourteen—a perfect figure, and although so young, her soft bosom was already budding into those proportions which delight the other sex. Her face was charming in its frankness; her breath sweet as the perfumes of Arabia, and, as I have always said, her skin as soft as velvet. Bella was evidently well aware of her good looks, and carried her head as proudly and as coquettishly as a queen. That she inspired admiration was not difficult to see by the wistful and longing glances which the young men, and sometimes also those of the more mature years, cast upon her. There was a general hush of conversation outside the building, and a turning of glances generally towards the pretty Bella, which told more plainly than words that she was the admired one of all eyes and the desired one of all hearts—at any rate among the male sex.

Paying, however very little attention to what was evidently a matter of every-day occurrence, the young lady walked sharply homewards with her Aunt, and after arrival at the neat and genteel residence, went quickly to her room. I will not say I followed her, but I "went with her," and beheld the gentle girl raise one dainty leg across the other and remove the tiniest of tight and elegant kid-boots.

I jumped upon the carpet and proceeded with my examinations. The left boot followed, and without removing her plump calf from off the other, Bella sat looking at the folded piece of paper which I had seen the young fellow deposit secretly in her hand.

Closely watching everything, I noted the swelling thighs, which spread upwards above her tightly fitting garters, until they were lost in the darkness, as they closed together at a point where her beautiful belly met them in her stooping position; and almost obliterated a thin and peach-like slit, which just shewed its rounded lips between them in the shade.

Presently Bella dropped her note, and being open, I took the liberty to read it.

"I will be in the old spot at eight o'clock to night," were the only words which the paper contained, but they appeared to have a special interest for Bella, who remained cogitating for some time in the same thoughtful mood.

My curiosity had been aroused, and my desire to know more of the interesting young being with whom chance had so promiscuously brought me in pleasing contact, prompted me to remain quietly ensconced in a snug though somewhat moist hiding place, and it was not until near upon the hour named that I once more emerged in order to watch the progress of events.

Bella had dressed herself with scrupulous care, and now prepared to betake herself to the garden which surrounded the country-house in which she dwelt.

I went with her.

Arriving at the end of a long and shady avenue the young girl seated herself upon a rustic bench, and there awaited the coming of the person she was to meet.

It was not many minutes before the young man presented himself whom I had seen in communication with my fair little friend in the morning.

A conversation ensued which, if I might judge by the abstraction of the pair from aught besides themselves, had unusual interest for both.

It was evening, and the twilight had already commenced: the air was warm and genial, and the young pair sat closely entwined upon the bench, lost to all but their own united happiness.

"You don't know how I love you Bella," whispered the youth, tenderly sealing his protestation with a kiss upon the pouting lips of his companion.

"Yes I do," replied the girl, naively, "are you not always telling me? I shall get tired of hearing it soon."

Bella fidgeted her pretty little foot and looked thoughtful.

"When are you going to explain and show me all those funny things you told me about?" asked she, giving a quick glance up, and then as rapidly bending her eyes upon the gravel walk.

"Now," answered the youth. "Now, dear Bella, while we have the chance to be alone and free from interruption. You know, Bella, we are no longer children?"

Bella nodded her head.

"Well, there are things which are not known to children, and which are necessary for lovers not only to know, but also to practice."

"Dear me," said the girl, seriously.

"Yes," continued her companion, "there are secrets

which render lovers happy, and which make them enjoy of loving and of being loved."

"Lord!" exclaimed Bella, "how, sentimental you have grown, Charlie; I remember the time when you declared sentiment was 'all humbug.'"

"So I thought it was, till I loved you," replied the youth.

"Nonsense," continued Bella, "but go on, Charlie, and tell me what you promised."

"I can't tell you without showing you as well," replied Charlie; "the knowledge can only be learnt by experience."

"Oh, go on then and show me," cried the girl, in whose bright eyes and glowing cheeks I thought I could detect a very conscious knowledge of the kind of instruction about to be imparted.

There was something catching in her impatience. The youth yielded to it, and covering her beautiful young form with his own, glued his mouth to hers and kissed it rapturously.

Bella made no resistance; she even aided and returned her lover's caresses.

Meanwhile the evening advanced: the trees lay in the gathering darkness, spreading their lofty tops to screen the waning light from the young lovers.

Presently Charlie slid on one side; he made a slight movement, and then without any opposition he passed his hand under and up the petticoats of the pretty Bella. Not satisfied with the charms which he found within the compass of the glistening silk stockings, he essayed to press on still further, and his wandering fingers now touched the soft and quivering flesh of her young thighs.

Bella's breath came hard and fast, as she felt the indelicate attack which was being made upon her charms. So far, however, from resisting, she evidently enjoyed the exciting dalliance.

"Touch it," whispered Bella, "you may."

Charlie needed no further invitation: indeed he was already preparing to advance without one and instantly comprehending the permission, drove his fingers forward.

The fair girl opened her thighs as he did so, and the next instant his hand covered the delicate pink lips of her pretty slit.

For the next ten minutes the pair remained almost motionless, their lips joined and their breathing alone marking the sensations which were overpowering them with the intoxication of wantonness. Charlie felt a delicate object, which stiffened beneath his nimble fingers, and assumed a prominence of which he had no experience.

Presently Bella closed her eyes, and throwing back her head, shuddered slightly, while her frame became supple and languid, and she suffered her head to rest upon the arm of her lover.

"Oh, Charlie," she murmured, "what is it you do? What delightful sensations you give me."

Meanwhile the youth was not idle, but having fairly explored all he could in the constrained position in which he found himself, he rose, and sensible of the need of assuaging the raging passion which his actions had fanned, he besought his fair companion to let him guide her hand to a dear object, which he assured her was capable of giving her far greater pleasure than his fingers had done.

Nothing loth, Bella's grasp was the next moment upon a new and delicious substance, and either giving way to the curiosity she simulated, or really carried away by her newly-roused desires, nothing would do, but she must bring out and into the light the standing affair of her friend.

Those of my readers who have been placed in a similar position will readily understand the warmth of the grasp and the surprise of the look which greeted the first appearance in public of the new acquisition.

Bella beheld a man's member for the first time in her life, in the full plenitude of its power, and although it was not, I could plainly see, by any means a formidable one, yet its white shaft and redcapped head, from which the soft skin retreated as she pressed it, gained her quick inclination to learn more.

Charlie was equally moved; his eyes shone and his hand continued to rove all over the sweet young treasure of which he had taken possession.

Meanwhile the toyings of the little white hand upon the youthful member with which it was in contact had produced effects common under such circumstances to all of so healthy and vigourous a constitution as that of the owner of this particular affair.

Enraptured with the soft pressures, the gentle and delicious squeezings, and artless way in which the young lady pulled back the folds from the rampant nut, and disclosed the ruby crest, purple with desire, and the tip, ended by the tiny orifice, now awaiting its opportunity to send forth its slippery offering, the youth grew wild with lust, and Bella, participating in sensations new and strange, but which carried her away in a whirlwind of passionate excitement, panted for she knew not what of rapturous relief.

With her beautiful eyes half closed, her dewy lips parted, and her skin warm and glowing with the unwonted impulse stealing over her, she lay the delicious victim of whomsoever had the instant chance to reap her favours and pluck her delicate young rose.

Charlie, youth though he was, was not so blind as to lose so fair an opportunity; besides, his now rampant passions carried him forward despite the dictates of prudence which he otherwise might have heard.

He felt the throbbing and well-moistened centre quivering beneath his fingers, he beheld the beautiful girl lying invitingly to the amorous sport, he watched the tender breathings which caused the young breast to rise and fall, and the strong sensual emotions which animated the glowing form of his youthful companion.

The full, soft and swelling legs of the girl were now exposed to his sensuous gaze.

Gently raising the intervening drapery, Charlie still further disclosed the secret charms of his lovely companion until, with eyes of flame, he saw the plump limbs terminate in the full hips and white palpitating belly.

Then also his ardent gaze fell upon the centre spot of attraction—on the small pink slit which lay half hidden at the foot of the swelling mount of Venus, hardly yet shaded by the softest down.

The titillation which he had administered, and the caresses which he had bestowed upon the coveted object had induced a flow of the native moisture which such excitement tends to provoke, and Bella lay with her peach-like slit well bedewed with nature's best and sweetest lubricant.

Charlie saw his chance. Gently disengaging her hand from its grasp upon his member, he threw himself frantically upon the recumbent figure of the girl.

His left arm wound itself round her slender waist, his hot breath was on her cheek, his lips pressed hers in one long, passionate and hurried kiss. His left hand, now free, sought to bring together those parts of both which are the active instruments of sensual pleasure, and with eager efforts he sought to complete conjunction.

Bella now felt for the first time in her life the magic touch of a man's machine between the tips of her rosy orifice.

No sooner had she perceived the warm contact which was occasioned by the stiffened head of Charlie's member, than she shuddered perceptibly, and already anticipating the delights of venery, gave down an abundance of proof of her susceptible nature.

Charlie was enraptured at his happiness, and eagerly strove to perfect his enjoyment.

But Nature, which had operated so powerfully in the development of Bella's sensual passions, left yet something to be accomplished, ere the opening of so early a rosebud could be easily effected.

She was very young, immature, certainly so in the sense of those monthly visitations which are supposed to mark the commencement of puberty; and Bella's parts, replete as they were with perfection and freshness, were as yet hardly prepared for the accommodation of even so moderate a champion as that which, with round intruded head, now sought to enter in and effect a lodgement.

In vain Charlie pushed and exerted himself to press into the delicate parts of the lovely girl his excited member.

The pink folds and the tiny orifice withstood all his attempts to penetrate the mystic grotto. In vain the pretty Bella, now roused into a fury of excitement and half mad with the titillation she had already undergone, seconded by all the means in her power the audacious attempts of her young lover.

The membrane was strong and resisted bravely until, with a desperate purpose to win the goal or burst everything, the youth drew back for a moment, and then desperately plunging forward, succeeded in piercing the obstruction and thrusting the head and shoulders of his stiffened affair into the belly of the yielding girl.

Bella gave a little scream, as she felt the forcible inroad upon her secret charms, but the delicious contact gave her courage to bear the smart in hopes of the relief which appeared to be coming.

Meanwhile Charlie pushed again and again, and proud of the victory which he had already won, not only stood his ground, but at each thrust advanced some small way further upon his road.

It has been said, "ce n'est que le premier coup qui coute," but it may be fairly argued that it is at the same time perfectly possible that "quelquefois il coute trop," as the reader may be inclined to infer with me in the present case.

Neither of our lovers, however, had strange to say, a thought on the subject, but fully occupied with the delicious sensations which had overpowered them, united to give effect to those ardent movements which both could feel would end in ecstasy.

As for Bella, with her whole body quivering with delicious impatience, and her full red lips giving vent to the short excursive exclamations which announced the extreme gratification, she gave herself up body and soul to the delights of the coition. Her muscular compressions upon the weapon which had now effectually gained her, the firm embrace in which she held the writhing lad, the delicate sides of the moistened, glove-like sheath, all tended to excite Charlie to madness. He felt himself in her body to the roots of his machine, until the two globes which tightened beneath the foaming champion of his manhood, pressed upon the firm cheeks of her white bottom. He could go no further and his sole employment was to enjoy—to reap to the full the delicious harvest of his exertions.

But Bella, insatiable in her passion, no sooner found the wished for junction completed, than relishing the keen pleasure which the stiff and warm member was giving her, became too excited to know or care further aught that was happening, and her frenzied excitement; quickly overtaken again by the maddening spasms of completed lust, pressed downwards upon the object of her pleasure, threw up her arms in passionate rapture, and then sinking back in the arms of her lover, with low groans of ecstatic agony and little cries of surprise and delight, gave down a copious emission, which finding a reluctant escape below, inundated Charlie's balls.

No sooner did the youth witness the delivering enjoyment he was the means of bestowing upon the beautiful Bella, and become sensible of the flood which she had poured down in such profusion upon his person, than he was also seized with lustful fury. A raging torrent of desire seemed to rush through his veins; his instrument was now plunged to the hilt in her delicious belly, then, drawing back, he extracted the smoking member almost to the head. He pressed and bore all before him. He felt a tickling, maddening feeling creeping upon him; he tightened his grasp upon his young mistress, and at the same instant that another cry of rapturous enjoyment issued from her heaving breast, he found himself gasping upon her bosom, and pouring into her grateful womb a rich tickling jet of youthful vigour.

A low moan of salacious gratification escaped the parted lips of Bella, as she felt the jerking gushes of seminal fluid which came from the excited member within her; at the same moment the lustful frenzy of emission forced from Charlie a sharp and thrilling cry as he lay with upturned eyes in the last act of the sensuous drama.

That cry was the signal for an interruption which was as sudden as it was unexpected. From out the bordering shrubs there stole the sombre figure of a man and stood before the youthful lovers.

Horror froze the blood of both.

Slipping from his late warm and luscious retreat, and essaying as best he could to stand upright, Charlie recoiled from the apparition as from some dreadful serpent.

As for the gentle Bella, no sooner did she catch sight of the intruder than, covering her face with her hands, she shrank back upon the seat which had been the silent witness of her pleasures, and too frightened to utter a sound, waited with what presence of mind she could assume to face the brewing storm.

Nor was she kept long in suspense.

Quickly advancing towards the guilty couple the newcomer seized the lad by the arm, while with a stern gesture of authority, he ordered him to repair the disorder of dress.

"Impudent boy," he hissed between his teeth, "what is it that you have done? To what lengths have your mad and savage passions hurried you? How will you face the rage of your justly offended father? How appease his angry resentment when in the exercise of my bounden duty, I apprise him of the mischief wrought by the hand of his only son."

As the speaker ceased, still holding Charlie by the wrist, he came forth into the moonlight and disclosed the figure of a man of some forty-five years of age, short, stout, and somewhat corpulent. His face, decidedly handsome, was rendered still more attractive by a pair of brilliant eyes, which, black as jet, threw around fierce glances of passionate resentment. He was habited in a clerical dress, the sombre shades and quiet unobstructive neatness of which drew out only more prominently his remarkably muscular proportions and striking physiognomy.

Charlie appeared, as well, indeed, he might, covered with confusion, when to his infinite and selfish relief, the stern intruder turned to the young partner of his libidinous enjoyment.

"For you, miserable girl, I can only express my utmost horror and my most righteous indignation. Forgetful alike of the precepts of the holy mother church, careless of your honour, you have allowed this wicked and presumptuous boy to pluck the forbidden fruit? What now remains for you? Scorned by your friends, and driven from your uncle's house, you will herd with the beasts of the field, and as Nebuchadnezar of old, shunned as contamination by your species, gladly gather a miserable sustenance in the highways. Oh, daughter of sin, child given up to lust and unto Satan. I say unto thee—"

The stranger had proceeded thus far in his abjuration of the unfortunate girl, when Bella, rising from her crouching attitude, threw herself at his feet, and joined her tears and prayers for forgiveness to those of her young lover.

"Say no more," at length continued the stern priest; "say no more. Confessions are of no avail, and humiliations do but add to your offence. My mind misgives me as to my duty in this sad affair, but if I obeyed the dictates of my present inclinations I should go straight to your natural guardians and acquaint them immediately with the infamous nature of my chance discovery."

"Oh, in pity, have mercy upon me," pleaded Bella, whose tears now coursed down her pretty cheeks, so lately aglow with wanton pleasure.

"Spare us, Father, spare us both. We will do anything in our power to make atonement. Six masses and several paters shall be performed on our account and our cost. The pilgrimage to the shrine of St. Engulphus, of which you spoke to me the other day, shall now surely be undertaken. I am willing to do anything, sacrifice anything, if you will spare this dear Bella."

The priest waved his hand for silence. Then he spoke, while accents of pity mingled with his naturally stern and resolute manner.

"Enough," said he, "I must have time. I must invoke assistance from the Blessed Virgin, who knew no sin, but who, without the carnal delights of mortal copulation, brought forth the babe of babes in the manger of Bethlehem. Come to me to-morrow in the sacristy, Bella. There in the precincts, I will unfold to you the Divine will concerning your transgression. At two o'clock I will expect you. As for you, rash youth, I shall reserve my judgment, and all action, until the following day, when at the same hour I shall likewise expect you."

A thousand thanks were being poured out by the united throats of the penitents, when the Father warned them both to part.

The evening had long ago closed in, and the dews of night were stealing upwards.

"Meanwhile, good night and peace; your secret is safe with me, until we meet again," he spoke and disappeared.

Mary Gaitskill

Bad Behavior

[1988]

They were staying in his grandmother's deserted apartment in Washington, D.C. The complex was a series of building blocks seemingly arranged at random, stuck together and painted the least attractive colours available. It was surrounded by bright green grass and a circular driveway, and placed on a quiet highway that led into the city. There was a drive-in bank and an insurance office next to it. It was enveloped in the steady, continuous noise of cars driving by at roughly the same speed.

"This is a horrible building," she said as they travelled up in the elevator.

The door slid open and they walked down a hall carpeted with dense brown nylon. The grandmother's apartment opened before them. Beth found the refrigerator and opened it. There was a crumpled package of French bread, a jar of hot peppers, several lumps covered with aluminum foil, two bottles of wine and a six-pack. "Is your grandmother an alcoholic?" she asked.

"I don't know." He dropped his heavy leather bag and her white canvas one in the living room, took off his coat and threw it on the bags. She watched him standing there, pale and gaunt in a black leather shirt tied at his waist with a leather belt. That image of him would stay with her for years for no good reason and with no emotional significance. He dropped into a chair, his thin arms flopping lightly on its arms. He nodded at the tray of whiskey, Scotch and liqueurs on the coffee table before him. "Why don't you make yourself a drink?"

She dropped to her knees beside the table and nervously played with the bottles. He was watching her quietly, his expression hooded. She plucked a bottle of thick chocolate liqueur from the cluster, poured herself a glass and sat in the chair across from his with both hands around it. She could no longer ignore the character of the apartment. It was brutally ridiculous, almost sadistic in its absurdity. The couch and chairs were covered with a floral print. A thin maize carpet zipped across the floor. There were throw rugs. There were artificial flowers. There was an abundance of small tables and shelves housing a legion of figures; grinning glass maidens in sumptuous gowns bore baskets of glass roses, ceramic birds warbled from the ceramic stumps they clung to, glass horses galloped across teakwood pastures. A ceramic weather poodle and his diamond-eyed kitty-cat companions silently watched the silent scene in the room.

"Are you all right?" he asked.

"I hate this apartment. It's really awful."

"What were you expecting? Jesus Christ. It's a lot like yours, you know."

"Yes. That's true, I have to admit." She drank her liqueur.

"Do you think you could improve your attitude about this whole thing? You might try being a little more positive."

Coming from him, this question was preposterous. He must be so pathologically insecure that his perception of his own behaviour was thoroughly distorted. He saw rejection everywhere, she decided; she must reassure him. "But I do feel positive about being here," she said. She paused, searching for the best way to express the extremity of her positive feelings. She invisibly implored him to see and mount their blue puff-ball bed. "It would be impossible for you to disappoint me. The whole idea of you makes me happy. Anything you do will be all right."

Her generosity unnerved him. He wondered if she realized what she was saying. "Does anybody know you're here?" he asked. "Did you tell anyone where you were going?"

"No." She had in fact told several people.

"That wasn't very smart."

"Why not?"

"You don't know me at all. Anything could happen to you."

She put her glass on the coffee table, crossed the floor and dropped to her knees between his legs. She threw her arms around his thighs. She nuzzled his groin with her nose. He tightened. She unzipped his pants. "Stop," he said. "Wait." She took his shoulders—she had a surprisingly strong grip—and pulled him to the carpet. His hovering brood of images and plans was suddenly upended, as though it had been sitting on a table that a rampaging crazy person had flipped over. He felt assaulted and invaded. This was not what he had in mind, but to refuse would make him seem somehow less virile than she. Queasily, he stripped off her clothes and put their bodies in a viable position. He fastened his teeth on her breast and bit her. She made a surprised noise and her body stiffened. He bit her again, harder. She screamed. He wanted to draw blood. Her screams were short and stifled. He could tell that she was trying to like being bitten, but that she did not. He gnawed her breast. She screamed sharply.

They screwed. They broke apart and regarded each other warily. She put her hand on his tentatively. He realized what had been disturbing him about her. With other women he had been with in similar situations, he had experienced a relaxing sense of emptiness within them that had made it easy for him to get inside them and, once there, smear himself all over their innermost territory until it was no longer theirs but his. His wife did not have this empty quality, yet the gracious way in which she emptied herself for him made her submission, as far as it went, all the more poignant. This exasperating girl, on the other hand, contained a tangible somethingness that she not only refused to expunge, but that seemed to willfully expand itself so that he banged into it with every attempt to invade her. He didn't mind the somethingness; he rather liked it, in fact, and had looked forward to seeing it demolished. But she refused to let him do it. Why had she told him she was a masochist? He looked at her body. Her limbs were muscular and alert. He considered taking her by the neck and bashing her head against the floor.

He stood abruptly. "I want to get something to eat. I'm starving."

She put her hand on his ankle. Her desire to abase herself had been completely frustrated. She had pulled him to the rug certain that if only they could fuck, he would enter her with overwhelming force and take complete control of her. Instead she had barely felt him, and what she had felt was remote and cold. Somewhere on her exterior he'd been doing some biting thing that meant nothing to her and was quite unpleasant. Despairing, she held his ankle tighter and put her forehead on the carpet. At least she could stay at his feet, worshipping. He twisted free and walked away. "Come on," he said.

Elizabeth Barrett Browning

Aurora Leigh

[1856]

But oh, the night! oh, bitter-sweet! oh, sweet!
O dark, O moon and stars, O ecstasy
Of darkness! O great mystery of love,—
In which absorbed, loss, anguish, treason's self
Enlarges rapture,—as a pebble dropt
In some full wine-cup, over-brims the wine!
While we to sate together, leaned that night
So close, my very garments crept and thrilled
With strange electric life; and both my cheeks
Grew red, then pale, with touches from my hair
In which his breath was; while the golden moon

Was hung before our faces as the badge
Of some sublime inherited despair,
Since ever to be seen by only one,—
A voice said, low and rapid as a sigh,
Yet breaking, I felt conscious, from a smile,—
'Thank God, who made me blind, to make me see!
Shine on, Aurora, dearest light of souls,
Which rule'st for evermore both day and night!
I am happy.'
    I flung closer to his breast,
As sword that, after battle, flings to sheathe;
And, in that hurtle of united souls,
The mystic motions which in common moods
Are shut beyond our sense, broke in on us,
And, as we sate, we felt the old earth spin,
And all the starry turbulence of worlds
Swing round us in their audient circles, till
If that same golden moon were overhead
Or if beneath our feet, we did not know.

Performance artist/writer **Kathy Acker** is the author of *Great Expectations, Empire of the Senseless* and a 1989 collection of novellas, *Young Lust*, from which "The Adult Life of Toulouse Lautrec" is taken.

Diane Ackerman's books include *A Natural History of the Senses* and the provocative *A Natural History of Love* (1994), which includes her thoughts on kissing.

The Autobiography of a Flea and Other Tart Tales **(Anonymous)** is probably the best-selling erotic novel ever written. The story of a flea who attaches itself to a tasty lass was first published in France in the 1880s.

The **Anonymous** *Account of the Visit Made to the Theatine Nuns* is taken from the state archives of Florence. It is thought to have been coaxed from Benedetta Carlini during a series of investigations in 1619.

The **Anonymous** ditty *Kitty's Atlantis for the Year 1766* originated in England.

The **Anonymous** *Melanesian Erotic Spell* was first recorded in Bronislaw Malinowski's *The Sexual Life of Savages* (1919). The spell frees a woman from unwanted sexual attention and is repeated while holding a coconut.

The Lustful Turk's **Anonymous** author penned this infamous account in 1828. It is thought to have originated in England.

Rey Anthony is the pseudonym of the author of *The Housewives' Handbook on Selective Promiscuity*. Anthony's colorful guide to "restrained" affairs was published in 1962.

English poet **Elizabeth Barrett Browning** is best known for her masterpiece *Sonnets from the Portuguese*, a collection of love sonnets written to her husband, Robert Browning. "Aurora Leigh" was written in 1856.

Emily Dickinson's "Wild Nights—Wild Nights" was originally written about 1861, but was not published until 30 years later. It can be found in her *Collected Poems*.

Mary Gaitskill is the author of *Two Girls, Fat and Thin* and a controversial debut novel, *Bad Behavior* (1988).

Anais Nin is equally known for her explicit personal diaries, as well as her two novels of erotica, *Little Birds* and *The Delta of Venus*.

Gabriella Parca's *Italian Women Confess* is an extraordinary collection of intimate interviews on love and sex, first published in 1963.

Pauline Réage's *The Story of O* is probably the most famous erotic novel in history. It was published in Paris in 1954, but (naturally) not in England until 1970.

Christina Rossetti's poems are known for their mysterious mystical moods. Her classic collection, *Goblin Market and Other Tales*, was published in 1862.

Sappho tutored young girls in the arts on the island of Lesbos. Legend says she flung herself into the sea in the throes of unrequited love. "It Seems to Me That Man is Equal to the Gods" dates to 600 B.C.

Sabina Sedgewick is a contributor to *Ladies Own Erotica* (1984), a collection of stories, poems, recipes and general fantasy culled by the The Kensington Ladies' Erotica Society.

Trotula, an English gynecologist, penned possibly the earliest health manual for women. It dates to about 1075.

"The Adult Life of Toulouse Lautrec" from *Young Lust* by Kathy Acker ©1986 by Kathy Acker. Reprinted by permission of Grove Press and International Creative Management.

"Sabina's Sauerkraut" by Sabina Sedgewick from *Ladies' Own Erotica* ©1984 by the Kensington Ladies' Erotica Society, by Permission of Ten Speed Press, P.O. Box 7123, Berkeley, CA 94707.

Excerpt from *The Story of O* by Pauline Réage ©1965 by Grove Press. Reprinted by permission of Grove Press and International Creative Management.

Excerpt from *Italian Women Confess,* edited by Gabriella Parca. Translation by Carolyn Gaiser ©1963 and renewed ©1991 by Farrar Straus & Giroux. Reprinted by permission of Farrar, Straus & Giroux.

Excerpt from "Artists and Models" in *Delta of Venus, Erotica,* ©1969 by Anaïs Nin, ©1977 by the Anaïs Nin Trust, reprinted by permission of Harcourt Brace & Company.

Excerpt from *The Housewives' Handbook on Selective Promiscuity* ©1962 by Rey Anthony. Reprinted by permission of the author.

"Kissing" from *The Natural History of Love* by Diane Ackerman ©1990, 1994 by Diane Ackerman. Reprinted by permission of Random House, Inc.

Excerpt from *Bad Behavior* reprinted with permission of Simon & Schuster. ©1988 by Mary Gaitskill.

THE

SEX
BOX

SEX

T H E

SEX
BOX

SEX

EDITED BY ANONYMOUS

CHRONICLE BOOKS

SAN FRANCISCO

Copyright © 1996 by John Miller. All rights reserved. No part of this book may be reproduced in any form without written permission from the publisher.

Page 168 constitutes a continuation of the copyright page.

To maintain the authentic style of each writer included herein, quirks of spelling and grammar remain unchanged from their original state.

Printed in Singapore.

ISBN 0-8118-1419-X

Library of Congress Cataloging-in-Publication Data available.

Book and cover design: Big Fish Books
Composition: Big Fish Books
Cover photograph: Frieze, circa 13th century, New Delhi, India.

Distributed in Canada by Raincoast Books,
8680 Cambie Street
Vancouver BC V6P 6M9

10 9 8 7 6 5 4 3 2 1

Chronicle Books
275 Fifth Street
San Francisco, CA 94103

To my angel, K

CONTENTS

Monique Wittig

We Descend

[1973]

We descend directly legs together thighs together arms entwined m/y hands touching your shoulders m/y shoulders held by your hands breast against breast open mouth against open mouth, we descend slowly. The sand swirls round our ankles, suddenly it surrounds our calves. It's from then on that the descent is slowed down. At the moment your knees are reached you throw back your head, *I* see your teeth, you smile, later you look at m/e you speak to m/e without interruption. Now the sand presses on the thighs. *I* shiver with gooseflesh, *I* feel your skin stirring, your nails dig into m/y shoulders, you look at m/e, you do not stop looking at m/e, the shape of your cheeks is changed by the greatest concern. The engulfment continues steadily, the touch of the sand is soft against m/y legs. You begin to sigh. When *I* am sucked down to m/y thighs *I* start to cry out, in a few moments *I* shall be unable to touch you, m/y hands on your shoulders your neck will be unable to reach your vulva, anguish grips m/e, the tiniest grain of sand between your belly and m/ine can separate us once for all. But your fierce joyful eyes shining hold m/e against you, you press m/y back with your large hands, *I* begin to throb in m/y eyelids, *I* throb in m/y brain, *I* throb in m/y thorax, *I* throb in m/y belly, *I* throb in m/y clitoris while you speak faster and faster clasping m/e *I* clasping you clasping each other with a marvellous strength, the sand is round our waists, at a given moment your skin splits from throat to pubis, m/ine in turn from below upwards, *I* spill m/yself into you, you mingle with m/e m/y mouth fastened on your mouth your neck squeezed by m/y arms, *I* feel our intestines uncoiling gliding among themselves, the sky darkens suddenly, it contains orange gleams, the outflow of the mingled blood is not perceptible, the most severe shuddering affects you affects m/e both together, collapsing you cry out, *I* love you m/y dying one, your emergent head is for m/e most adorable and most fatal, the sand touches your cheeks, m/y mouth is filled.

Chin P'ing Mei

Hsi-men's Adventures

[1800s]

Hsi-men sat on the bed and made the Lady of the Vase place herself upon the cushions and play the flute for him. Grasping Hsi-men's treasure, she wished she could suckle it the whole night through. She tickled the jade-scepter with her lips and fondled it for hours, ever unsatisfied. She held it firmly in her mouth, drawing in and out continuously. Hsi-men was delighted and cried, "Let the essence flow," and she sucked as it shot into her mouth. She was not able to drink it quickly enough.

The red lips open wide; the slender fingers
Play their part daintily.
Deep in, deep out. Their hearts are wild with passion.
There are no words to tell the ecstasy that thrills
     their souls.

Hsi-men lay down on the bed, took down his trousers, lifted his limpo, and told the woman to take it into her mouth while he himself enjoyed some wine. "Suck this well for me," he said, "and I'll give you a gorgeous gown to wear on the next festival day."

"To be sure," answered the woman; "I wish to suck it all night long."

Her slender fingers were playing with the drooping warrior between his legs, pressing it to her cheeks, fondling it with her hands; and finally she put it between her lips and kissed its head. Instantly the warrior was inflamed with fury and arose; its head was as hard as a nail, its eye was wide open, its jowls bristled with bushy hair, and its body stood perfectly stiff.

Neither of them wasted any words. His lust for the woman was great; and she spread her legs, opened her yellow blossom with her fingers, and let the man invade her to the furthest recess. Warm liquid flowed out of her and wet his clothes. Hsi-men placed a considerable amount of red powder upon the head of his member, and then holding fast to the bedsides with both hands, he thrust so vigorously that the woman opened her eyes wide and called him "Darling."

When he finally withdrew, he wished to wipe his weapon on his trousers; but the woman stopped him and said: "I don't want you to wipe it. I will suck it for you." Hsi-men wishing for nothing sweeter, she bent over, seized his treasure in both her hands, and sucked it until it was clean. Then the man put it back in his trousers.

Hsi-men wished to enjoy the delights of love with his new lady. He knew that she played the flute exquisitely. With tender fingers she opened his trousers, took out his treasure, and stroked it passionately until it rose up rigid and became a superb purple color. The man asked her to mouth it.

She lay back upon the bed and put his jade-scepter between her ruby-red lips. "It's so enormous," she said, "it hurts my mouth." Then she suckled, and tickled the head with her tongue, and began licking up and down. His giant became longer and thicker. With smooth fingers she seized it and entirely devoured it, soon letting it drop dead from her mouth.

At dawn, Golden Lotus and Hsi-men Ch'ing awoke. Golden Lotus saw that his weapon stood upright like a ramrod. "Darling," she said, "you must forgive me, but I can stand it no longer. I want to suckle it!"

"Suckle it," said Hsi-men. "If you can soften it, good for you." The woman seized and received his member between her lips. She sucked for a whole hour, but it did not die. Hsi-men, placing his hands on her dazzling white neck, began to move his weapon about, now pushing it in and anon pulling it out of her mouth with all his might. Soon her lips were dripping, and she slowly drank it down.

Havelock Ellis

Foot-Fetichism

[1919]

O f all forms of erotic symbolism the most frequent is that which idealizes the foot and the shoe. The phenomena we here encounter are sometime so complex and raise so many interesting questions that it is necessary to discuss them somewhat fully.

It would seem that even for the normal lover the foot is one of the most attractive parts of the body. Stanley Hall found that among the parts specified as most admired in the other sex by young men and women who answered a *questionnaire* the feet came fourth (after the eyes, hair, stature and size).[1] Casanova, an acute student and lover of women who was in no degree a foot fetichist, remarks that all men who share his interest in women are attracted by their feet; they offer the same interest, he considers, as the question of the particular edition offers to the book-lover.[2]

At the same time it is scarcely unusual for the normal lover, in most civilized countries to-day, to attach primary importance to the foot, such as he very frequently attaches to the eyes, though the feet play a very conspicuous part in the work of certain novelists.[3]

In a small but no inconsiderable minority of persons, however, the foot or the boot becomes the most attractive part of a woman, and in some morbid cases the woman herself is regarded as a comparatively unimportant appendage to her feet or her boots. The boots under civilized conditions much more frequently constitute the sexual symbol than do the feet themselves; this is not surprising since in ordinary life the feet are not often seen.

It is usually only under exceptionally favoring conditions that foot-fetichism occurs, as in the case recorded by Marandon de Montyel of a doctor who had been brought up in the West Indies. His mother had been insane and he himself was subject to obsessions, especially of being incapable of urinating; he had had nocturnal incontinence of urine in childhood. All the women of the people in the West Indies go about with naked feet, which are often beautiful. His puberty evolved under this influence, and foot-fetichism developed. He especially admired large, fat, arched feet, with delicate skin and large, regular toes. He masturbated with images of feet. At 15 he had relations with a colored chambermaid, but feared to mention his fetichism, though it was the touch of her feet that chiefly excited him. He now gave up masturbation, and had a succession of mistresses, but was always ashamed to confess his fancies until, at the age of 33, in Paris, a very intelligent woman who had become his mistress discovered his mania and skillfully enabled him to yield to it without shock to his modesty. He was devoted to this mistress, who had very beautiful feet (he had been horrified by the feet of Europeans generally), until she finally left him. (*Archives de Neurologie*, October, 1904.)

Probably the first case of shoe-fetichism ever recorded in any detail is that of Restif de la Bretonne (1734–1806), publicist and novelist, one of the most remarkable literary figures of the later eighteenth century in France. Restif was a neurotic subject, though not to an extreme degree, and his shoe-fetichism, though distinctly pronounced, was not pathological; that is to say, that the shoe was not itself an adequate gratification of the sexual impulse, but simply a highly important aid to tumescence, a prelude to the natural climax of detumescence; only occasionally, and *faute de mieux*, in the absence of the beloved person, was the shoe used as an adjunct to masturbation.

Perhaps the chief passion of Restif's life was his love for Colette Parangon. He was still a boy (1752), she was the young and virtuous wife of the printer whose apprentice Restif was and in whose house he lived. Madam Parangon, a charming woman, as she is described, was not happily married, and she evidently felt a tender affection for the boy whose excessive love and reverence for her were not always successfully concealed. "Madonna Parangon," he tells us, "possessed a charm which I could never resist, a pretty little foot; it is a charm which arouses more than tenderness. Her shoes, made in Paris, had that voluptuous elegance which seems to communicate soul and life. Sometimes Colette wore shoes of simple white drugget or with silver flowers; sometimes rose-colored slippers with green heels, or green with rose heels; her supple feet, far from deforming her shoes, increased their grace and rendered the form more exciting." One day, on entering the house, he saw Madame Parangon elegantly dressed and wearing rose-colored shoes with tongues, and with green heels and a pretty rosette. They were new and she took them off to put on green slippers with rose heels and borders which he thought equally exciting. As soon as she had left the room, he continues, "carried away by the most impetuous passion and idolizing Colette, I seemed to see her and touch her in handling what she had just worn; my lips pressed one of these jewels, while the other, deceiving the sacred end of nature, from excess of exaltation replaced the object of sex (I cannot express myself more clearly). The warmth which she had communicated to the insensible object which had touched her still remained and gave a soul to it; a voluptuous cloud covered my eyes." He adds that he would kiss with rage and transport whatever had come in close contact with the woman he adored, and on one occasion eagerly pressed his lips to her cast-off underlinen, *vela secretiora penetralium.*

At this period Restif's foot-fetichism reached its highest point of development. It was the aberration of a highly sensitive and very precocious boy. While the preoccupation with feet and shoes persisted throughout life, it never became a complete perversion and never replaced the normal end of sexual desire. His love for Madam Parangon, one of the deepest emotions in his whole life, was also the climax of his shoe-fetichism. She represented his ideal woman, an ethereal sylph with wasp-waist and a child's feet; it was always his highest praise for a woman that she should resemble Madame Parangon, and he desired that her slipper should be buried with him. (Restif de la Bretonne, *Monsieur Nicolas*, vols. i–iv, vol., xiii, p. 5; *id*, *Mes Inscriptions*, pp. ci-cv.)

To suppose that a fetichistic admiration of his mistress's foot is due to a lover's latent desire to be kicked, is as unreasonable as it would be to suppose that a fetichistic admiration for her hand indicated a latent desire to have his ears boxed. In determining whether we are concerned with a case of foot fetichism or of masochism we must take into consideration the whole of the subject's mental and emotional attitude. An act, however definite, will not suffice as a criterion, for the same act in different persons may have altogether different implications. To amalgamate the two is the result of inadequate psychological analysis and only leads to confusion.

It is, however, often very difficult to decide whether we are dealing with a case which is predominantly one of masochism or of foot-fetichism. The nature of the action desired, as we have seen, will not suffice to determine the psychological character of the perversion. Krafft-Ebing believed that the desire to be trodden on, very frequently experienced by masochists, is absolutely symptomatic of masochism.[4] This is scarcely the case. The desire to be trodden on may be fundamentally an erotic symbolism, closely approaching foot-fetichism, and such slight indications of masochism as appear may be merely a parasitic growth on the symbolism, a growth perhaps more suggested by the circumstances involved in the gratification of the abnormal desire than inherent in the innate impulse of the subject. This may be illustrated by the interesting case of a very intelligent man with whom I am well acquainted.

C. P., aged 38. Heredity good. Parents both healthy and normal. Several children of the marriage, all sexually normal as far as is known. C. P. is the youngest of the family and separated from the others by an interval of many years. He was a seven-months' child. He has always enjoyed good health and is active and vigorous, both mentally and physically.

From the age of 9 or 10 to 14 he masturbated occasionally for the sake of physical relief, having discovered the act for himself. He was, however, quite innocent and knew nothing of sexual matters, never having been initiated either by servants or by other boys.

"When I encounter a woman who very strongly attracts me and whom I very greatly admire," he writes, "my desire is never that I may have sexual connection with her in the ordinary sense, but that I may lie down upon the floor on my back and be trampled upon by her. This curious desire is seldom present unless the object of my admiration is really a lady, and of fine proportions. She must be richly dressed—preferably in an evening gown, and wear dainty high-heeled slippers, either quite open so as to show the curve of the instep, or with only one strap or 'bar' across. The skirts should be raised sufficiently to afford me the pleasure of seeing her feet and a liberal amount of ankle, but in no case above the knee, or the effect is greatly reduced. Although I often greatly admire a woman's intellect and even person, sexually no other part of her has any serious attraction for me except the leg, from the knee downwards, and the foot, and these must be exquisitely clothed. Given this condition, my desire amounts to a wish to gratify my sexual sense by contact with the (to me) attractive part of the woman. Comparatively few women have a leg or foot sufficiently beautiful to my mind to excite any serious or compelling desire, but when this is so, or I suspect it, I am willing to spend any time or trouble to get her to tread upon me and am anxious to be trampled on with the greatest severity.

"The treading should be inflicted for a few minutes all over the chest, abdomen and groin, and lastly on the penis, which is, of course, lying along the belly in a violent state of erection, and consequently too hard for the treading to damage it. I also enjoy being nearly strangled by a woman's foot.

"If the lady finally stands facing my head and places her slipper upon my penis so that the high heel falls about where the penis leaves the scrotum, the sole covering most of the rest of it and with the other foot upon my abdomen, into which I can *see* as well as feel it sink as she shifts her weight from one foot to the other, orgasm takes place almost at once. Emission under these conditions is to me an agony of delight, during which practically the lady's whole weight should rest upon the penis.

"One reason for my special pleasure in this method seems to be that first the heel and afterwards the sole of the slipper as it treads upon the penis greatly check the passage of the semen and consequently the pleasure is considerably prolonged. There is also a curious mental side to the affair. I love to imagine that the lady who is treading upon me is my mistress and I her slave, and that she is doing it to punish me for some fault, or to give *herself* (not me) pleasure.

"It follows that the greater the contempt and severity with which I am 'punished,' the greater becomes my pleasure. The idea of 'punishment' or 'slavery' is seldom aroused except when I have great difficulty in accomplishing my desire and the treader is more than usually handsome and heavy and the trampling mercilessly inflicted. I have been trampled so long and so mercilessly several times, that I have flinched each time the slipper pressed its way into my aching body and have been black and blue for days afterwards. I take the greatest interest in leading ladies on to do this for me where I think I will not offend, and have been surprisingly successful. I must have lain beneath the feet of quite a hundred women, many of them of good social position, who would never dream of permitting any ordinary sexual intercourse, but who have been so interested or amused by the idea as to do it for me—many of them over and over again. It is perhaps needless to say that none of my own or the ladies' clothing is ever removed, or disarranged, for the accomplishment of orgasm in this manner. After a long and varied experience, I may say that my favorite weight is 10 to 11 stone, and that black, very high-heeled slippers, in combination with tan silk stockings, seem to give me the greatest pleasure and create in me the strongest desires.

"Boots, or outdoor shoes, do not attract me to anything like the same degree, although I have, upon several occasions, enjoyed myself fairly well by their use. Nude women repel me, and I find no pleasure in seeing a woman in tights. I am not averse to normal sexual connection and occasionally employ it. To me, however, the pleasure is far inferior to that of being trampled upon. I also derive keen pleasure—and usually have a strong erection—from seeing a woman, dressed as I have described, tread upon anything which yields under her foot—such as the seat of a carriage, the cushions of a punt, a footstool, etc., and I enjoy seeing her crush flowers by treading upon them. I have often strolled along in the wake of some handsome lady at a picnic or a garden party for the pleasure of seeing the grass upon which she has trodden rise slowly again after her foot has pressed it. I delight also to see a carriage sway as a woman leaves or enters it—anything which needs the pressure of the foot.

"To pass now to the origin of this direction of my feelings.

"Even in early childhood I admired pretty feminine foot-gear, and in the contemplation of it experienced vague sensations which I now recognize as sexual. When a lad of 14 or so, I stayed a good deal at the house of some intimate friends of my parents, the daughter of the house—an only child—a beautiful and powerful girl, about six years my senior, being my special chum. This girl was always daintily dressed, and having most lovely feet and ankles not unnaturally knew it. Whenever possible she dressed so as to show off their beauty to the best advantage—rather short skirts and usually little high-heeled slippers—and was not averse to showing them in a most distractingly coquettish manner. She seemed to have a passion for treading upon things which would scrunch or yield under her foot, such as flowers, little windfallen apples and pears, acorns, etc., or heaps of hay, straw or cut grass. As we wandered about the gardens—for we were left to do exactly as we liked—I got quite accustomed to seeing her hunt out and tread upon such things, and used to chaff her about it. At that time I was—as I am still—fond of lying at full length on a thick hearthrug before a good fire. One evening as I was lying in this way and we were alone, A. crossed the room to reach a bangle from the mantelpiece. Instead of reaching over me, she playfully stepped upon my body, saying that she would show me how the hay and straw felt. Naturally I fell in with the joke and laughed. After standing upon me a few moments she raised her skirt slightly and, holding on to the mantelpiece for support, stretched out one dainty foot in its brown silk stocking and high-heeled slipper to the blaze to warm, while looking down and laughing at my scarlet, excited face. She was a perfectly frank and charming girl, and I feel pretty certain that, although she evidently enjoyed my excitement and the feeling of my body yielding under her feet, she did not on this first occasion clearly understand my condition; nor can I remember that, though the desire for sexual gratification drove me nearly mad, it appeared to awaken in her any reciprocal feeling. I took hold of her raised foot and, after kissing it, guided it by an absolutely irresistible impulse on to my penis, which was as hard as wood and seemed almost bursting. Almost at the moment that her weight was thrown upon it, orgasm took place for the first time in my life thoroughly and effectively. No description can give any idea of what I felt—I only know that from that moment my distorted sexual focus was fixed forever. Numberless times, after that evening, I felt the weight of her dainty slippers, and nothing will ever cause the memory of the pleasure she thus gave me to fade. I know that A. came to enjoy treading upon me, as much as I enjoyed having her do it. She had a liberal dress allowance and, seeing the pleasure they gave me, she was always buying pretty stockings and ravishing slippers with the highest and most slender Louis heels she could find and would show them to me with the greatest glee, urging me to lie down that she might try them on me. She confessed that she loved to see and feel them sink into my body as she trod upon me and enjoyed the crunch of the muscles under her heels as she moved about. After some minutes of this, I always guided her slipper on to my penis, and she would tread carefully, but with her whole weight—probably about 9 stone—and watch me with flashing eyes, flushed cheeks, and quivering lips, as she felt—as she must have done plainly—the throbbing and swelling of my penis under her foot as emission took place. I have not the smallest doubt that orgasm took place simultaneously with her, though we never at any time spoke openly of it. This went on for several years on almost every favorable opportunity we had, and after a month or two of separation sometimes four or five times during a single day. Several times during A.'s absence I masturbated by getting her slipper and pressing it with all my strength against the penis while imagining that she was treading upon me. The pleasure was, of course, very inferior to her attentions. There was never at any time between us any question of normal sexual intercourse, and we were both well content to let things drift as they were.

The foregoing history, while it very distinctly brings before us a case of erotic symbolism, is not strictly an example of shoe-fetichism. The symbolism is more complex. The focus of beauty in a desirable woman is transferred and concentrated in the region below the knee; in that sense we have foot-fetichism. But the act of coitus itself is also symbolically transferred. Not only has the foot become the symbol of the vulva, but trampling has become the symbol of coitus; intercourse takes place symbolically *per pedem*. It is a result of this symbolization of the foot and of trampling that all acts of treading take on a new and symbolical sexual charm. The element of masochism—of pleasure in being a woman's slave—is a parasitic growth; that is to say, it is not founded in the subject's constitution, but chances to have found a favorable soil in the special circumstances under which his sexual life developed. It is not primary, but secondary, and remains an unimportant and merely occasional element.

It may be instructive to bring forward for comparison a case in which also we have a symbolism involving boot-fetichism, but extending beyond it. In this case there is a basis of inversion (as is not infrequent in erotic symbolisms), but from the present point of view the psychological significance of the case remains the same.

A. N., aged 29, unmarried, healthy, though not robust, and without any known hereditary taint. Has followed various avocations without taking great interest in them, but has shown some literary ability.

"I am an Englishman," his own narrative runs, "the third of three children. At my birth my father was 41 and my mother 34. My mother died of cancer when I was 15. My father is still alive, a reserved man, who still nurses his sorrow for his wife's death. I have no reason to believe my parents anything but normal and useful members of society. My sister is normal and happily married. My brother I have reason to believe to be an invert.

"A horoscope case for me describes me in a way I think correct, and so do my friends: 'A mild, obliging, gentle, amiable person, with many fine traits of character;

timid in nature, fond of society, loving peace and quietude, delighting in warm and close friendships. There is much that is firm, steadfast and industrious, some self-love, a good deal of diplomacy, a little that is subtle, or what is called finesse. You are reserved with those you dislike. There is a serious and sad side to your character; you are very thoughtful and contemplative when in these moods. But you are not pessimistic. You have superior abilities, for they are intuitively intellectual. There is a cold reticence which restrains generous impulses and which inclines to acquisitiveness; it will make you deliberate, inventive, adding self-esteem, some vanity.'

"At an early age I was left much alone in the nursery and there contracted the habit of masturbation long before the age of puberty. I use the word 'masturbation' for want of a better, though it may not quite describe my case. I have never used my hand to the penis. As far back as I can remember I have had what a Frenchman has described as 'le fetichisme de la chaussure,' and in those early days, before I was 6 years old, I would put on my father's boots, taken from a cupboard at hand, and then tying or strapping my legs together would produce an erection, and all the pleasurable feelings experienced, I suppose by means of masturbation. I always did this secretly, but couldn't tell why. I continued this practice on and off all my boyhood and youth. When I discovered the first emission I was much surprised. I always did this thing without loosening my trousers. As to how these feelings arose I am totally unable to say. I can't remember being without such feelings, and they seem to me perfectly normal. The sight, or even thought, of high boots, or leggings, especially if well polished or in patent leather, would set all my sexual passions aflame, and does yet. As a boy my great desire was to wear these things. A soldier in boots and spurs, a groom in tops, or even an errand-boy in patent leather leggings, fascinated me, and to this day, despite reason and everything else. The sight of such things produced an erection. An emission I could always produce by tightly tying my legs together, but only when wearing boots, and preferably leggings, which when I had pocket money I bought for this purpose. (At the present moment I have five pairs in the house and two pairs of high boots, quite unjustified by ordinary use.) This habit I lapse into yet at times. The smell of leather affects me, but I never know how far this may be due to the association with boots; the smell suggests the image. Restraint by a leather strap is more exciting than by cords. Erotic dreams always take the form of restraint on the limbs when booted.

"Uniforms and liveries have a great temptation for me, but only when of a tight-fitting nature and smart, as soldiers', grooms', etc., but not sailors'; most powerfully when the person is in boots or leggings and breeches."

This case, while it concerns a person of quite different temperament, with a more innate predisposition to specific perversions, is yet in many respects analogous to the previous case. There is boot-fetichism; nothing is felt to be so attractive as the foot-gear, and there is also at the same time more than this; there is the attraction of repression and constraint developed into a sexual symbol. In C. P.'s case that symbolism arises from the experience of an abnormal heterosexual relationship; in A. N.'s case it is founded on auto-erotic experiences associated with inversion; in both alike the entire symbolism has become diffused and generalized.

In another class of cases a purely ideal symbolism may be present by means of a fetich which acts as a powerful stimulus without itself being felt to possess any attraction. A good illustration of this condition is furnished by a case which has been communicated to me by a medical correspondent in New Zealand.

"The patient went out to South Africa as a trooper with the contingent from New Zealand, throwing up a good position in an office to do so. He had never had any trouble as regards connection with women before going to South Africa. While in active service at the front he sustained a nasty fall from his horse, breaking his leg. He was unconscious for four days, and was then invalided down to Cape Town. Here he rapidly got well, and his accustomed health returning to him he started having what he terms 'a good time.' He repeatedly went to brothels, but was unable to have more than a temporary erection, and no ejaculation would take place. In one of these places he was in company with a drunken trooper, who suggested that they should perform the sexual act with their boots and spurs (only) on. My patient, who was also drunk, readily assented, and to his surprise was enabled to perform the act of copulation without any difficulty at all. He has repeatedly tried since to perform the act without any spurs, but is quite unable to do so; with the spurs he has no difficulty at all in obtaining all the gratification he desires. His general health is good. His mother was an extremely nervous woman, and so is his sister. His father died when he was quite young. His only other relation in the colony is a married sister, who seems to enjoy vigorous health."

The consideration of the cases here brought forward may suffice to show that beyond those fetichisms which find their satisfaction in the contemplation of a part of the body or a garment, there is a more subtle symbolism. The foot is a center of force, an agent for exerting pressure, and thus it furnishes a point of departure not alone for the merely static sexual fetich, but for a dynamic erotic symbolization. The energy of its movement becomes a substitute for the energy of the sexual organs themselves in coitus, and exerts the same kind of fascination. The young girl "who seemed to have a passion for treading upon things which would scrunch or yield under her foot," already possessed the germs of an erotic symbolism which, under the influence of circumstances in which she herself took an active part, developed into an adequate method of sexual gratification.[5] The youth who was her partner learned, in the same way, to find an erotic symbolism in all the pressure reactions of attractive feminine feet, the swaying of a carriage beneath their weight, the crushing of flowers on which they tread, the slow rising of the grass which they have pressed. Here we have a symbolism which is altogether different from that fetichism which adores a definite object; it is a dynamic symbolism finding its gratification in the spectacle of movement which ideally recall the fundamental rhythm and pressure reactions of the sexual process.

We may trace a very similar erotic symbolism in an absolutely normal form. The fascination of clothes in the lover's eyes is no doubt a complex phenomenon, but in part it rests on the aptitudes of a woman's garments to express vaguely a dynamic symbolism which must always remain indefinite and elusive, and on that account always possess fascination. No one has so acutely described this symbolism as Herrick, often an admirable psychologist in matters of sexual attractiveness. Especially instructive in these respect are his poems, "Delight in Disorder," "Upon Julia's Clothes," and notably "Julia's Petticoat." "A sweet disorder in the dress," he tells us, "kindles in clothes a wantonness;" it is not on the garment itself, but on the character of its movement that he insists; on the "erring lace," the "winning wave" of the "tempestuous petticoat;" he speaks of the "liquefaction" of clothes, their "brave vibration each way free," and of Julia's petticoat he remarks with a more specific symbolism still,

> "Sometimes 'twould pant and sigh and heave,
> As if to stir it scarce had leave;
> But having got it, thereupon,
> 'Twould make a brave expansion."

In the play of the beloved woman's garment, he sees the whole process of the central act of sex, with its repressions and expansions, and at the sight is himself ready to "fall into a swoon."

---

[1] G. Stanley Hall, *Adolescence*, vol, ii, p. 113. It will be noted that the hand does not appear among the parts of the body which are normally of supreme interest. An interest in the hand is by no means uncommon (it may be noted, for instance, in the course of History XII in Appendix B to vol. iii of these *Studies*), but the hand does not possess

the mystery which envelops the foot, and hand-fetichism is very much less frequent that foot-fetichism, while glove-fetichism is remarkably rare. An interesting case of hand fetichism, scarcely reaching morbid intensity, is recorded by Binet, *Etudes de Psychologie Expérimentale*, pp. 13–19; and see Krafft-Ebing, *Op. cit.*, pp. 214 *et. seq.*

2 *Mémoires*, vol i, Chapter VII.

3 Among leading English novelists Hardy shows an unusual but by no means predominant interest in the feet and shoes of his heroines; see, *e.g.*, the observations of the cobbler in *Under the Greenwood Tree*, Chapter III. A chapter in Geothe's *Wahlverwandschaften* (Part I, Chapter II) contains an episode involving the charm of the foot and the kissing of the beloved's shoe.

4 Yet some of the cases he brings forward, (*e.g.*, Coxe's as quoted by Hammond) show no sign of masochism, since, according to Krafft-Ebing's own definition (*Psychopathia Sexualis*, English translation of tenth edition, p. 116), the idea of subjugation by the opposite sex is of the essence of masochism.

5 Her actions suggest that there is often a latent sexual consciousness in regard to the feet in women, atavistic or pseudo-atavistic, and corresponding to the sexual attraction which the feet formerly aroused, almost normally, in men. This is also suggested by the case, referred to by Shufeldt, of an unmarried woman, belonging to a family exhibiting in a high degree both erotic and neurotic traits, who had "a certain uncontrollable fascination for shoes. She delights in new shoes, and changes her shoes all day long at regular intervals of three hours each. She keeps this row of shoes out in plain sight in her apartment." (R. W. Shufeldt, "On a Case of Female Impotency," 1896, p. 10.)

Nell Port

Tantric Sex

[1984]

Directions for Tantric sex:

1. Man and woman sit nude on floor, facing each other. The woman moves as close to the man as possible and puts her legs over the man's legs and around his body. The man circles her body with his legs. The arms are relaxed on the partners' hips. Both take several deep breaths, rest their gaze on the left eye of the other and meditate together, eyes open, for 5 to 10 minutes.

2. The partners move closer, and the woman puts her mouth near the man's left ear. Feeling the movement of his breath, she replicates the rhythm in his ear, breathing his breath. (Do this meditation for 5 minutes.) They move their heads to the other side and the man replicates the rhythm of the woman's breath. (Do for 5 minutes.) They shift heads again. Starting with their individual rhythms, the partners slowly arrive at a common rhythm, "breathing the one breath." (Continue this meditation for as long as is enjoyable.)

3. After gentle loveplay, the woman introduces the erect penis into her well-lubricated vagina, in the same posture described in exercises 1 and 2. Through periodic contractions of her vaginal muscles and occasional slight movements by the man, both partners attempt to keep the penis erect without thrusting. Both breathe deeply and are sensitive to the flow of energy between them.[1]

I felt very lusty and the children were all gone. It was late in the afternoon. I told him I wanted to try Tantric sex.

"What's that?"

"It's when you don't move, and I'm not sure if you're supposed to have an orgasm."

So we got completely undressed, sat down on the floor, and began.

Step number one was very strange for me. The position was easy enough to assume, but "resting my gaze on the left eye of the other and meditating, eyes open, for 5 to 10 minutes" made me very uncomfortable. It was as though that eye had been disembodied and was free-floating. It could as easily have been a stranger or a statue I was gazing at. I always seek eye contact with people to whom I'm speaking, but this was different, bizarre. Maybe I could learn to like it.

Step number two started off very badly. While replicating the rhythm of his breath in my ear, my stomach kept sending little gurgles upward to my throat—it was very distracting and very unerotic. I really tried hard not to laugh.

We shifted right away to "breathing the one breath." For me this was an extremely profound experience.

The sensation of being nude, sitting about as close together as two people can, arms around one another, in daylight, was novel and very exciting. We breathed together like this for a long time. I think I felt a little dizzy. It transcended any verbal communication we have ever had. It was probably the closest I have ever come to having a spiritual experience. I did feel our spirits merging together in a way that was entirely different from joining together sexually.

Then, as though in a dream and in slowest motion, the spiritual closeness dissolved and merged into a physical union as body parts slipped together gently, quietly, and almost motionless. The feeling of transcendence remained with me. I was being taken out of my body. But the pulsing and throbbing was a reminder of our two very real bodies joined together, almost still, but with a powerful energy flowing between us. The heat and the accelerated throbbing in my groin reduced me once again (or should I say expanded me once again?) into a purely physical being. I resisted the overwhelming desire to move—to grind—but the throbbings were growing into contractions now, which were out of control. The contractions continued to grow and swell until they were so mighty that they broke loose. My body stiffened and rocked back and forth for several long seconds, then sighed and slumped, exhausted.

I returned rather quickly to the quiet house and the afternoon.

[1] Reprinted with permission of Stella Resnick, Ph.D., from her article "The Erotic Lifestyle: Being Turned On," published in *New Age*, August 1978.

Thomas Rowlandson

Pretty Little Games

[1800s]

New feats of horsemanship

Well mounted on a mettled steed,
Famed for his strength as well as speed,
Corrinna and her favorite buck
Are pleas'd to have a flying fuck.
While o'er the downs the courser strains,
With fiery eye and loosened reins,
Around his neck her arms she flings,
Behind her buttocks move like springs.
While Jack keeps time to every motion,
And pours in loves delicious potion.

The county squire new mounted

The County squire to London came,
And left behind his dogs and game;
Yet finer sport he has in view,
And hunts the hare and cony too.
The lovely lass her charms displays
She tips the hint and he obeys,
Within a tavern view the fair,
Each leg supported on a chair,
Her buttocks on the table seated
By which the squires joys compleated.

The hairy prospect or the Devil in a fright

Once on a time the Sire of evil,
In plainer English call'd the devil,
Some new experiment to try
At Chloe cast a roguish eye;
But she who all his arts defied,
Pull'd up and shew'd her sexes pride:
A thing all shagg'd about with hair,
So much it made old Satan stare,
Who frightened at the grim display,
Takes to his heels and runs away.

A. Cooke

The Honey-moon

[1880]

The subject, then, owes its origin to the "honey-moon;" but the honey-moon must be. Where, then, is the remedy? We propose to speak very plainly on this point, for it were of little service to portray the disease unless we could also indicate the specific, which, under Providence, we hope to do clearly and unequivocally. It were well if the treatment could begin with the earliest manifestations of the malady, with the first dawning of the indomitable passion in the boy, and follow him through the dangerous years whose progress in a former Chapter, we have sufficiently traced. But as this is impracticable, in the actual state of things, we must take him as he is when he closes the door of the nuptial chamber—mayhap a "reformed rake"—and say to him, with all the import of a solemn warning, "Hold!" In your keeping are now placed the destinies of that shrinking woman, for wedded happiness or wedded woe; your own tranquillity and peace of mind, perhaps your honor as a husband and father hang upon your decision now. Be cautious how you thread the mysterious path before you. You have need of all the fortitude and self-control you can possibly summon to your aid, in this great emergency. You may talk of the instincts of nature, but in you these instincts are brutalized; in her they are artificially suppressed. You have the double task of curbing the former and of developing the latter. Undoubtedly the "instincts of nature" would make the marriage consummation a very awkward proceeding, sufficiently protracted for all practical purposes; but society has gotten these instincts sadly out of tune for both of you. By proper caution and delicacy on your part they may yet be harmonized. And perfect accord be thus secured. Your first words should be those of re-assurance and sympathy. Assure her most positively that her apprehensions are groundless, that no consummation shall occur this night, or, indeed, at all, until on that, as you trust on all other subjects, your wishes and hers shall exactly harmonize; above all, inform her that whenever your happy marriage shall be consummated, neither violence nor suffering shall attend it, but perfect and reciprocal happiness shall crown the act. You should know that gentleness, moderation, but more than all, due and reasonable *cultivation* of her womanly passion will enable you to fulfill your pledge to the very letter. You should know that in rare cases days or even weeks must elapse before *entire* consummation can be effected, but that when it does occur the slight pain she will suffer will be of such a character as shall increase, rather than diminish her pleasure. You will also discover, by experience, that with due deliberation and prudence, Nature will cooperate in your favor to relieve you of nearly all the trouble you anticipate.

We can not be more explicit than this, but you will readily comprehend our meaning when you obey these instructions. The slightest intimation of pain or fear should warn you to desist, being determined that under no circumstances shall more violence be used than is obviously invited and *shared*. In a word, beware of committing a veritable outrage on the person of her whom God has given you for a companion. From all that we can learn, and the instances from which we derive our conclusions are very numerous, the first conjugal act is little else than a legalized *rape*, in most cases. Let nothing interfere with your determination to wait for and obtain entire reciprocity of thought and desire, and let this always be your guide, not only during the honey-moon, but also throughout your married existence. Thus will you secure not only happiness and love for yourself, but that perfect confidence and gratitude from your wife which shall make her literally a sharer in your joys, as she must needs be in your sorrows. You should never forget that this passion is ordinarily slower of growth and more tardy of excitation in women than in men, but when fairly aroused in them it is incomparably stronger and more lasting. This, of course, with due allowances for differences of individual temperaments. Therefore be careful to avoid a most common error of unphilosophical man, that of undue haste and precipitation on these occasions throughout your wedded career. Be always assured that your wife is at least in entire sympathy with your own condition. It is rare that two natures are so exactly in harmony with each other that love and desire are always equal in both, but the rule should be for the *one who loves the most to measure his ardor by that of the one who loves the least.*

We are now led to anticipate the question, "How frequently does health or prudence permit the repetition of the marital act?" No positive rule can be stated on this subject, dependent, as it is, on so great a variety of conditions, as individual temperaments, state of health at the moment, etc., but general principles can be clearly stated, from which may be readily deduced rules for particular instances. Regard must always be had to instructions already stated; namely, that nothing should induce a man to gratify his own desires at the expense of his wife's comfort or inclination; that the lawful pleasures of wedlock should never be permitted to degenerate into mere animal lust; that the rule should be, in all cases, to keep within, but never to exceed the limits of fond desire. Franklin's rule for eating, always to rise from the table with an appetite for more, can wisely be applied to the conjugal act—never repeat it so frequently but that the ability on both sides exists for further indulgence.

Perhaps most men learn this lesson soon enough for themselves, but a strongly passionate woman may well-nigh ruin a man of feebler sexual organization than her own, and so it is important that the woman also should be familiarized with the "physiology of matrimony," sufficiently, at least, to refrain from too exacting or frequent demands. Whatever may be her feelings, she should always remember that delicacy, as well as prudence and common sense, require her to await the advances of her companion before she manifests her willingness for his approaches. If, on the one hand, he is bound to respect her temperamental conditions, she, on her part, is equally bound to preserve towards him such an amount of womanly reserve and continence as shall prove, at the same time, her most alluring attribute, as well as her most successful guarantee of continued conjugal happiness. Something should always be held in reserve, no less of her capacity for bestowing and receiving enjoyment, than of her personal and peculiar charms. The imagination should always be left to occupy itself in depicting those treasures which it has enjoyed but never beheld; and thus the husband will remain the lover, and the courtship continue until *death do them part*. Drapery but enhances the estimation in which men hold the female attractions of person, and the rustle of a woman's garment is more potent to charm than the lavish exposure of the proportions of a Venus.

"These violent delights have violent ends,
And in their triumph die; like fire and powder,
Which, as they kiss, consume: the sweetest honey
Is loathsome in his own deliciousness,
And in the taste confounds the appetite:
Therefore, love moderately; long love doth so;
Too swift arrives as tardy as too slow."

From once to thrice a month may be stated as a fair average frequency for the indulgence during the comparative youth and health of both parties, and when no circumstances exist to render abstinence a necessity.

There are but two legitimate methods of avoiding increase of family, and these should be adopted only for legitimate reasons, such as *bona fide* considerations of health, or clearly established peculiarities of constitution. No sordid calculations of economy should have a feather's weight in the adoption of either. Whom the Lord endows with existence He provides for, according to the needs of His children, and no mere human foresight can discover whether economy lies in the increase or diminution in the number of children. The first and incomparably the most judicious method of avoiding off-spring is entire continence during the time it is desirable or necessary to remain exempt. The second method is at the same time less positive and of more doubtful propriety. We allude here to the law of partial continence; that is, absolute avoidance of the conjugal act for the term of fourteen days after the cessation of the last monthly period. This is the extreme limit, and in certain cases may be shortened by two or even four days, but these are exceptional cases, and there are no practical means of ascertaining with positiveness the exceptions to the rule. All other methods of prevention of offspring are disgusting, beastly, positively wrongful, as well as unnatural, and *physically injurious.* Some of them are so revolting that it is impossible to imagine how persons with the least pretensions to decency can adopt them. Any deliberate preparations with such an object savor too much of cold-blooded calculation to be even possible with pure-minded people. At best, the conjugal act should be spontaneous, and directly in accordance with the promptings of Nature. A husband who can coolly lay his plans with reference to future performances of this character, is guilty of practicing the seducer's art in relation to his own marriage bed; he is the unclean bird that literally befouls his own nest. It is then impossible that those who are guilty of such practices can be ignorant of their wicked and criminal nature, and the woman who consents, equally with the man who organizes the method, is a willful and premeditated criminal. We are not writing for the benefit of such persons. We can positively assert, however, that, without a single exception, they are certainly productive of disastrous consequences to health. But there is a practice so universal that it may well be termed a national vice, so common that it is unblushingly acknowledged by its perpetrators, for the commission of which the husband is even eulogized by his wife, and applauded by her friends, a vice which is the scourge and desolation of marriage; it is the crime of *Onan*. "He spilled his seed upon the ground, lest children should be born. And therefore the Lord slew him, because he did a detestable thing."

Who can doubt that Almighty God, in this terrible punishment, wished to impart to man a positive moral instruction which should endure to the end of time, for the crime of Onan will have imitators while the world endures—as what crimes will not? But that these should be found among men of respectability would surpass belief, if the thing were not notoriously true. At any rate, the conjugal onanists in this age and country are more numerous than the exceptions. Ministers of the Gospel, prominent Church members, the very élite of society, well-nigh monopolize the art, for it is far less common to find repugnance to offspring in the lower classes than in "upper-tendom."

This enormous crime is not in all cases confined to the husband; the wife too often becomes affected with the diabolical mania, and not only by consent, but often by voluntary effort, facilitates its accomplishment. The writer knows of cases in which this conduct has been the cause of domestic discord, through remonstrances on the part of the husband. In these instances the woman only was guilty of the crime. One example must suffice.

We were consulted by a gentleman of the highest respectability, who complained that his wife had not only never borne him any children, but was so constituted that she seemed incapable of permitting full completion of the conjugal act. On inquiry, it appeared that she had acted by the instigations of her own mother, who had instructed her in the execution of a certain maneuver too indecent to describe, by which she "could avoid the dangers of child-birth." Yet this monstrous mother is a zealous member of an "orthodox" Church, and not only believes in hell-fire, but indicates without scruple the very souls who, in her opinion, will be consigned to it. It is a comfort to add that the machinations of the old she-devil were readily thwarted by proper medical advice, and the parties now glory in the possession of children and connubial bliss.

Anonymous

Ancient Egyptian Love Lyric

[1085-570 B.C.]

I

Is there anything sweeter than this hour?
　　for I am with you, and you lift up my heart—
　　　　for is there not embracing and fondling
when you visit me
　　and we give ourselves up to delights?
　　If you wish to caress my thigh,
　　then I will offer you my breast also—it won't
　　　　thrust you away!

Will you leave because you are hungry?
> —are you such a man of your belly?

Would you leave because you need something to wear?
> —I have a chestful of fine linen!

Would you leave because you wish something to drink?
> Here, take my breasts! They are full to
>> overflowing, and all for you!

Glorious is the day of our embracings;
I treasure it a hundred thousand millions!

II

Your love has gone all through my body
> like honey in water,
> as a drug is mixed into spices,
> as water is mingled with wine.

Oh that you would speed to see your sister
> like a charger on a battlefield, like a bull to
>> his pasture!

For the heavens are sending us love like a flame spreading
through straw
and desire like the swoop of the falcon!

Vatsyayana

The Kama Sutra

[100]

On Biting, and the Means to be Employed With Regard to Women of Different Countries

All the places that can be kissed are also the places that can be bitten, except the upper lip, the interior of the mouth, and the eyes.

The qualities of good teeth are as follows: They should be equal, possessed of a pleasing brightness capable of being coloured, of proper proportions, unbroken, and with sharp ends.

The defects of teeth on the other hand are that they are blunt, protruding from the gums, rough, soft, large, and loosely set.

The following are the different kinds of biting:

The hidden bite

The swollen bite

The point

The line of points

The coral and the jewel

The line of jewels

The broken cloud

The biting of the boar

The biting, which is shown only by the excessive redness of the skin that is bitten, is called the 'hidden bite'.

When the skin is pressed down on both sides, it is called the 'swollen bite'.

When a small portion of the skin is bitten with two teeth only, it is called the 'point'.

When such small portions of the skin are bitten with all the teeth, it is called the 'line of points'.

The biting, which is done by bringing together the teeth and the lips, is called the 'coral and the jewel'. The lip is the coral, and the teeth the jewel.

When biting is done with all the teeth, it is called the 'line of jewels'.

The biting, which consists of unequal risings in a circle, and which comes from the space between the teeth, is called the 'broken cloud'. This is impressed on the breasts.

The biting, which consists of many broad rows of marks near to one another, and with red intervals, is called the 'biting of a boar'. This is impressed on the breasts and the shoulders; and these two last modes of biting are peculiar to persons of intense passion.

The lower lip is the place on which the 'hidden bite', the 'swollen bite', and the 'point' are made; again the 'swollen bite' and the 'coral and the jewel' bite are done on the cheek. Kissing, pressing with the nails, and biting are the ornaments of the left cheek, and when the word cheek is used it is to be understood as the left cheek.

Both the 'line of points' and the 'line of jewels' are to be impressed on the throat, the arm pit, and the joints of the thighs; but the 'line of points' alone is to be impressed on the forehead and the thighs.

The marking with the nails, and the biting of the following things—an ornament of the forehead, an ear ornament, a bunch of flowers, a betel leaf, or a tamala leaf, which are worn by, or belong to the woman that is beloved—are signs of the desire of enjoyment.

Here end the different kinds of biting.

In the affairs of love a man should do such things as are agreeable to the women of different countries.

The women of the central countries (i.e. between the Ganges and the Jumna) are noble in their character, not accustomed to disgraceful practices, and dislike pressing the nails and biting.

The women of the Balhika country are gained over by striking.

The women of Avantika are fond of foul pleasures, and have not good manners.

The women of the Maharashtra are found of practising the sixty-four arts, they utter low and harsh words, and like to be spoken to in the same way, and have an impetuous desire of enjoyment.

The women of Pataliputra (i.e., the modern Patna) are of the same nature as the women of the Maharashtra, but show their likings only in secret.

The women of the Dravida country, though they are rubbed and pressed about at the time of sexual enjoyment, have a slow fall of semen, that is they are very slow in the act of coition.

The women of Vanavasi are moderately passionate, they go through every kind of enjoyment, cover their bodies, and abuse those who utter low, mean and harsh words.

The women of Avanti hate kissing, marking with the nails, and biting, but have a fondness for various kinds of sexual union.

The women of Malwa like embracing and kissing, but not wounding, and they are gained over by striking.

The women of Abhira, and those of the country

about the Indus and five rivers (i.e. the Punjab), are gained over by the Auparishtaka or mouth congress.

The women of Aparatika are full of passion, and make slowly the sound 'Sit'.

The women of the Lat country have even more impetuous desire, and also make the sound "Sit'.

The women of the Stri Rajya, and Koshola (Oude), are full of impetuous desire, their semen falls in large quantities, and they are fond of taking medicine to make it do so.

The women of the Andhra country have tender bodies, they are fond of enjoyment, and have a liking for voluptuous pleasures.

The women of Ganda have tender bodies, and speak sweetly.

Now Suvarnanabha is of opinion that that which is agreeable to the nature of a particular person, is of more consequence than that which is agreeable to a whole nation, and that therefore the peculiarities of the country should not be observed in such cases. The various pleasures, the dress, and the sports of one country are in time borrowed by another, and in such a case these things must be considered as belonging originally to that country.

Among the things mentioned above, viz. embracing, kissing, etc., those which increase passion should be done first, and those which are only for amusement or variety should be done afterwards.

There are also some verses on this subject as follows:

'When a man bites a woman forcibly, she should angrily do the same to him with double force. Thus a "point" should be returned with a "line of points" and a "line of points" with a "broken cloud", and if she be excessively chafed, she should at once begin a love quarrel with him. At such time she should take hold of her lover by the hair, and bend his head down, and kiss his lower lip, and then, being intoxicated with love, she should shut her eyes and bite him in various places. Even by day, and in a place of public resort, when her lover shows her any mark that she may have inflicted on his body, she should smile at the sight of it, and turning her face as if she were going to chide him, she should show him with an angry look the marks on her own body that have been made by him. Thus if men and women act according to each other's liking, their love for each other will not be lessened even in one hundred years.'

Of the Different Ways of Lying Down, and Various Kinds of Congress

Of the occasion of a 'high congress' the Mrigi (Deer) woman should lie down in such a way as to widen her yoni, while in 'low congress' the Hastini (Elephant) woman should lie down so as to contract hers. But in an 'equal congress' they should lie down in the natural position. What is said above concerning the Mrigi and the Hastini applies also to the Vadawa (Mare) woman. In a 'low congress' the woman should particularly make use of medicine, to cause her desires to be satisfied quickly.

The Deer-woman has the following three ways of lying down:

The widely opened position
The yawning position
The position of the wife of Indra

When she lowers her head and raises her middle parts, it is called the 'widely opened position'. At such a time a man should apply some unguent, so as to make the entrance easy.

When she raises her thighs and keeps them wide apart and engages in congress, it is called the 'yawning position'.

When she places her thighs with her legs doubled on them upon her sides, and thus engages in congress, it is called the position of Indrani and this is learnt only by practice. The position is also useful in the case of the 'highest congress'.

The 'clasping position' is used in 'low congress', and in the 'lowest congress', together with the 'pressing position', the 'twining position', and the 'mare's position'.

When the legs of both the male and the female are stretched straight out over each other, it is called the 'clasping position'. It is of two kinds, the side position and the supine position, according to the way in which they lie down. In the side position the male should invariably lie on his left wide, and cause the woman to lie on her right side, and this rule is to be observed in lying down with all kinds of women.

When, after congress has begun in the clasping position, the woman presses her lover with her thighs, it is called the 'pressing position'.

When the woman places one of her thighs across the thigh of her lover it is called the 'twining position'.

When a woman forcibly holds in her yoni the lingam after it is in, it is called the 'mare's position'. This is learnt by practice only, and is chiefly found among the women of the Andhra country.

The above are the different ways of lying down, mentioned by Babhravya. Suvarnanabha, however, gives the following addition:

When the female raises both of her thighs straight up, it is called the 'rising position'.

When she raises both of her legs, and places them on her lover's shoulders, it is called the 'yawning position'.

When the legs are contracted, and thus held by the lover before his bosom, it is called the 'pressed position'.

When only one of her legs is stretched out, it is called the 'half pressed position'.

When the woman places one of her legs on her lover's shoulder, and stretches the other out, and then places the latter on his shoulder, and stretches out the other, and continues to do so alternately, it is called the 'splitting of a bamboo'.

When one of her legs is placed on the head, and the other is stretched out, it is called the 'fixing of a nail'. This is learnt by practice only.

When both the legs of the woman are contracted and placed on her stomach, it is called the 'crab's position'.

When the thighs are raised and placed one upon the other, it is called the 'packed position'.

When the shanks are placed one upon the other, it is called the 'lotus-like position'.

When a man, during congress, turns round, and enjoys the woman without leaving her, while she embraces him round the back all the time, it is called the 'turning position', and is learnt only by practice.

Thus, says Suvarnanabha, these different ways of lying down, sitting, and standing should be practiced in water, because it is easy to do so therein. But Vatsyayana is of opinion that congress in water is improper, because it is prohibited by the religious law.

When a man and a woman support themselves on each other's bodies, or on a wall, or pillar, and thus while standing engage in congress, it is called the 'supported congress'.

When a man supports himself against a wall, and the woman, sitting on his hands joined together and held underneath her, throws her arms round his neck, and putting her thighs alongside his waist, moves herself by her feet, which are touching the wall against which the man is leaning, it is called the 'suspended congress'.

When a woman stands on her hands and feet like a quadruped, and her lover mounts her like a bull, it is called the 'congress of a cow'. At this time everything that is ordinarily done on the bosom should be done on the back.

In the same way can be carried on the congress of a dog, the congress of a goat, the congress of a deer, the forcible mounting of an ass, the congress of a cat, the jump of a tiger, the pressing of an elephant, the rubbing of a boar, and the mounting of a horse. And in all these cases the characteristics of these different animals should be manifested by acting like them.

When a man enjoys two women at the same time, both of whom love him equally, it is called the 'united congress'.

When a man enjoys many women altogether, it is called the 'congress of a herd of cows'.

The following kids of congress—sporting in water, or the congress of an elephant with many female elephants which is said to take place only in the water, the congress of a collection of goats, the congress of a collection of deer—take place in imitation of these animals.

In Gramaneri many young men enjoy a woman that may be married to one of them, either one after the other, or at the same time. Thus one of them holds her, another enjoys her, a third uses her mouth, a fourth holds her middle part, and in this way they go on enjoying her several parts alternately.

The same things can be done when several men are sitting in company with one courtesan, or when one courtesan is alone with many men. In the same way this can be done by the women of the king's harem when they accidentally get hold of a man.

The people in the Southern countries have also a congress in the anus, that is called the 'lower congress'.

Thus ends the various kinds of congress. There are also two verses on the subject as follows:

'An ingenious person should multiply the kinds of congress after the fashion of the different kinds of beasts and of birds. For these different kinds of congress, performed according to the usage of each country, and the liking of each individual, generate love, friendship, and respect in the hearts of women'.

Of the Various Modes of Striking, and the Sounds Appropriate to Them

Sexual intercourse can be compared to a quarrel, on account of the contrarieties of love and its tendency to dispute. The place of striking with passion is the body, and on the body the special places are:

> The shoulders
> The head
> The space between the breasts
> The back
> The jaghana, or middle part of the body
> The sides

Striking is of four kinds:

Striking with the back of the hand
Striking with the fingers a little contracted
Striking with the fist
Striking with the open palm of the hand

On account of its causing pain, striking gives rise to the hissing sound, which is of various kinds, and to the eight kinds of crying:

The sound Hin
The thundering sound
The cooing sound
The weeping sound
The sound Phut
The sound Phât
The sound Sût
The sound Plât

Besides these, there are also words having a meaning, such as 'mother', and those that are expressive of prohibition, sufficiency, desire of liberation, pain or praise, and to which may be added sounds like those of the dove, the cuckoo, the green pigeon, the parrot, the bee, the sparrow, the flamingo, the duck, and the quail, which are all occasionally made use of.

Blows with the first should be given on the back of the woman while she is sitting on the lap of the man, and she should give blows in return, abusing the man as if she were angry, and making the cooing and the weeping sounds. While the woman is engaged in congress the space between the breasts should be struck with the back of the hand, slowly at first, and then proportionately to the increasing excitement, until the end.

At this time the sounds Hin and others may be made, alternately or optionally, according to habit. When the man, making the sound Phât, strikes the woman on the head, with the fingers of his hand a little contracted, it is called Prasritaka, which means striking with the fingers of the hand a little contracted. In this case the appropriate sounds are the cooing sound, the sound Phât and the sound Phut in the interior of the mouth, and at the end of congress the sighing and weeping sounds. The sound Phât is an imitation of the sound of bamboo being split, while the sound Phut is like the sound made by something falling into water. At all times when kissing and such things are begun, the woman should give a reply with a hissing sound. During the excitement when the woman is not accustomed to striking, she continually utters words expressive of prohibition, sufficiently, or desire of liberation, as well as the words 'father', 'mother', intermingled with the sighing, weeping and thundering sounds.[1] Towards the conclusion of the congress, the breasts, the jaghana, and the sides of the woman should be pressed with the open palms of the hands, with some force, until the end of it, and then sounds like those of the quail or the goose should be made.

There are two verses on the subject as follows:

'The characteristics of manhood are said to consist of

roughness and impetuosity, while weakness, tenderness, sensibility, and an inclination to turn away from unpleasant things are the distinguishing marks of womanhood. The excitement of passion, and peculiarities of habit may sometimes cause contrary results to appear, but these do not last long, and in the end the natural state is resumed.'

The wedge of the bosom, the scissors on the head, the piercing instrument on the cheeks, and the pinchers on the breasts and sides, may also be taken into consideration with the other four modes of striking, and thus give eight ways altogether. But these four ways of striking with instruments are peculiar to the people of the southern countries, and the marks caused by them are seen on the breasts of their women. They are local peculiarities, but Vatsyayana is of opinion that the practice of them is painful, barbarous, and base, and quite unworthy of imitation.

In the same way anything that is a local peculiarity should not always be adopted elsewhere, and even in the place where the practice is prevalent, excess of it should always be avoided. Instances of the dangerous use of them may be given as follows. The king of the Panchalas killed the courtesan Madhavasena by means of the wedge during congress. King Satakarni Satavahana of the Kuntalas deprived his great Queen Malayavati of her life by a pair of scissors, and Naradeva, whose hand was deformed, blinded a dancing girl by directing a piercing instrument in a wrong way.

There are also two verses on the subject as follows:

'About these things there cannot be either enumeration or any definite rule. Congress having once commenced, passion alone gives birth to all the acts of the parties.'

'Such passionate actions and amorous gesticulations or movements, which arise on the spur of the moment, and during sexual intercourse, cannot be defined, and are as irregular as dreams. A horse having once attained the fifth degree of motion goes on with blind speed, regardless of pits, ditches, and posts in his way; and in the same manner a loving pair become blind with passion in the heat of congress, and go on with great impetuosity, paying not the least regard to excess. For this reason one who is well acquainted with the science of love, and knowing his own strength, as also the tenderness, impetuosity, and strength of the young women, should act accordingly. The various modes of enjoyment are not for all times or for all persons, but they should only be used at the proper time, and in the proper countries and places.'

---

[1]Men who are well acquainted with the act of love are well aware how often one woman differs from another in her sighs and sounds during the time of congress. Some women like to be talked to in the most loving way, others in the most lustful way, others in the most abusive way, and so on. Some women enjoy themselves with closed eyes in silence, others make a great noise over it, and some almost faint away. The great art is to ascertain what gives them the greatest pleasure, and what specialties they like best.

Isabel Gowdie

Eyewitness Account of Sex with the Devil

[1662]

First as I was going between the towns of Druwdewin and The Headis, the Devil met with me and there I covenanted with him and promised to meet him in the night time, in the Kirk of Aulderne, which I did. He stood at the reader's desk, and a black book in his hand, where I came before him and renounced Jesus Christ and my baptism; and all between the sole of my foot and the crown of my head. I got up freely and went over to the Devil. Margaret Brodie, in Aulderne, held me up to the Devil, until he re-baptized me, and marked me in the shoulder, and with his mouth sucked out my blood at that place, and spouted it in his hand, and sprinkling it upon my head and face, he said, "I baptize ye, Janet, to my self, in my own name!" Within a while, we all left.

And within a few days, he came to me, in the New Ward's of Inshoch, and there had carnal copulation with me. He was a very huge, black, rough man, very cold; and I found his nature [semen] within me all cold as spring well water. He will lie all heavy upon us, when he has carnal dealing with us, like a sack of barley malt. His member is exceedingly great and long; no man's member is so long and big as his. He would be among us like a stud horse among mares. He would lie with us in the presence of the multitude; neither of us had any kind of shame; but especially he has no shame at all. He would lie and have carnal dealing with all, at every time, as he pleased. He would have carnal dealing with us in the shape of a deer or any other shape that he would be in. We would never refuse him. He would come to my house-top in the shape of a crow, or like a deer, or in any other shape now and then.

I would recognize his voice, at the first hearing of it, and would go forth to him and have carnal copulation with him. The youngest and lustiest women will have very great pleasure in their carnal copulation with him, yea much more than with their own husbands; and they will have an exceedingly great desire for it with him, as much as he can give them and more, and never think shame of it. He is abler for us that way than any man can be (Alas! that I should compare him to any man!) only he is heavy like a sack of barley malt; a huge nature [outpouring of semen], very cold as ice.

Margaret Mead

Arapesh Marriage

[1935]

A man must approach his wife gently, he must make "good little talk," he must be sure that she is well prepared to receive his advances. Otherwise even she, who has been reared by his side, on his food, may become a stranger, the inimical one. There is no emphasis upon satisfaction in sex-relations; the whole emphasis for both men and women is the degree of preparedness, the completeness of the expectancy. Either man or wife may make the tentative advance that crystallizes a latent consciousness of the other into the sex act. It is as customary for the woman as for the man to say, "Shall I lay the bed?" or, "Let us sleep." The verb "to copulate" may be used either with a male subject and a female object, or with a female subject and a male object. More often the phrase "They played together" or "They slept" is used. Women express their preferences for men in terms of ease and lack of difficulty of sex-relationships, not in terms of ability to satisfy a specific desire. There is no recognition on the part of either sex of a specific climax in women, and climax in men is phrased simply as loss of tumescence. The emphasis upon mutual readiness and mutual ease is always the dominant one.

The oral sensitivity so highly developed in childhood and early adolescence is continued into adult sex life. It will be remembered that this oral play has been checked in boys at adolescence, and in spite of the partial substitution of arecanut chewing and smoking, this requires a certain amount of self-control. At the same time, the taboo upon any careless handling of the genitals has prevented the development of masturbation. The boy comes to marriage, therefore, with his oral sensitivity somewhat muted, a strong taboo upon any mixture of oral and genital contacts, and some feeling against any type of tactual stimulation. The girl has not been dealt with so stringently; she has been permitted to bubble her lips right up to her marriage, and if she wishes, she is permitted to continue the comforting practice until she substitutes a child at her breast. The rigorous hygienic practices of the menstrual hut have insured her against feeling even first intercourse as painful. She shares with her husband the taboo against combining oral and genital contacts. It is probably that among a people in whom oral sensitivity is permitted such a highly specialized development, the existence of this taboo has very definite results in ensuring a complete genital expression of sex in adult life. The highly prized oral stimulation falls into place as foreplay, and it is interesting and significant that the Arapesh, unlike most primitive people, possess the true kiss, that is, lip-contact that is punctuated by a sharp implosion of the breath.

Anonymous

Turko-Persian Bab Nameh (Book of Lust)

[DATE UNKNOWN]

A woman may be enjoyed by two men at the same time. The performance would doubtless require an extension of parts; but whoever reflects on their proverbial extensive quality will not doubt of their admitting with ease two guests, after a trial or two and with sufficiency of natural or artificial lubrication, provided themselves could accommodate their entrance to the convenience of each other.

And in the way above alluded to, I am confident that this might be effected. The woman must lie straight, on either side, and the man who attacks her in front must, after entering her, lift her uppermost leg on his buttock. The antagonist in the rear must then accommodate himself to her posture, and glide in likewise.

The men may knock her as hard as they will; so long as the woman is careful to keep herself exactly straight, and not to withdraw from one or the other, their violent shocks will only serve to make her more fixed and steady.

John Cleland

Fanny Hill

[1748]

Nor was this worthy act of justice long delayed: I had it too much at heart. Mr H— had, about a fortnight before, taken into his service a tenant's son, just come out of the country, a very handsome young lad, scarce turned nineteen, fresh as a rose, well shaped and clever-limbed: in short, a very good excuse for any woman's liking, even though revenge had been out of the question; any woman, I say, who was disprejudiced and had wit and spirit enough to prefer a point of pleasure to a point of pride.

Mr H— had clapped a livery upon him; and his chief

employ was, after being shown my lodgings, to bring and
carry letters or messages between his master and me; and
as the situation of all kept ladies is not the fittest to
inspire respect even to the meanest of mankind, and perhaps less of it from the most ignorant, I could not help
observing that this lad, who was, I suppose, acquainted
with my relation to his master by his fellow servants,
used to eye me in that bashful confused way, more expressive, more moving, and readier caught at by our sex than
any other declarations whatever: my figure had, it seems,
struck him, and modest and innocent as he was, he did
not himself know that the pleasure he took in looking at
me was love, or desire; but his eyes, naturally wanton,
and now inflamed by passion, spoke a great deal more
than he durst have imagined they did. Hitherto, indeed, I
had only taken notice of the comeliness of the youth, but
without the least design. My pride alone would have
guarded me from a thought that way, had not Mr H—'s
condescension with my maid, where there was not half
the temptation in point of person, set me a dangerous

example; but now I began to look on this stripling as every way a delicious instrument of my designed retaliation upon Mr H—, of an obligation for which I should have made a conscience to die in his debt.

In order then to pave the way for the accomplishment of my scheme, for two or three times that the young fellow came to me with messages, I managed so as without affectation to have him admitted to my bedside, or brought to me at my toilet, where I was dressing; and by carelessly showing or letting him see as if without meaning or design, sometimes my bosom rather more bare than it should be; sometimes my hair, of which I had a very fine head, in the natural flow of it while combing; sometimes a neat leg, that had unfortunately slipped its garter, which I made no scruple of tying before him, easily gave him the impressions favourable to my purpose, which I could perceive to sparkle in his eyes and glow in his cheeks. Then certain slight squeezes by the hand, as I took letters from him, did this business completely.

When I saw him thus moved and fired for my purpose, I inflamed him yet more, by asking him several leading questions; such as had he a mistress?—was she prettier than me?—could he love such a one as I was?—and the like; to all which the blushing simpleton answered to my wish, in a strain of perfect nature, perfect undebauched innocence, but with all the awkwardness and simplicity of country breeding.

When I thought I had sufficiently ripened him for the laudable point I had in view, one day that I expected him at a particular hour, I took care to have the coast clear for the reception I designed him. And, as I had laid it, he came to the dining-room door, tapped at it, and, on my bidding him come in, he did so and shut the door after him. I desired him then to bolt it on the inside, pretending it would not otherwise keep shut.

I was then lying at length on that very couch, the scene of Mr H—'s polite joys, in an undress which was with all the art of negligence flowing loose, and in a most tempting disorder: no stays, no hoop—no encumbrance whatever; on the other hand, he stood at a little distance that gave me a full view of a fine featured, shapely, healthy, country lad, breathing the sweets of fresh blooming youth; his hair, which was of a perfect shining black, played to his face in natural side-curls and was set out with a smart tuck-up behind; new buckskin breeches that, clipping close, showed the shape of a plump well-made thigh, white stockings, garter-laced livery, shoulder-knot, altogether composed a figure in which the beauties of pure flesh and blood appeared under no disgrace from the lowness of a dress, to which a certain spruce neatness seems peculiarly fitted.

I bid him come towards me and give me his letter, at the same time throwing down carelessly a book I had in my hands. He coloured, and came within reach of delivering me the letter, which he held out awkwardly enough for me to take, with his eyes riveted on my bosom, which was, through the designed disorder of my handkerchief, sufficiently bare and rather shaded than hidden.

I, smiling in his face, took the letter, and immediately

catching gently hold of his shirt-sleeve, drew him towards me, blushing and almost trembling; for surely his extreme bashfulness and utter inexperience called for at least these advances to encourage him. His body was now conveniently inclined towards me, and just softly chucking his smooth beardless chin, I asked him, if he was afraid of a lady?—and with that taking and carrying his hand to my breasts, I pressed it tenderly to them. They were now finely furnished and raised in flesh, so that, panting with desire, they rose and fell, in quick heaves, under his touch: at this, the boy's eyes began to lighten with all the fires of inflamed nature, and his cheeks flushed with a deep scarlet; tongue-tied with joy, rapture, and bashfulness, he could not speak, but then his looks, his emotion, sufficiently satisfied me that my train had taken, and that I had no disappointment to fear.

My lips, which I threw in his way, so as that he could not escape kissing them, fixed, fired and emboldened him, and now, glancing my eyes toward that part of his dress which covered the essential object of enjoyment, I plainly discovered the swell and commotion there, and as I was now too far advanced to stop in so fair a way, and was indeed no longer able to contain myself or wait the slower progress of his maiden bashfulness (for such it seemed, and really was), I stole my hand upon his thighs, down one of which I could both see and feel a stiff hard body, confined by his breeches, that my fingers could discover no end to. Curious then, and eager to unfold so alarming a mystery, playing, as it were, with his buttons, which were bursting ripe from the active force within, those of his waistband and foreflap flew open at a touch, when out it started; and now, disengaged from the shirt, I saw with wonder and surprise, what? not the plaything of a boy, not the weapon of a man, but a maypole of so enormous a standard that, had proportions been observed, it must have belonged to a young giant; its prodigious size made me shrink again. Yet I could not, without pleasure, behold and even ventured to feel such a length! such a breadth of animated ivory, perfectly well turned and fash-ioned, the proud stiffness of which distended its skin, whose smooth polish and velvet softness might vie with that of the most delicate of our sex, and whose exquisite whiteness was not a little set off by a sprout of black curling hair round the root, through the jetty sprigs of which the fair skin showed as, in a fine evening, you may have remarked the clear light ether, through the branchwork of distant trees, overtopping the summet of a hill. Then the broad and bluish-casted incarnate of the head and blue serpentines of its veins altogether composed the most striking assemblage of figure and colours in nature; in short, it stood an object of terror and delight.

But what was yet more surprising, the owner of this natural curiosity (through the want of occasions in the strictness of his home breeding, and the little time he had been in town not having afforded him one) was hitherto an absolute stranger, in practice at least, to the use of all that manhood he was so nobly stocked with; and it now fell to my lot to stand his first trial of it, if I could resolve to run the risks of its disproportion to that tender part of me in which such an over-sized machine was very fit to lay in ruins.

But it was now of the latest to deliberate; for by this time, the young fellow, overheated with the present objects, and too high-mettled to be longer curbed in by that modesty and awe which had hitherto restrained him, ventured, under the stronger impulse and instructive promptership of nature alone, to slip his hands, trembling with eager impetuous desires, under my petticoats, and seeing, I suppose, nothing extremely severe in my looks to stop, or dash him, he feels out and seizes gently the centre-spot of his ardours. Oh then! the fiery touch of his fingers determines me, and my fears melting away before the growing intolerable heat, my thighs disclose of themselves and yield all liberty to his hand; and now, a favourable movement giving my petticoats a toss, the avenue lay too fair, too open to be missed; he is now upon me. I had placed myself with a jet under him, as commodious and open as possible to his attempts, which were untoward enough, for his machine, meeting with no inlet, bore and battered stiffly against me in random pushes, now above, now below, now beside its point, till, burning with impatience from its irritating touches, I guided gently with my hand this furious fescue to where my young novice was now to be taught his first lesson of pleasure. Thus he nicked at length the warm and insufficient orifice; but he was made to find no breach practicable, and mine, though so often entered, was still far from wide enough to take him easily in.

By my direction, however, the head of this unwieldy machine was so crucially pointed that, feeling him foreright against the tender opening, a favourable motion from me met his timely thrust, by which the lips of it, strenuously dilated, gave way to his thus assisted impetuosity, so that we might both feel that he had gained a lodgment; pursuing then his point, he soon, by violent and, to me, most painful piercing thrusts, wedges himself at least so far in as to be now tolerably secure of his entrance: here he stuck; and I now felt such a mixture of pleasure and pain as there is no giving a definition of. I dreaded, alike, his splitting me farther up or his withdrawing: I could not bear either to keep or part with him;

the sense of pain, however, prevailing, from his prodigious size and stiffness, acting upon me in those continued rapid thrusts with which he furiously pursued his penetration, made me cry out gently: 'Oh, my dear, you hurt me!' This was enough to check the tender respectful boy, even in his mid-career; and he immediately drew out the sweet cause of my complaint, whilst his eyes eloquently expressed at once his grief for hurting me and his reluctance at dislodging from quarters of which the warmth and closeness had given him a gust of pleasure that he was now desire-mad to satisfy; and yet too much a novice not to be afraid of my withholding his relief, on account of the pain he had put me to.

But I was myself far from being pleased with his having too much regarded my tender exclaims, for now more and more fired with the object before me, as it still stood with the fiercest erection, unbonneted and displaying its broad vermillion head, I first gave the youth a re-encouraging kiss, which he repaid me with a fervour that seemed at once to thank me and bribe my farther compliance, and I

soon replaced myself in a posture to receive, at all risks, the
renewed invasion, which he did not delay an instant; for,
being presently remounted, I once more felt the smooth
hard gristle forcing an entrance, which he achieved rather
easier than before. Pained, however, as I was, with his
efforts of gaining a complete admission, which he was so
regardful as to manage by gentle degrees, I took care not to
complain. In the meantime, the soft strait passage gradually
loosens, yields, and stretched to its utmost bearing by the
stiff, thick, in-driven engine, sensible at once to the ravishing pleasure of the feel and the pain of the distension, let
him in about half way, when all the most nervous activity
he now exerted to further his penetration gained him not
an inch of his purpose; for whilst he hesitated there, the
crisis of pleasure overtook him, and the close compressure
of the warm surrounding fold drew from him the ecstatic
gush, even before mine was ready to meet it, kept up by the
pain I had endured in the course of the engagement, from
the unsufferable size of his weapon, though it was not as
yet in above half its length.

I expected then, but without wishing it, that he would draw, but well pleasingly disappointed; for he was not to be let off so. The well-breathed youth, hot-mettled and flush with genial juices, was now fairly in for making me know my driver. As soon, then, as he had made a short pause, waking, as it were, out of a trance of pleasure (in which every sense seemed lost for a while, whilst, with his eyes shut and short quick breathings, he had yielded down his maiden tribute), he still kept his post, yet unsated with enjoyment, and solacing in these so new delights, till his stiffness, which had scarce perceptibly remitted, being thoroughly recovered to him, who had not once unsheathed, he proceeded afresh to cleave and open to himself an entire entry into me, which was not a little made easy to him by the balsamic injection with which he had just plentifully moistened the whole internals of the passage. Redoubling, then, the active energy of his thrusts, favoured by the fervid appetency of my motions, the soft oiled wards can no longer stand so effectual a picklock, but yield and open him an entrance: and now, with conspiring nature and my industry, strong to aid him, he pierces, penetrates, and at length, winning his way inch by inch, gets entirely in, and finally, a home-made thrust, sheathes it up to the guard; on the information of which, from the close jointure or our bodies (insomuch that the hair on both sides perfectly interweaved and encurled together), the eyes of the transported youth sparkled with more joyous fires, and all his looks and motions acknowledged excess of pleasure, which I now began to share, for I felt him in my very vitals! I was quite sick with delight! stirred beyond bearing with its furious agitations within me, and gorged and crammed even to a surfeit: thus I lay gasping, panting, under him, till his broken breathings, faultering accents, eyes twinkling with humid fires, lunges more furious, and an increased stiffness gave me to hail the approaches of the second period:—it came—and the sweet youth, over-powered with ecstasy, died away in my arms, melting in a flood that shot in genial warmth into the innermost recesses of my body, every conduit of which, dedicated to that pleasure, was on flow to mix with it. Thus we continued for some instants, lost, breathless, senseless of everything and in every part but those favourite ones of nature, in which all that we enjoyed of life and sensation was now totally concentered.

When our mutual trance was a little over, and the young fellow had withdrawn that delicious stretcher with which he had most plentifully drowned all thoughts of revenge in the sense of actual pleasure, the widened wounded passage refunded a stream of pearly liquids, which flowed down my thighs, mixed with streaks of blood, the marks of the ravage of that monstrous machine of his, which had now triumphed over a kind of second maidenhead. I stole, however, my handkerchief to those parts and wiped them as dry as I could, whilst he was readjusting, and buttoning up.

I made him now sit down by me, and as he had gathered courage from such extreme intimacy, he gave me an aftercourse of pleasure, in a natural burst of tender gratitude and joy, at the new scenes of bliss I had opened to him; scenes positively so new that he had never before had the least acquaintance with that mysterious mark, the cloven stamp of female distinction, though nobody better qualified than he to penetrate into its deepest recesses or do it nobler justice. But when, by certain motions, certain unquietness of his hands, that wandered not without design, I found he languished for satisfying a curiosity natural enough, to view and handle those parts which attract and concentre the warmest force of imagination, charmed as I was to have any occasion of obliging and humouring his young desires, I suffered him to proceed as he pleased, without check or control, to the satisfaction of them.

Easily, then, reading in my eyes the full permission of myself to all his wishes, he scarcely pleased himself more than me, when, having insinuated his hands under my petticoat and shift, he presently removed those bars to the sight by slily lifting them upwards, under favour of a thousand kisses, which he thought, perhaps, necessary to divert my attention to what he was about. All my drapery being now rolled up to my waist, I threw myself into such a pos‑ ture upon the couch as gave up to him, in full view, the whole region of delight, and all the luxurious landscape round it. The transported youth devoured everything with his eyes and tried with his fingers to lay more open to his sight the secrets of that dark and delicious deep: he opens the folding lips, the softness of which, yielding entry to anything of a hard body, close round it, and oppose the sight; and feeling further, meets with, and wonders at, a soft fleshy excrescence, which, limber and relaxed after the late enjoyment, now grew, under the touch and examina‑ tion of his fiery fingers, more and more stiff and consider‑ able, till the titillating ardours of that so sensible part made me sigh as if he had hurt me. On which he withdrew his curious probing fingers, asking me pardon, as it were, in a kiss that rather increased the flame *there*.

Novelty ever makes the strongest impressions, and in pleasures especially: no wonder then that he was swal‑ lowed up in raptures of admiration of things so interest‑ ing by their nature, and now seen and handled for the first time. On my part, I was richly overpaid for the pleasure I gave him, in that of examining the power of those objects thus abandoned to him, naked and free to his loosest wish, over the artless, natural stripling: his eyes streaming fire, his cheeks glowing with a florid red, his fervid frequent sighs, whilst his hands convulsively squeezed, opened, pressed together again the lips and sides of that deep flesh-wound or gently twitched the over-growing moss; and all proclaimed the excess, the riot of joys, in having his wantonness thus humoured. But he did not long abuse my patience, for the objects before him had now put him by all his, and coming out with that formidable machine of his, he lets the fury loose, and pointing it directly to the pouting-lipped mouth that bids him sweet defiance in dumb-show, squeezes in the head, and driving with refreshed rage, breaks in and plugs up the whole passage of that soft pleasure-conduit, where he makes all shake again, and put once more all within me into such an uproar as nothing could still but a fresh inundation from the very engine of those flames, as well as from all the springs with which nature floats that reservoir of joy, when risen to its floodmark.

I was now so bruised, so battered, so spent with this over-match that I could hardly stir or raise myself, but lay palpitating, till the ferment of my senses subsiding by degrees, and the hour striking at which I was obliged to dispatch my young man, I tenderly advised him of the necessity there was for parting, which I felt as much displeasure at as he could do, who seemed eagerly disposed to keep the field, and to enter on a fresh action; but the danger was too great, and after some hearty kisses of leave and recommendations of secrecy and discretion, I forced myself to force him away, not without assurances of seeing him again, to the same purpose, as soon as possible, and thrust a guinea into his hands; not more, lest, being too flush of money, a suspicion or discovery might arise from thence, having everything to fear from the dangerous indiscretion of that age in which young fellows would be too irresistible, too charming, if we had not that terrible fault to guard against.

Gabriel García Márquez

Love in the Time of Cholera

[1988]

One night during the war, when he was drifting, not knowing what direction his life should take, the celebrated Widow Nazaret took refuge in his house because hers had been destroyed by cannon fire during the siege by the rebel general Ricardo Gaitán Obeso. It was Tránsito Ariza who took control of the situation and sent the widow to her son's bedroom on the pretext that there was no space in hers, but actually in the hope that another love would cure him of the one that did not allow him to live. Florentino Ariza had not made love since he lost his virginity to Rosalba in the cabin on the boat, and in this emergency it seemed natural to him that the widow should sleep in the bed and he in the hammock. But she had already made the decision for him. She sat on the edge of the bed where Florentino Ariza was lying, not knowing what to do, and she began to speak to him of her inconsolable grief for the husband who had died three years earlier, and in the meantime she removed her widow's weeds and tossed them in the air until she was not even wearing her wedding ring. She took off the taffeta blouse with the beaded embroidery and threw it across the room onto the easy chair in the corner, she tossed her bodice over her shoulder to the other side of the bed, with one pull she removed her long ruffled skirt, her satin garter belt and funeral stockings, and she threw everything on the floor until the room was carpeted with the last remnants of her mourning. She did it with so much joy, and with such well-measured pauses, that each of her gestures seemed to be saluted by the cannon of the attacking troops, which shook the city down to its foundations. Florentino Ariza tried to help her unfasten her stays, but she anticipated him with a deft maneuver, for in five years of matrimonial devotion she learned to depend on herself in all phases of love, even the preliminary stages, with no help from anyone. Then she removed her lace panties, sliding them down her legs with the rapid movements of a swimmer, and at last she was naked.

She was twenty-eight years old and had given birth three times, but her naked body preserved intact the giddy excitement of an unmarried woman. Florentino Ariza was never to understand how a few articles of penitential clothing could have hidden the drives of that wild mare who, choking on her own feverish desire, undressed him as she had never been able to undress her husband, who would have thought her perverse, and tried, with the confusion and innocence of five years of conjugal fidelity, to satisfy in a single assault the iron abstinence of her mourning. Before that night, and from the hour of grace when her mother gave birth to her, she had never been in the same bed with any man other than her dead husband.

She did not permit herself the vulgarity of remorse. On the contrary. Kept awake by the gunfire whizzing over the roofs, she continued to evoke her husband's excellent qualities until daybreak, not reproaching him for any disloyalty other than his having died without her, which was mitigated by her conviction that he had never belonged to her as much as he did now that he was in the coffin nailed shut with a dozen three-inch nails and two meters under the ground.

"I am happy," she said, "because only now do I know for certain where he is when he is not at home."

That night she stopped mourning once and for all, without passing through the useless intermediate stage of blouses with little gray flowers, and her life was filled with love songs and provocative dresses decorated with macaws and spotted butterflies, and she began to share her body with anyone who cared to ask for it. When the troops of General Gaitán Obeso were defeated after a sixty-three day siege, she rebuilt the house that had been damaged by cannon fire, adding a beautiful sea terrace that overlooked the breakwater where the surf would vent its fury during the stormy season. That was her love nest, as she called it without irony, where she would receive only men she liked, when she liked, how she liked, and without charging one red cent, because in her opinion it was the men who were doing her the favor. In a very few cases she would accept a gift, as long as it was not made of gold, and she managed everything with so much skill that no one could have presented conclusive evidence of improper conduct. On only one occasion did she hover on the edge of public scandal, when the rumor circulated that Archbishop Dante de Luna had not died by accident after eating a plate of poisonous mushrooms but had eaten them intentionally because she threatened to expose him if he persisted in his sacrilegious solicitations. As she used to say between peals of laughter, she was the only free woman in the province.

The Widow Nazaret never missed her occasional appointments with Florentino Ariza, not even during her busiest times, and it was always without pretensions of

loving or being loved, although always in the hope of finding something that resembled love, but without the problems of love. Sometimes he went to her house, and then
they liked to sit on the sea terrace, drenched by salt spray,
watching the dawn of the whole world on the horizon.
With all his perseverance, he tried to teach her the tricks
he had seen others perform through the peepholes in the
transient hotel, along with the theoretical formulations
preached by Lotario Thugut on his nights of debauchery.
Her persuaded her to let themselves be observed while
they made love, to replace the conventional missionary
position with the bicycle on the sea, or the chicken on the
grill, or the drawn-and-quartered angel, and they almost
broke their necks with the cords snapped as they were
trying to devise something new in a hammock. The
lessons were to no avail. The truth is that she was a fear-
less apprentice but lacked all talent for guided fornication.
She never understood the charm of serenity in bed, never
had a moment of invention, and her orgasms were inop-
portune and epidermic: an uninspired lay. For a long time

Florentino Ariza lived with the deception that he was the
only one, and she humored him in that belief until she
had the bad luck to talk in her sleep. Little by little, listening to her sleep, he pieced together the navigation
chart of her dreams and sailed along the countless islands
of her secret life. In this way he learned that she did not
want to marry him, but did feel joined to his life because
of her immense gratitude to him for having corrupted
her. She often said to him:

"I adore you because you made me a whore."

Said in another way, she was right. Florentino Ariza
had stripped her of the virginity of a conventional marriage, more pernicious than congenital virginity or the
abstinence of widowhood. He had taught her that nothing one does in bed is immoral if it helps to perpetuate
love. And something else that from that time on would be
her reason for living: he convinced her that one comes
into the world with a predetermined allotment of lays,
and whoever does not use them for whatever reason,
one's own or someone else's, willingly or unwillingly,

loses them forever. It was to her credit that she took him at his word. Still, because he thought he knew her better than anyone else, Florentino Ariza could not understand why a woman of such puerile resources should be so popular—a woman, moreover, who never stopped talking in bed about the grief she felt for her dead husband. The only explanation he could think of, one that could not be denied, was that the Widow Nazaret had enough tenderness to make up for what she lacked in the marital arts. They began to see each other with less frequency as she widened her horizons and he exploited his, trying to find solace in other hearts for his pain, and at last, with no sorrow, they forgot each other.

Anonymous

Yoruba Erotic Chorus

[1964]

Solo: *Teacher's penis*
Chorus: *Mistress's [school mistress] vagina.*
Solo: *Ijebu's vagina*
Chorus: *Like a drinking cup.*
Solo: *Ijebu's penis*
Chorus: *Like a rafter.*

Louis Berman

The Glands That Regulate Sexuality

[1921]

It has been demonstrated that the injection of an ounce or two of the blood, which means the internal secretion mixture, of a starving animal, into one not starving, increased the signs of hunger and the accompanying hunger contractions of the stomach. There can be no doubt that hunger is the expression of certain specific conditions of the blood. When these, in the cycle of metabolism, become sufficiently great, the stomach is stimulated to contract in a way which augments the pressure within it to a point at which the feeling of hungriness, and the wish to satisfy it, or to get rid of it, becomes imperative, the dominant of consciousness.

Without doubt the sexual cravings are likewise to be determined. Sex libido is an expression of a certain concentration, a definite amount peculiar to the individual, of the substance manufactured by the interstitial cells, circulating in the blood. It arouses its effects probably by (1) increasing the amount of reproductive material in the sex glands in a direct chemically stimulating effect upon the germinative cells, and so raising the internal pressure within them, (2) stimulating the involuntary muscles within the walls and canals of the sex glands, and so by augmenting the senses of the muscles, elevating the total intravisceral pressure, (3) by a direct chemical and indirect nervous effect upon the brain, the muscles, the heart, as well as the other glands of internal secretions stimulating the organism as a whole. Though the isolation in pure form of the substance or substances involved has never been scientifically achieved, their inference is entirely justified. It is indeed the only comprehensible mechanism conceivable that will fit all the known facts about the matter.

Li Yu

The Carnal Prayer Mat

[c. 1652]

She's beginning to show a little interest, thought Vesperus. I was planning to start at once, but this is the first time her desires have been aroused and her appetite is still quite undeveloped. If I give her a taste of it now, she'll be like a starving man at the sight of food—she'll bolt it down without savouring it and so miss the true rapture; I think I'll tantalize her a little before mounting the stage.

Pulling up an easy chair, he sat down and drew her onto his lap, then opened the album and showed it to her picture by picture. This album differed from others in that the first page of each leaf contained the erotic picture and the second page a comment on it. The first part of the comment explained the activity depicted, while the rest praised the artist's skill. All the comments were in the hand of famous writers.

Vesperus told Jade Scent to try to imagine herself in the place of the people depicted and to concentrate on their expressions so that she could imitate them later on. While she looked at the pictures, he read out the comments:

Picture Number One. The Releasing the Butterfly in Search of Fragrance position. The woman sits on the Lake Tai rock with her legs apart while the man sends his jade whisk into her vagina and moves it from side to side seeking the heart of the flower. At the moment depicted, the pair are just beginning and have not reached the rapturous stage, so their eyes are wide open and their expressions not much different from normal.

Picture Number Two. The Letting the Bee Make Honey position. The woman is lying on her back on the brocade quilt, bracing herself on the bed with her hands and raising her legs aloft to meet the jade whisk and let the man know the location of the heart of the flower so that he will not thrust at random. At the moment depicted, the woman's expression is almost ravenous, while the man seems so nervous that the observer feels anxiety on his behalf. Supreme art at its most mischievous.

Picture Number Three. The Lost Bird Returns to the Wood position. The woman leans back on the embroidered couch with her legs in the air, grasping the man's thighs and driving them directly downward. She appears to have entered the state of rapture and is afraid of losing her way. The couple are just at the moment of greatest exertion and show extraordinary vitality. This scene has the marvellous quality of 'flying brush and dancing ink.'

Picture Number Four. The Starving Horse Races to the Trough position. The woman lies flat on the couch with her arms wrapped around the man as if to restrict his movements. While he supports her legs on his shoulders, the whole of the jade whisk enters the vagina, leaving not a trace behind. At the moment depicted, they are on the point of spending; they are about to shut their eyes and swallow each other's tongues, and their expressions are identical. Supreme art indeed.

Picture Number Five. The two Dragons Who Fight Till They Drop position. The woman's head rests beside the pillow and her hands droop in defeat, as soft as cotton floss. The man's head rests beside her neck, and his whole body droops too, also as soft as cotton floss. She has spent, and her soul is about to depart on dreams of the future. This is a state of calm after furious activity. Only her feet, which have not been lowered but still rest on the man's shoulders, convey any trace of vitality. Otherwise, he and she would resemble a pair of corpses, which leads the observer to understand their rapture and think of lovers entombed together.

By the time Jade Scent reached this page, her sexual desires were fully aroused and could no longer be held in check. Vesperus turned the page and was about to show her the next picture when she pushed the book away and stood up.

'A fine book this is!' she exclaimed. 'It makes one uncomfortable just to look at it. Read it yourself if you want to. I'm going to lie down.'

Vesperus caught her in his arms. 'Dear heart, there are more good ones. Let's look at them together and then go to bed.'

'Don't you have any time tomorrow? Why do you have to finish today?'

Vesperus knew she was agitated, and he put his arms around her and kissed her. When kissing her before, he had tried to insert his tongue in her mouth but her tightly clenched teeth always prevented him. As a result, she was still unacquainted with his tongue after more than a month of marriage. But on this occasion he had no sooner touched her lips than that sharp soft tongue of his had somehow slipped past her teeth and entered her mouth.

'Dear heart,' said Vesperus, 'there's no need to use the bed. Why don't we take this easy chair as our rock and imitate the picture in the album. What do you say?'

Jade Scent pretended to be angry. 'People don't *do* things like that!'

'You're right,' said Vesperus, 'people don't do them. Immortals do! Let's be immortals for a little while.' He put out his hand and undid her belt. Jade Scent's heart was willing, even if her words were not and she simply hung on his shoulder and offered no resistance. Taking off her trousers, Vesperus noticed a large damp patch in the seat caused by her secretions while she was looking at the pictures.

Vesperus took off his own trousers and pulled her over to the chair, where he made her sit with her legs apart. He then inserted his jade whisk into her vagina before removing the clothes from her upper body.

Dubravka Ugresic

A Hot Dog in a Warm Bun

[1981]

I

On the twenty-fifth of March a truly unbelievable thing took place in Zagreb. Nada Matic, a young doctor specializing in plastic surgery, awoke in her room and looked at the clock. It was 6:15. Nada jumped out of bed, jumped into the shower, squatted under the stream of water, then, lighting a cigarette, jumped into a terrycloth robe. It was 6:25. She pulled on her grey spring suit, daubed some rouge on her cheeks, and grabbed her bag. It was half past six. She locked the door, finished the cigarette in the elevator, and hurried off to catch her tram.

By the time Nada Matic stepped off the tram, it was ten to seven. And just then, right in the middle of the square, Nada Matic was overcome by a sudden, unusually intense hunger. She rushed over to the Skyscraper Cafeteria, which served hot dogs in warm buns, nervously called out to the waitress, "More mustard, please!" greedily grabbed the hot dog, and impatiently threw away the napkin. (This is what Nada Matic did. This is what I do too: I always dispose of those unnecessary and shamefully tiny scraps of paper waitresses use to wrap hot dogs.)

Then she set off across the square. She was about to bring the hot dog to her lips, when—was it some dark sense of foreboding or a ray of the March morning sun alighting on the object in question, illuminating it with its own special radiance? In either case, to make a long story short—she glanced down at the fresh pink hot dog and her face convulsed in horror. For what did she see peering through the longish bun and ocherish mustard foam but a genuine, bona fide . . . ! Nada came to a complete and utter halt. No, there could be no doubt. *Glans, corpus, radix, cor-*

pora cavernosa, corpora spongiosa, praeputium, frenulum, scrotum, our heroine, Nada Matic, thought, running through her totally useless anatomy class knowledge and still not believing her eyes. No, that thing in the bun was most definitely not a hot dog!

Utterly shaken, Nada resumed her journey to the Municipal Hospital at a much slower pace. It had all come together in a single moment: the anatomy lesson, plastic surgery, the desire to specialize in aesthetic prosthetics— it had all flashed before her eyes like a mystical sign, a warning, the finger of fate, a finger that, if we may be forgiven the crudeness of our metaphor, peered out of the bun in so tangible, firm, fresh, and pink a state as to be anything but an illusion.

Nada Matic decided to give the "hot dog" issue top priority. Taking the "hot dog" to the laboratory and dropping it in a bottle of Formalin would have been the simplest solution, of course, but what would her colleagues have said? Nada looked here and there for a litter basket; but there were none in sight. As she'd thrown the napkin away and had no paper tissues, she tried to hide the "hot dog" by coaxing it into the bun with her finger, but smooth, slippery, and springy as it was, it kept sliding out, the head gleaming almost maliciously in Nada's direction.

It then occurred to Nada that she might drop into a cafe and just happen to leave the "hot dog" on the lower shelf of one of the tables she often stood beside—she had said goodbye to three umbrellas that way—but in the end she lost her nerve. For the first time in her life Nada felt what it was like to be a criminal.

Oh, before I forget, I ought to tell you a few things about our heroine. Nada Matic is the kind of shortish, plumpish blonde that men find attractive. But her generous, amicable, amorous character kept getting in her way, and men disappeared from her life, poor thing, without her ever quite understanding why. Abandoned by no fault of her own, she naturally and periodically found herself involved in hot and heavy escapades with married medical personnel of the male sex.

Suddenly Nada felt terribly sorry for herself: her

whole life seemed to have shrunk into that grotesque symbol of bun-*cum*-relay-race baton. No, she'd better take care
of it at once. She gave the bun an unconscious squeeze
and the hot dog peeked out at her again, turning her self-
pity to despair. And just as she noticed a broken basement
window and was about to toss it away, bun and all, who
should pass by with a cold nod but one of the surgeons,
Otto Waldinger. Quick as lightning, Nada stuffed the
"hot dog" into her pocket, smearing gooey mustard all
over her fingers. The bastard! Scarcely even acknowledg-
ing her, while not so long ago . . . !

And then she spied a mercifully open drain. She
removed the "hot dog" from her pocket with great care
and flung it into the orifice. It got stuck in the grating.
She nudged it with her foot, but it refused to budge. It
was too fat.

At that point up sauntered a young, good-looking
policeman.

"Identity papers, please."

"What for?" Nada mumbled.

"Jaywalking."

"Oh," said Nada, rummaging frenetically through her bag.

"What's the matter?" asked the policeman, looking down at the grating. "Lost your appetite?" A good inch and a half of the "hot dog" was sticking out of the bun. Nada Matic went pale.

But at this point everything becomes so enveloped in mist that we cannot tell what happened next.

II

Mato Kovalic, a writer (or, to be more specific, a novelist and short story writer), awoke rather early and smacked his lips, which he always did when he awoke though he could not for the life of him explain why. Kovalic stretched, moved his hand along the floor next to the bed until it found his cigarettes, lit one, inhaled, and settled back. There was a full-length mirror on the opposite wall, and Kovalic could see his bloated grey face in it.

During his habitual morning wallow in bed he was

wont to run through the events of the previous day. The thought of the evening's activities and Maja, that she-devil of an invoice clerk, called forth a blissful smile on his face and his hand willy-nilly slid under the covers . . . Unbelievable! No, absolutely impossible!

Kovalic flung back the blanket and leaped up as if scalded. There he felt only a perfectly smooth surface. Kovalic rushed over to the mirror. He was right. There he saw only an empty, smooth space. He looked like one of those naked, plastic dummies in the shop windows. He pinched and pulled at himself several times; he slapped his face to see whether he was awake; he jumped in place once or twice; and again he placed his hand on the spot where only the night before there had been a bulge. . . . No, *it* was gone!

But here we must say a few words about Kovalic and show the reader what sort of man our hero is. We shall not go into his character, because the moment one says something about a writer all other writers take offense. And to point out that Kovalic was a writer who divided all prose into two categories, prose *with balls* and prose *without* (he was for the former), would be quite out of place in these circumstances and might even prompt the reader to give a completely erroneous and vulgar interpretation to the whole incident. Let us therefore say instead that Kovalic greatly valued—and wished to write—novels that were true to life, down to earth. What he despised more than anything were symbols, metaphors, allusions, ambiguities, literary frills; what he admired was authenticity, a razor-edged quality where every word meant what it meant and not God knows what else! He was especially put off by intellectualizing, attitudinizing, high-blown flights of fancy, genres of all kinds (life is too varied and unpredictable to be forced into prefabricated molds, damn it!), and—naturally—critics! Who but critics, force-fed on the pap of theory, turned works of literature into paper monsters teeming with hidden meanings?

Kovalic happened to be working on a book of stories called *Meat*, the kingpin of which was going to be about his neighbour, a retired butcher positively in love with his trade. Kovalic went on frequent drinking bouts with the man for the purpose of gathering material: nouns (brisket, chuck, flank, knuckle, round, rump, saddle, shank, loin; weinerwurst, weisswurst, liverwurst, bratwurst, blood pudding, etc.), verbs (pound, hack, gash, slash, gut, etc.), and whole sentences: "You shoulda seen me go through them—the slaughterhouse ain't got nothing on me!" "A beautiful way to live a life—and earn a pile!" "My knives go with me to the grave." Kovalic intended to use the latter, which the old man would say with great pathos, and end the story with a wallop.

We might add that Kovalic was a good-looking man and much loved by women, about which he had no qualms whatsoever.

Well, now the reader can judge for himself the state our hero was in when instead of his far from ugly bulge he found a smooth, even space.

Looking in the mirror, Kovalic saw a broken man. God, he thought, why me? And why not my arms or legs? Why not my ears or nose, unbearable as it would have been . . . . What good am I now. . . ? Good for the dump, that's what! If somebody had chopped it off, I wouldn't have made a peep. But to up and disappear on me, vanish into thin air. . . ? No, it's impossible! I must be dreaming, hallucinating. And in his despair he started pinching the empty space again.

Suddenly, as if recalling something important, Kovalic pulled on his shoes and ran out into the street. It was a sunny day, and he soon slowed his pace and began to stroll. In the street he saw a child peeling a banana, and in a bar he saw a man pouring beer from a bottle down his gullet, in a doorway he saw a boy with a plastic pistol in his hand come running straight at him; he saw a jet cross the sky, a fountain in a park start to spurt, a blue tram come round a bend, some workers block traffic dragging long rubber pipes across the road, two men walking toward him, one of whom was saying to the other, "But for that you really need balls. . . ."

God! thought Kovalic, compulsively eyeing the man's trousers. Can't life be cruel!

Queer! the cocky trousers sneered, brushing past him.

I must, I really must do something, thought Kovalic, sinking even deeper into despair. And then he had a lifesaver of a thought . . . Lidija! Of course! He'd go and see Lidija.

III

You never know what's going to happen next, thought Vinko K., the young, good-looking policeman, as he jay-walked across the square. Pausing in front of a shop window, he saw the outline of his lean figure and the shadow of the truncheon dangling at his side. Through the glass he saw a young woman with dark, shining eyes making hot dogs. First she pierced one half of a long roll with a heated metal stake and twisted it several times; then she poured some mustard into the hollow and stuffed a pink hot dog into it. Vinko K. was much taken with her dexterity. He went in and pretended to be waiting his turn, while in fact he was watching the girl's pudgy hands and absentmindedly twirling his billy.

"Next!" her voice rang out.

"Me? Oh, then I might as well have one," said a flustered Vinko K., "as long as . . ."

"Twenty!" her voice rang out like a cash register.

Vinko K. moved over to the side. He subjected the bun to a close inspection: it contained a fresh hot dog. Meanwhile, two more girls had come out of a small door, and soon all three were busy piercing rolls and filling them with mustard and hot dogs.

Vinko K. finished off his hot dog with obvious relish and then walked over to the girls.

"Care to take a little break, girls?" he said in a low voice. "Can we move over here?" he added, even more softly. "Yes, this is fine. . . ."

Squeezed together between cases of beverages and boxes of hot dogs, a sink, a bin, and a broom, Vinko K. and the waitresses could scarcely breathe.

"I want you to show me all the hot dogs you have on the premises," said a calm Vinko K.

The girl opened all the hot dog boxes without a murmur.

The hot dogs were neatly packed in cellophane wrappers.

"Hm!" said Vinko K. "Tell me, are they all vacuumed-packed?"

"Oh, yes!" all three voices rang out. "They're all vacuum-packed!"

A long, uncomfortable silence ensued. Vinko K. was thinking. You never knew what would happen next in his line. You could never tell what human nature had in store.

Meanwhile the girls just stood there, huddled together like hot dogs in a cellophane wrapper. All at once Vinko K.'s fingers broke into a resolute riff on one of the cardboard boxes and, taking a deep breath, he said, as if giving a password, "Fellatio?"

"Aaaaah?!" the girls replied, shaking their heads, and though they did not seem to have understood the question they kept up a soft titter.

"Never heard of it?" asked Vinko K.

"Teehee! Teehee! Teehee!" they tittered on.

"Slurp, slurp?" Vinko K. tried, sounding them out as best he could.

"Teehee! Teehee! Teehee!" they laughed pleasantly, like the Chinese.

Vinko K. was momentarily nonplussed. He thought of using another word with the same meaning but it was so rude he decided against it.

"Hm!" he said instead.

"Hm!" said the girls, rolling their eyes and bobbing their heads.

Vinko K. realized his case was lost. He sighed. The girls sighed compassionately back.

By this time there was quite a crowd waiting for hot dogs. Vinko K. went outside. He stole one last glance at the first girl. She glanced back, tittered, and licked her lips. Vinko K. smiled and unconsciously bobbed his billy. She, too, smiled and vaguely nodded. Then she took a roll and resolutely rammed it onto the metal stake.

But at this point everything becomes so enveloped in mist again that we cannot tell what happened next.

IV

"Entrez!" Lidija called out unaffectedly, and Kovalic collapsed into her enormous, commodious armchair with a sigh of relief.

Lidija was Kovalic's best friend; she was completely, unhesitatingly devoted to him. Oh, he went to bed with her all right, but out of friendship; she went to bed with *him* out of friendship too. They didn't do it often, but they had stuck with it for ages—ten years by now. Kovalic knew everything there was to know about Lidija; Lidija knew everything there was to know about Kovalic. And they were never jealous. But Kovalic the writer—much as he valued sincerity in life and prose—refused to admit to himself that he had once seen their kind of relationship in a film and found it highly appealing, an example (or so he thought) of a new, more humane type of rapport between a man and a woman. It was in the name of this ideal that he gave his all to her in bed even when he was not particularly up to it.

They had not seen each other for quite some time, and Lidija started in blithely about all the things that had happened since their last meeting. She had a tendency to end each sentence with a puff, as if what she had just produced was less a sentence than a hot potato.

Lidija had soon trotted out the relevant items from the pantry of her daily life, and following a short silence—and a silent signal they had hit upon long before—the two of them began to undress.

"Christ!" cried Lidija, who in other circumstances was a translator to and from the French.

"Yesterday . . ." said Kovalic, crestfallen, apologetic. "Completely disappeared . . ."

For a while Lidija simply stood there, staring wide-eyed at Kovalic's empty space; then she assumed a serious and energetic expression, went over to her bookcase, and took down the encyclopedia.

"Why bother?" asked Kovalic as she riffled the pages. "Castration, castration complex, coital trophy—it's all beside the point! It's just disappeared, understand? Dis-appeared!"

"*Bon Dieu de Bon Dieu!*" Lidija muttered. "And what are you going to do now?"

"I don't know," Kovalic whimpered.

"Who were you with last?"

"Girl named Maja . . . But that's every bit as much beside the point."

"Just wondering," said Lidija, and said no more.

As a literary person in her own right, Lidija had often cheered Kovalic up and on with her gift for the apt image. But now her sugar-sweet sugar beet, her pickle in the middle, her poor withered mushroom, her very own Tom Thumb, her fig behind the leaf, her tingaling dingaling, her Jack-in-the-box had given way to—a blank space!

All of a sudden Lidija had a divine inspiration. She threw herself on Kovalic and for all the insulted, humiliated, oppressed, for all the ugly, impotent, and sterile, for all the poor in body, hunched in back, and ill in health— for every last one she gave him her tenderest treatment, polishing, honing him like a recalcitrant translation, fondling, caressing, her tongue as adroit as a keypunch, kneading his skin with her long, skilful fingers, moving lower and lower, seeking out her Jack's mislaid cudgel, picking and pecking at the empty space, fully expecting the firm little rod to pop out and give her cheek a love tap. Kovalic was a bit stunned by Lidija's abrupt show of passion, and even after he began to feel signs of arousal he remained prostate, keeping close tabs on the pulsations as they proceeded from pitpat to rat-tat-tat to boomety-boom, waiting for his Jack to pump, his rubber-gloved Tom to thump, he didn't care who, as long as he came out into the open!

Kovalic held his breath. He felt the blank space ticking off the seconds like an infernal machine; he felt it about to erupt like a geyser, a volcano, an oil well; he felt himself swelling like soaked peas, like a tulip bulb, like a cocoon; felt it coming, any time now, any second now, any—pow! boo-oo-oom! cra-a-a-sh-sh-sh!

Moaning with pleasure, Kovalic climaxed, climaxed to his great surprise—in the big toe of his left foot!

Utterly shaken, Kovalic gave Lidija a slight shove and peered down at his foot. Then, still refusing to believe that what happened had happened, he fingered the toe. It gave him a combination of pleasure and mild pain—and just sat there, potatolike, indifferent. Kovalic stared at it, mildly offended by its lack of response.

"Idiot!" said Lidija with a French intonation, and stood up, stalked out, and slammed the door.

Kovalic stretched. The smooth space was still hideously smooth. He wiggled his left toe, then his right. The left one struck him as perceptibly fatter and longer.

It did happen, thought Kovalic. There's no doubt about it. It actually happened. Suddenly he felt grateful to Lidija. The only thing was, did he really climax in his toe or was his mind playing tricks on him? Kovalic leaned over and felt the toe again, then went back to the smooth space, and finally, heaving a worried sigh, lit a cigarette.

"Anyone for a nice homemade sausage?" asked a conciliatory Lidija, peering in from the kitchen.

Kovalic felt all the air go out of him: Lidija's proposition was like a blow to the solar plexus; it turned him into the butt of a dirty joke.

Kovalic was especially sensitive to clichés; he avoided

them in both literature and life. And now he was terribly upset. By some absurd concatenation of events his life had assumed the contours of a well-established genre (a joke of which he was the punch line). How could life, which he had always thought of as vast—no, boundless—how could life give in to the laws of a genre? And with nary a deviation! Kovalic was so distressed he felt tears welling in his eyes. How he loved—literature! It was so much better, more humane, less predictable, more fanciful. In a well-written story Lidija would have offered him nothing less than a veal cutlet; in the low genre of life, Lidija, she gives him—a sausage!

Suddenly Kovalic felt hungry.

V

On Saturday, the seventh of April, Nada Matic awoke from a nightmare she had had for many nights. She would dream she was working in her office at Plastic Surgery. It was crammed with anatomical sketches, plaster molds, and plastic models—all of "hot dogs" of the most varied dimensions. Suddenly, in trooped a band of students who tore them all to pieces, laughing and pointing at her all the while. Nada thought she would die of shame, and to make matters worse she felt something sprouting on her nose—an honest-to-goodness sausage! At that point the scene would shift to the operating room, where she—Nada—and Dr. Waldinger were performing a complex procedure. But there was a round hole in the white sheet covering the patient, and she couldn't stop staring through it at his hideous smooth space. Then the scene would shift again, and she and Otto Waldinger were in a field pulling out a gigantic beet. She was holding Otto around the waist when suddenly she was attacked by a gigantic mouse! She could feel its claws on her thighs.

Nada Matic was drinking her morning coffee, smoking a cigarette, and leafing through the evening paper. She would seem to have acquired the fine habit of perusing the Saturday classifieds. Suddenly an item in the "Lost and Found" column caught her eye. She did a double take, stunned by a wild but logical thought: If someone were to lose something like that, it would only be natural for him to try to find it!

> On the twenty-fifth of March, I left a collapsible umbrella in the Skyscraper Cafeteria. Would the finder please return it. No questions asked. Phone xyz and ask for Milan.

Nada jumped out of her seat. The ad was perfectly clear! The umbrella was obviously a respectable substitution for *that*. The fact that it was collapsible made the whole thing absolutely unambiguous!

Nada grabbed the telephone and dialled the number. The conversation was to the point: That's right. Five o'clock. See you there. Good-bye.

At five o'clock that afternoon Nada Matic rang the doorbell of a Dalmatinska Street apartment. A dark man of about thirty opened the door.

He could be the one, thought Nada and said, "Hello, my name is Nada Matic."

"And mine is Milan Misko. Come in."

"Are you the one who lost his umbrella?"

"That's right."

"At the cafeteria?"

"The Skyscraper."

"Collapsible?"

"Yes, yes," said Milan Misko, the owner of the lost umbrella, in an amiable voice. "Do come in." Nada went in.

They sat down. The owner of the collapsible umbrella brought out a bottle of wine and two glasses.

"So, you're the one who lost it," Nada said tellingly and took a sip of the wine.

"That's right."

"God, how thick can he be?" thought Nada, beginning to feel annoyed. She took a long look at *that* place, but could make nothing out. She had to put it into words! But how?

"It must have been hard for you . . ." she said, trying a more direct approach.

"With all the spring showers, you mean? I'd have picked up another one, but you do get attached to your own . . ."

"What was it like? Your umbrella, I mean," she asked its owner nonchalantly.

"Oh, nothing special . . . . You mean, what colour, how long?"

"Yes," said Nada, swallowing hard, "how long. . . ?"

"Oh, standard size," he said, as calm as could be. "You know—collapsible." And he looked over at Nada serenely. "The kind that goes in and out."

Now there could be no doubt. Nada resolved to take the plunge and call a spade a spade, even if it meant humiliating herself. After all, she had played her own bitter part in the affair. So she took the sort of deep breath she would have taken before a dive, half-shut her eyes, stretched out her arms in a sleepwalker's pose, and—jumped! I'm wrong, she thought as she flew mentally through the air, terribly, shamefully wrong. But it was too late to retreat.

And though at this point everything becomes enveloped in mist again, we can guess exactly what happened.

VI

The waitress switched off the light and shut the door after the other girls. For some reason she didn't feel like going with them. She sat down for a short rest and looked through the window at the passersby and the brand names atop the buildings. As she bent over to take off the slippers she wore at work, her hand happened to graze her knee. She let her hand rest on the knee and froze in that position as if listening for something. Then, heaven knows why, she thought of the dark handsome guy who'd left his umbrella in the cafeteria a week or so before and that young, good-looking policeman with the funny, kinky questions—both of them so attractive and somehow connected. . . . Or had she noticed them and had they registered with her mainly because they had—of that she was sure—noticed *her*?

Sheltered by the darkness, the cartons, and the glass, the girl sat with her legs slightly parted, relaxed, peering out of the window at the passersby, when suddenly her hands reached by themselves for one of the cardboard boxes, pulled out a few packages of hot dogs, and started tugging feverishly at the cellophane wrappers. God, what was she doing? What was she doing? What if somebody saw her? Nobody saw her.

She slowly brought a raw hot dog to her lips and quickly stuffed it into her mouth. The hot dog slid down her throat, leaving practically no taste behind. She grabbed a second and quickly chewed it up. Then a third, a fourth, a fifth . . .

There in the heart of the city, enslaved by the darkness, the cartons, and the glass, sat a waitress with her legs slightly parted and her dark, shining eyes peering out at the passersby while she greedily downed hot dog after hot dog. At one point the image of a gigantic, ravenous female mouse flashed through her mind, but she immediately forgot it. She was following the movements of her jaws and listening in on her gullet.

VII

In the afternoon of the seventh of April there was a nervous ring at Kovalic's door. Kovalic was a bit taken aback to see a young, good-looking policeman carrying an unusual-looking bundle.

"Are you Mato Kovalic the writer? Or, rather, the novelist and short story writer?"

"I am," said Kovalic with a tremor in his voice.

"Well, this is yours. Sign here."

"But . . ." Kovalic muttered.

"Good-bye," said the policeman and, with a knowing wink, added, "and good luck!"

"But officer . . . !" Kovalic cried out. It was too late. The policeman had disappeared into the elevator.

Kovalic unwrapped the bundle with trembling hands. Out of the paper fell a bottle filled with a clear liquid, and floating in that liquid was his very own . . . ! Unbelievable! Kovalic was beside himself. For several moments he stood stock-still; then he went back and cautiously removed the object from the bottle and started inspecting it.

That's it, all right—the real thing! Kovalic thought aloud. He'd have recognized it anywhere! And he jumped for joy—though carefully grasping it in his hands.

Since, however, it is a well-known fact that nothing on this earth lasts for very long, our hero suddenly frowned. He had had a terrifying thought. What if it wouldn't go back on?

With indescribable terror in his heart Kovalic walked over to the mirror. His hands were trembling. He carefully returned the object to its former place. Panic! It refused to stick! He brought it up to his lips, warmed it with his breath, and tried again. No luck!

"Come on, damn you!" Kovalic grumbled. "Stick! Stick, you stupid fool!" But the object fell to the floor with a strange, dull, corklike thud. "Why won't it take?" Kovalic wondered nervously. And though he tried again and again, his efforts were in vain.

Crushed, Kovalic was left holding his own, his very own and now very useless part. And much as Kovalic stared at it, it clearly remained indifferent to his despair and lay there in his hand like a dead fish.

"Ba-a-a-a-astard!" Kovalic screamed in a bloodcurdling voice and flung the object into a corner and himself onto his bed. "No, I'm not dreaming," Kovalic whispered into his pillow. "This can't be a dream. This is madness, lunacy . . ." And with that he fell asleep.

VIII

Lidija typed out the word *maladie* and paused. She was still on page one. The translation of the report was due on Monday morning at the Department of Veterinary Medicine.

She stood up, stretched, and switched on the light. She glanced out of the window. It was still day, but the street was grey and empty and smooth from the rain.

Lidija went into the kitchen and opened the refrigerator door out of habit. She peered in without interest and slammed it shut.

Then she went into the bathroom, turned on the tap, and put her wrist under a jet of cold water. It felt good. She glanced up at the mirror. All at once she felt like licking it.

She moved in close to its smooth surface. Her face with tongue hanging out flashed into sight. She drew back slowly. A smooth and empty gesture. Like her life. "Smooth, empty, empty, smooth . . ." she murmured on her way back to the kitchen.

On the kitchen table Lidija noticed a few dried-out bits of bread. She touched them. She like the way dry crumbs pricked the pulp of her fingers. She moistened her finger with saliva, gathered up the crumbs, and went into the combined bedroom and living room. Again she looked out at the street, preoccupied, nibbling on the crumbs from her finger and on the finger itself. The street was empty.

And then she noticed a young, good-looking policeman. He had a limber way about him and was crossing the smooth street, or so it seemed to Lidija, as if it were water. Suddenly she opened the window, breathed deeply, pursed her lips for a whistle, and stopped. What was she doing, for heaven's sake? What had gotten into her?

The policeman looked up. In a well-lit window he saw an unusual-looking woman standing stock-still and staring at him. His glance came to a rest on her full, slightly parted lips. He noticed a crumb on the lower one. Or was he just imagining it? Suddenly he had a desire to remove that real or imagined crumb with his own lips.

"What if she really . . ." flashed through his mind as he noiselessly slipped into the main door. But what happened next we really have no idea.

IX

Kovalic awoke with a vague premonition. His head felt fuzzy, his body leaden. He lay completely motionless for a while when all at once he felt an odd throbbing sensation. He tore off the blanket, and low and behold!—*it* was back in place.

Kovalic couldn't believe his eyes. He reached down and fingered it—yes, it was his, all right! He gave it a tug just to make sure—yes, it popped out of his hand, straight, taut, elastic. Kovalic jumped for joy and leapt out of bed, rushing over to the mirror for a look. No doubt about it: there it stood, rosy, shiny, and erect—and just where it had been before. Kovalic cast a worried glance at the bottle. He saw a little black catfish swimming about as merrily as you please. Intent on engineering clever turns within its narrow confines, it paid him no heed.

"Oh!" Kovalic cried out in amazement.

Then he looked back down below. Situation normal: stiff and erect! Trembling with excitement, Kovalic raced to the phone.

At this point, however, the events are temporarily misted over by censorship, and the reader will have to deduce what happened from the following lines.

Exhausted and depressed, her eyes circled in black, her mouth dry, Maja the invoice clerk lay on her back apathetically staring at that horrid black fish. It was making its two-thousand-one-hundred-and-fifty-first turn in the bottle. At last she picked herself up slowly and started gathering her clothes the way an animal licks its wounds. Suddenly her eyes lit on a slip of paper lying next to her left shoe. The paper contained a list of names in Kovalic's handwriting. *Vesna, Branka, Iris, Goga, Ljerka, Visnja,*

Maja, Lidija. All the names but Lidija's (hers too!) had lines through them.

"Monster!" she said in a hoarse, weary voice, and slammed the door.

Kovalic stared apathetically at the lower half of his body. *It* was in place, sprightly, and erect as ever. He flew into a rage, bounded out of bed, bolted to the bottle, and smashed it to the floor. The catfish flipped and flopped for a while, then calmed down. Kovalic gleefully watched the gill contractions subside. But *it* was still erect.

"Down, monster!" Kovalic shouted and gave it a mean thwack. It swayed and reddened, but then spryly, with a rubberlike elasticity, sprang back into place and raised its head at Kovalic almost sheepishly.

"Off with you, beast!" Kovalic screamed. The object refused to budge.

"I'll strangle you!" Kovalic bellowed. The object stared straight ahead, curtly indifferent.

"I wish you'd never been found," Kovalic whimpered, and flung himself onto the bed in despair. "You bastard, you! I'll get you yet!" And he burst into sobs, mumbling incoherent threats into the pillow. Then, wiping his tears, he raised his fist into the air, heaven knows why, and muttered, "I'll put you through the meat grinder!" And all of a sudden the old butcher's saying went off like an alarm in his brain: *My knives go with me to the grave!*

And the fear and trembling caused by this new piece of data sent Kovalic reeling—and into a dead faint.

X

Well, dear readers, now you see the sort of thing that happens in our city! And only now, after much reflection, do I realize how much in it is unbelievable—starting from the alienation of the object in question from its rightful owner. Nor is it believable that authors should choose such things to write stories about. First, they are of no use either to literature or to the population, and second, they are of no use . . . well, either. And yet, when all is said and done, there is hardly a place you won't find similar incongruities. No, say what you will, these things do happen—rarely, but they do.

For my part, I have a clear conscience. I have stuck to the plot. Had I given myself free rein, well, I don't know where things would have ended! And even so, what happened to Nada Matic? Who is Milan Misko? What became of Vinko K.? And Lidija and the waitress and the butcher? To say nothing of our hero Mato Kovalic? Is he doomed to spend his life getting it—down?

But I repeat: I have stuck to the plot. Though if the truth be told, I did insert two nightmares from my own childhood, to wit: 1) the sausage dream ("Watch out or a sausage will sprout on your nose," my grandfather used to say when he got angry with me), and 2) the beet dream (I can recall no more terrifying story from my childhood than the one in which a whole family gathered to pull out a big, beautiful, and completely innocent beet!).

In connection with said plot may I suggest the following points as worthy of further consideration:

1. How did the object alienated from its owner, Mato Kovalic, find its way into the bun?
2. How did Vinko K. discover its owner?

3. Miscellaneous.

All that is merely by-the-by, of course, in passing. I myself have no intention of taking things any further. . . . But if you, honoured readers, decide to do so, I wish you a merry time of it and a hearty appetite!

Anonymous

Gumbo Ya-Ya

[1945]

Black Art Used to Influence People to Win Love
(fetishes and charms used by men)

Take some of the desired one's hair and sleep with it under the pillow.

Rub love oil into the palm of your right hand.

Carry a piece of weed called 'John the Conqueror' in your pocket.

Charms Used by Women

Write the man's name and yours on separate pieces of paper. Pin them together in the form of a cross with yours on top. Put them in a glass of water containing sugar and orange-flower water and burn a red candle before this glass for nine days.

Place the man's picture behind a mirror.

Wrap a thimble in a small piece of silk and carry this in your pocket for three days. Every time you enter or leave the house, make a wish regarding your sweetheart. Your wish will come true in three months.

To Make a Love Powder

Gut live hummingbirds. Dry the heart and powder it. Sprinkle the powder on the person you desire.

A Love Fetish

Put a live frog in an ant's nest. When the bones are clean, you will find one flat, heart-shaped, and one with a hook. Secretly hook this into the garment of your beloved, and keep the heart-shaped one. If you should lose the heart-shaped bone, he will hate you as much as he loved you before.

Prostitute's Lure

Essences of vanilla, verbena, Jack honeysuckle, wintergreen, rosebud, and 'follow-me-boy' water. Scrub place and sprinkle mixture from front to back. Mix thyme seed, popcorn, and brown sugar in a jar, place three lighted candles over it, then fling the last mixture in the four corners of the room. (Marie Contesse method.)

The **Anonymous** Ancient Egyptian Love Lyric is a fragment from a series of poems dating between 1085 and 570 B.C. It is translated by Joseph Kaster.

The **Anonymous** *Gumbo Ya-Ya* is a rollicking collection of swamp tales, ghost stories and magic charms, all assembled for the Works Project Administration in 1945.

The **Anonymous** Turko-Persian *Bab Nameh*, or Book of Lust, dates to ancient times. Our excerpt is from "The Philosophy of Love" section.

The **Anonymous** *Yoruba Erotic Chorus* is sung during the Festival of Oke Ibadan in Central Africa. Naked twelve-year-olds parade the streets and chant praises to the god of the Ibadan hills.

New York chemist **Louis Berman** published his then-shocking *The Glands that Regulate Sexuality* in 1921.

The infamous *Fanny Hill* was written by **John Cleland** in 1748, while he was imprisoned for bad debt.

A. Cooke's insights in "The Honey-moon" are excerpted from his stormy tract *Satan and Society*, which he privately published in 1880.

Havelock Ellis's detailed history of Foot-Fetichism was recorded in his volume *Psychology of Sex* (1919).

Isabel Gowdie's *Eyewitness Account of Sex with the Devil* is a transcript from a 1662 Scottish witch trial.

Colombian novelist **Gabriel García Márquez**'s sultry tales of magic realism include *One Hundred Years of Solitude*, *Chronicle of a Death Foretold* and *Love in the Time of Cholera*. García Márquez won the Nobel Prize for Literature in 1982.

Anthropologist **Margaret Mead** spent her life studying primitive peoples and their sexual relations. Her surprising results were published in several books, including *Coming of Age in Samoa* and *Growing Up in New Guinea*. "Arapesh Marriage" is from the seminal *Sex and Temperament in Three Primitive Societies* (1935).

Chin P'ing Mei's writings on the adventures of Hsi-men date from the 19th century. While most are not available in English, a few appear in an obscure 1962 anthology, *The Cradle of Erotica*.

Nell Port is a contributor to *Ladies Own Erotica* (1984), a collection of stories, poems, recipes and general fantasy culled by the The Kensington Ladies' Erotica Society.

Thomas Rowlandson was a 19th-century English printmaker. Poems such as "New Feats of Horsemanship" were commonly found scribbled in the lower corners of his work.

Dubravka Ugresic published *In the Jaws of Life* in 1981. The short story "A Hot Dog in a Warm Bun" is from that collection. The translation is by Michael Henry Heim.

The vividly detailed erotic manual, *Kama Sutra* (literally love-science) is thought to have been written by the Indian sage **Vatsyayana** in the 1st century. This 1883 translation from Richard Burton is still considered a classic.

Monique Wittig is the author of three novels, *The Opoponax, Les Guerillieres* and the 1973 *The Lesbian Body*, from which "We Descend" is taken. This translation is by Peter Owen.

Nothing is known of the mysterious Chinese essayist and sage **Li Yu**. His erotic writing, including *The Carnal Prayer Mat*, dates to the mid 1600s.

"We Descend" from *The Lesbian Body* by Monique Wittig ©1973 by Monique Wittig. Reprinted by permission of the author.

"Tantric Sex" by Nell Port from *Ladies' Own Erotica* ©1984 by the Kensington Ladies' Erotica Society, by Permission of Ten Speed Press, P.O. Box 7123, Berkeley, CA 94707.

Excerpt from *Sex and Temperament* by Margaret Mead ©1935, 1950, 1963 by Margaret Mead. Reprinted by permission of William Morrow and Company, Inc.

"A Hot Dog in a Warm Bun" from *In the Jaws of Life* by Dubravka Ugresic, ©1981 by Dubravka Ugresic. Reprinted by permission of Virago Press.

Excerpt from *Love in the Time of Cholera* by Gabriel García Márquez, trans., Edith Grossman ©1988 by Alfred A. Knopf, Inc. Reprinted by permission of the publisher.